ADVANCE PRAISE

"What happens when you lose everything? This radiant debut gets at the dark beating heart of survival, set against a backdrop of differing geography, beliefs, cultures, and races, in prose as intricate as a jazz fugue. Blazingly original and fiercely smart, *A Narrow Bridge* shows that who we love is really who we are."
— Caroline Leavitt, *The New York Times*–bestselling author of *Cruel Beautiful World* and *Pictures of You*

"*A Narrow Bridge* is a moving story about the intersection between love and loss and an unsentimental exploration of the role of faith in healing. I held my breath until the very last word of this cinematic, compassionate, and compelling debut."
— Michelle Brafman, author of *Bertrand Court* and *Washing the Dead*

"A beautifully written, imaginative, and poignant testimony to the power of love and the limits of faith."
— Steven Z. Leder, senior rabbi at Wilshire Boulevard Temple in Los Angeles and author of *The Extraordinary Nature of Ordinary Things*

"A gripping, heartbreaking, ultimately uplifting story of two broken people and the healing power of love. Beautifully drawn, the writing keeps you riveted page after fast-turning page."
—Jeffrey Richman, six-time Emmy-winning executive producer of *Modern Family* and *Frasier*

Published by Prospect Park Books
2359 Lincoln Avenue
Altadena, California 91001
www.prospectparkbooks.com

Distributed by Consortium Book Sales & Distribution
www.cbsd.com

Library of Congress Cataloging in Publication Data
Names: Gesher, J. J., author.
Title: A narrow bridge / J.J. Gesher.
Description: Altadena, California : Prospect Park Books, 2017.
Identifiers: LCCN 2016020624 | ISBN 9781938849824 (paperback)
Subjects: LCSH: Jewish men--Fiction. | Alabama--Fiction. | Domestic fiction. | BISAC: FICTION / Family Life. | FICTION / Jewish.
Classification: LCC PS3607.E86 N37 2017 | DDC 813/.6--dc23
LC record available at https://lccn.loc.gov/2016020624

Cover design by David Ter-Avanesyan
Layout by Amy Inouye, Future Studio
Printed in the United States of America

A NARROW BRIDGE

J.J. GESHER

PROSPECT
·PARK·
BOOKS

CHAPTER 1

The first time Jacob Fisher saw someone shoot up he was twelve years old. He was sitting on the couch in Lenny's basement apartment, eating the only snack Lenny ever provided, saltine crackers. Lenny was the superintendent of the Brooklyn building where the Fisher family lived. All of the people in Jacob's life were observant Jews and lifelong New Yorkers. Lenny was other, an older African American with a hint of the South about him.

Most everyone Jacob knew rushed words, determined to avoid someone else's selfish interruption. Lenny's cadence was different. He never hurried his thoughts or opinions. He listened when Jacob spoke, nodding his head, encouraging further response. When Lenny found out that Jacob studied piano, he made a point of sharing his love of the blues and jazz. Although Jacob's parents were unaware of the frequent visits, he stole time to visit Lenny in the musty apartment with the peculiar smell. Today, a sandalwood candle burned in an attempt to neutralize the odor of fried fish and beans.

Jacob polished off his wax-paper sleeve of crackers while he listened to Lenny ramble a twenty-minute love letter to Billie Holiday's imperfect genius. As he spoke, Lenny loaded one of her records onto an old-fashioned turntable, and a mournful plea for love flooded the small space. Lenny, arms stretched wide, greeted her voice. As if Jacob were invisible, Lenny poured a small envelope of powder into a bent spoon and held it over the lit candle until the powder turned into an amber liquid. Suddenly, Lenny announced to the walls and furniture that he was diabetic and that the injection was insulin. He sat on a kitchen chair, loaded a syringe, and injected the fluid into a protruding vein in his ankle. The only time he lifted his head from the task at hand was to tap an air bubble out of the syringe. He never made eye contact. Jacob knew he was lying. His uncle was diabetic, and the insulin came out of a small glass bottle.

The top of Lenny's bent head shone dark brown through his gray close-cropped curls. His body swayed with the recording's seductive, hypnotic melody. As soon as he injected the liquid, Lenny looked completely happy, like someone who had just tasted the most delicious chocolate cake. He took a deep, satisfied breath and dozed off with his eyes half open.

Out of respect, Jacob stayed on the couch until the last notes faded. Handling the vinyl like Lenny had taught him, touching only the paper disc in the center and the rim where there was no groove, he removed the record from the turntable and carefully slipped it back into its cardboard cover. Quietly, he let himself out. Ever since that day, Jacob couldn't listen to Billie Holiday without thinking of saltines, Lenny, and heroin.

—◦—

Jacob's hand cradled a sheet of sandpaper as he finished the fine details on the bookcase he was building. At thirty-two, he was a man at ease with his body: long, well-muscled limbs, deeply intelligent blue eyes, thick, dark hair and beard. His even strokes matched the rhythm of Ray Charles's "Come Rain or Come Shine" wafting gently from a speaker. The pain in the cry of a minor key resonated deep within him like an untold secret. Indeed, for all these years, the blues had to be a secret. The world of Orthodox Judaism forbade him to listen; the rabbis condemned any music that wasn't related to prayer as *narishkeit*. In Yiddish, that meant foolishness.

There was no higher insult for a learned man than to be labeled a fool, but Jacob didn't care what anyone else thought about his taste in music. He defiantly ignored the rabbis' judgment. He felt a primal connection to the sound of the blues.

When he was a child, Jacob's parents had marked him as difficult. He was a constant drip of disappointment, the son who'd openly defied religious rules and scoffed at tradition. Some rebellion was expected in all religious homes, but Jacob had relished any opportunity to challenge the status quo. Obstinately, he'd watch television on the Sabbath to follow his beloved Yankees, and he'd openly neglect to say mandatory prayers. He'd provoke, prod, and irritate until he got a response. When his father accused him of being intentionally argumentative, he wore the label like a compliment.

Even with the comfort of his music and his woodwork, Jacob couldn't get Trench McGinnis out of his mind. Only this afternoon he thought he'd spotted him on the street. He hadn't laid eyes on Trench in the fourteen years since he got clean. But the instant he registered his face, a tinny taste in his mouth forced him to remember the feeling of smack entering his body. Ever since the sighting, that tinny taste kept popping in uninvited. He focused on the music to get rid of the sensation.

Jacob sang a quiet duet with Ray Charles as the angled work light revealed the hand-carved details of his latest piece of furniture. The light illuminated him as well. On his head, a *kipah*, the skullcap that marked him as an observant Jew. He hunched, alone and diligent, over the unfinished bookcase, coaxing it into beauty. The repeated back-and-forth of the #2 sandpaper smoothed the surface of the wood. Soon, it could be stained. His sweat mingled with the vaguely acrid smell of the freshly scraped lumber, enveloping him in a cloud of testosterone familiarity.

Years ago, when he was at the rehab program in Israel, he'd learned to work with wood. He grew to appreciate the marbled grains, the sensuous textures, and the life to be charmed from something no longer alive. This skill had proven essential. In his Orthodox community, being a scholar and cantor was well respected, but he never earned enough money to provide for his family. The woodworking filled the gaps.

Finishing a piece comforted him; all intrusive thoughts dissipated, and his concentration narrowed. Gone were the minutia of daily obligations, the needs and wants of his three young children, the meticulous lesson plans for the classes he taught at the yeshiva, the politics of his religious community. This piece of wood and this moment in time were all that mattered.

Jacob was unaware that his wife, Julia, had quietly opened the door to the back room that masqueraded as a wood shop. She stood there, barefoot, a full-length cotton nightgown skimming the floor, her body outlined through the fabric by the soft glow of the hall light. There were curves to this woman, but not those of too much food and too little exercise—rather, the soft contours of childbearing and health. In every way she was a woman best described as ripe. Her intellect was honed; her features, pleasing, eyes wide, lips full, rounded breasts and hips willing to welcome husband and child.

Now was the time for husband.

Julia's soft voice intruded on Jacob's meditation. "Come to bed, Jacob. You've been hiding in here for hours."

His attention never leaving the wood, his rhythm never faltering, Jacob responded. "I promised Mrs. Shapiro I'd have this finished by the weekend."

Julia gently entered the room and moved to his side. "It's beautiful," she whispered, one hand on his shoulder, the other moving lightly over the finely carved details.

There was need in her touch. The way her hand moved from his shoulder to the back of his neck spoke of animal hunger. It would be impossible for him to finish now.

"It has to be stained," Jacob said, drawing out the seduction. Julia leaned in to share her veiled invitation. "Not now. I can't sleep without you in bed...it's cold." She leaned over him to turn off the music. Jacob's breath stopped in his throat. He was filled with wonder and gratitude as he absorbed the feel of her lips against his ear, the brush of her breasts against his arm. After nine years of married life, he still longed for her.

The bookshelf could wait.

⸺◦⸺

The morning sun forced Jacob to squint as he stepped out of his modest Williamsburg row house and headed for the synagogue. His fedora, white shirt, dark suit, and black shoes were his unofficial uniform. The threads of his *tsitses*, the fringed undergarment worn by observant Jews, peeked from beneath his suit. The clothing helped the Orthodox recognize one another and stand apart from secular society.

Morning rush hour in Brooklyn was better than a cup of coffee. Within minutes of his front door, Jacob was keenly aware of all his senses. He was greeted by the pungent smell of the Korean market, where ducks hung by their feet, and salsa music blasting from the corner bodega. Turban-swathed Sikhs waited for fares in their cabs while hipsters, punksters, and gangsters weaved in and out in their choreographed daily migration. As Jacob moved with the herd, he passed a corner newsstand and stopped to read a *New York Post* headline: "Fear of Homegrown Terrorism Escalates." He handed the wizened news jockey a dollar as he flipped the paper under his arm. Unlike most of his generation, Jacob preferred the feel of newsprint to electronic scrolling.

"Morning."

"Same to you, Rabbi," the man growled over the cigar stub in his mouth.

Jacob was surprised. He bought the paper here often, yet

today this grizzled old man had chosen to speak to him for the first time.

"I'm not a rabbi, I'm a cantor," Jacob answered politely.

The guardian of the news flashed a yellow-toothed grin and removed the stogie. "What's the difference?"

Jacob momentarily debated if the effort of an answer was worthwhile. He decided to continue the civility.

"One talks, the other sings...I'm the singer."

The old man slipped the cigar back in place, leaned on a stack of newspapers, and challenged him. "Oh yeah? So sing something."

Instantly, Jacob's eyebrows arched, and the corners of his mouth hinted at a private joke waiting to be delivered. Jacob turned up the portable radio on the newsstand's back shelf. In a pure tenor voice he sang along with the Rolling Stones.

You can't always get what you wa-ant.
No, you can't always get what you wa-ant.
But if you try sometime,
You just might find,
You get what you need.

The old man rumbled a smoker's laugh. "Love those oldies."

Jacob tipped his fedora. "Me too."

Newspaper under his arm, he stood at a crosswalk waiting for the light to change. A swarm of Orthodox men poured out of a nearby synagogue. Across the street he spotted Trench Mc-Ginnis—this time he was sure. Jacob was amazed that Trench was still alive. He must have moved back to the neighborhood. Trench was an anomaly in the sea of Orthodox men—a bright red baseball cap bobbing among black fedoras. The cap was only part of the reason Jacob recognized him. Trench was tiny, maybe five foot one, and wiry. He walked quickly, darting between the other pedestrians. Jacob lifted his hand to wave but changed his mind, pretending to adjust his hat instead. What could he say to Trench after all these years?

And why should he want to connect again? Trench had been the one to lead him into drugs, a slow march from weed, to oxycontin, to heroin. Trench wasn't a dealer...just a user. The phrase *just a user* made Jacob shake his head in wry disbelief. They met in a jazz club. Trench had recognized Jacob's musical gift—from a trained classical pianist to a self-taught player of blues and jazz. He encouraged him to pursue his talent, dragging him to basement clubs in the outer boroughs, pretending not to notice Jacob's nervous performances. Trench had fed him and let him crash on his couch when Jacob's father kicked him out. Trench was the one who taught him about the opposite sex, even smoothing the way for his first experience.

There were a lot of firsts under Trench's tutelage. The first time Trench showed him how to smoke heroin was a casual transition. There was no nodding off like he remembered with Lenny, no gutless, drooling junkie behavior like he'd seen on television. The first time he did heroin, all he felt was content. He was on top of the "bads" that happened in everyday life: his disappointments, his ineptitudes, his failures. Heroin tricked him into believing that he was the person he wished he were. Jacob could do heroin and still create music, still perform in clubs. He felt alive and the world was beautiful. And heroin was cheap—ten, maybe twenty dollars and he was set for the weekend. But the drug was insidious. Soon the ten-dollar hit didn't work the same. He needed more of the drug each time and that was costly. Smoking heroin no longer put him in the right place. Shooting it did.

The next steps were a blur: dealers, back alleys, asking his mother for money, stealing from relatives and friends. Trench redeemed himself by calling 911 and Jacob's parents on the night he overdosed. That saved his life. He owed Trench for that.

Jacob could have yelled Trench's name. He could have grinned and offered a casual " 'sup?" Trench would laugh his ass off when he recognized him under the beard. Trench's laugh was easy and contagious, and even after all these years, Jacob could conjure the sound.

The light changed, and the pedestrians upstream and downstream flowed by one another. Jacob resisted the impulse to connect with his old friend, watching him enter a building next to the Tip Top Cleaners. When Jacob got straight, he'd learned that all the old friends had to go. Best not to poke the dragon.

CHAPTER 2

Julia hadn't always been an Orthodox Jew; until she met Jacob, she hadn't been religious at all. Fresh out of college and working as a speech therapist in the public schools, she was on the morning subway when she noticed, sitting across from her, a shockingly handsome man reading a folded newspaper. Her attraction was immediate. She only realized what he was wearing—that he was an observant Jew—*after* she found him appealing. Julia knew staring was rude, but she couldn't stop herself. The fantasy was instantaneous. What would it be like to make love to this man? Her thoughts leapfrogged, and the intensity of her imaginings flashed in quick succession—his chest, shoulders, thighs. She wanted him to touch her. Without conscious consent, the most private parts of her body readied themselves for intimacy, and she blushed with secret embarrassment.

Had common decency not prevailed, she would have kissed him then and there. These feelings were unnerving; she'd never felt the urge to throw herself at a strange man before. She stared at him so intently that he, as if compelled by some greater force, looked up. Nature took over. Julia did not look away, and neither did the stranger. They both flushed red, aware of the breach of conduct, and yet their eyes stayed locked.

Relieved that the train had arrived at her stop, she gathered her bag and stood, breaking their contact. As the subway doors closed behind her, Julia stood on the platform and rummaged through her purse for her cellphone. Unexpectedly, the man from the train appeared next to her.

"Excuse me...is your mother Jewish?"

Julia was caught off guard and then instantly annoyed. She knew Orthodox Jews believed that religious identity was passed on through the mother, but how could a total stranger ask such a personal question?

Still, she answered him politely. "Yes."

"Good. My name is Jacob Fisher. I think we are meant to know each other."

Jacob and Julia began to meet at parks or coffee shops after work. He wanted to spend time alone with her, but it had to be in a public place. According to his Orthodox beliefs, an unmarried man and a woman could not be alone together, nor could they touch. Once, a group of rowdy kids passed them on the sidewalk. The kids, absorbed in their own antics, crowded Julia, forcing her to bump into Jacob's shoulder. Less than a second of unintentional touch, yet they both blushed. She wouldn't have thought twice about accidental physical contact with any other man, but she knew that for Jacob, touching was forbidden.

One Sunday, Julia put on a strapless sundress, threw a cardigan over her shoulders, and went to meet Jacob. By this time, she knew something about the laws of modesty, and she didn't want to offend him. As they walked through Central Park, the sun beat down and, without thinking, she took off her sweater and tied it around her waist. He didn't comment—in fact, he hardly looked at her. He was expounding on some point about the relationship between the stock market and the global economy when she could no longer hide her frustration.

"Why don't you look at me when you talk?"

"I can't," he stammered. "The way you're dressed makes me uncomfortable."

"Uncomfortable?" she responded sharply.

"You're not modest."

"Modest? I'm dressed like every other normal twenty-five-year-old New Yorker out for an afternoon with her..." She couldn't finish the sentence. What was Jacob to her? A teacher? A spiritual guide? A boyfriend?

Jacob stopped in his tracks. "I don't look because I respect you, Julia. When you dress like that, you are not respecting yourself."

Julia fumed. "This is the twenty-first century. We dress for the weather, to be comfortable in our bodies. Showing my shoulders is not a sin..."

Jacob countered somberly. "You mustn't give in to the sexual excesses of the society that surrounds us."

"You make sexuality sound like a disease," she rebutted. She was flustered and exasperated. All of a sudden she had a powerful craving for a cold beer in a dark tavern, far away from this self-righteous jerk. She turned and walked toward the subway. "Forget it. This is never going to work."

Jacob chased after her. He stood in front of her and touched her arm. "Don't go."

She looked down at his hand. His touch burned with electricity. She knew he was breaking one of his many rules.

"Let me explain." He pulled back, but she could still feel the heat of his handprint, like a thermal image on her skin. "The Torah teaches that our physical acts can help us achieve spiritual greatness. Our job is to take the gifts of the everyday world and make them sacred."

Jacob searched her face while his mind struggled for the words that would convince her to stay. "Making love to your wife is beautiful. Sex for the sake of temporary satisfaction is not."

The subtext of the lesson was clear. He wanted her not for a casual relationship, but forever. If she wanted Jacob in her life, she would have to be the one to change.

Because Julia was born a Jew, she didn't have to convert. But her unobservant past presented a problem. According to the Talmud, she wasn't raised with the proper guidance of Jewish law and ritual. However, if she demonstrated her commitment to an observant way of life, she'd be considered a *Ba'al T'shuva*, someone who returns to the fold and is fully accepted in the community.

———

Six months after that chance meeting on the subway, after much conversation and no physical contact, and in accordance with all the rules of Orthodoxy, they were married.

The wedding night did not disappoint. After months of chaste courtship, Julia had controlled her expectations. She feared that Jacob would be awkward and that she'd have to teach him. When they got to the hotel room, the two of them sat separately, joyfully rehashing the evening's events. They laughed at her father's slightly inebriated and emotional toast. They became sentimental, wishing that their deceased grandparents and Jacob's late father could have been there. During the spirited *hora*, Jacob's mother, Hava, had leaned in to Julia and declared that they were dancing on Hitler's grave. When Julia told Jacob what his mother had said, a moment of gravity descended. Jacob crossed the room to her.

He stood in front of her, cleared his throat, and straightened his posture. She had the absurd notion that he was going to ask her to slow dance, as if they were a couple in a 1950s movie about teenagers. Instead, he took her hand and kissed her palm, and then enclosed her hand in both of his. He studied the veins on the back of his own hand so intently that Julia looked, too. Was he trying to show her something? She waited for him to speak.

"There are things about my past that..." he began, but he couldn't seem to find more words.

Julia could see that he was struggling to confine his emotions to his throat.

"Let it be. We both have a past," she said simply. "Weren't you the one who taught me that a *Ba'al T'shuva* is a master of personal change? Maybe we're both *Ba'al T'shuva*."

Jacob smiled. "The student has become the teacher."

With natural dignity, he pulled her in close and kissed her. She was relieved that he kissed so well. He gently undressed her, caressing each newly revealed part of her body as if he had been gifted an extraordinary present. Julia allowed herself to be seduced. He knew what to do and how to please her. There was nothing pious or Orthodox in their lovemaking.

Julia found the transition to religious married life less difficult than she'd imagined. The adherence to the daily laws of Judaism, the ritual baths, and even the required head covering all became second nature. She found herself welcoming the sense of tradition and purpose that was at the core of her observant life. Here, within the boundaries of the rules, it was easy to lean, easy to ask for help.

Jacob's community enveloped her in warmth, and she felt a belonging that she hadn't even known she was missing. If a family was dealing with difficulties, there was the comfort of food and company. If there was cause for celebration, the community threw itself into preparations and festivities. When each of her children was born—a boy, Yossi, followed by two girls, Miriam and Sarah—friends appeared with advice, casseroles, housekeeping, and babysitting. Within the community, the expectations for her were as clear as her role: valued wife and mother. Although Julia embraced her new life, she still saw her old friends at art-house movies, still managed to look quirky and fashionable, and still chortled at the off-color joke or double entendre.

Julia worried about the bills, but finances rarely troubled Jacob, who always spouted some version of "God will provide."

When she was irritated by the constant commotion in their home, he'd tell her that crying babies and sick children were really blessings, signs of God's goodness in granting them such robust children. That was easy for him to say. He could sleep through a baby's cry, the children fighting, and her frustration. He never deviated from his observance, nor did he allow any negativity to penetrate his contentment.

Sometimes, she saw a shadow of melancholy settle on his face. Riding on the subway or in the middle of a dinner conversation, he would tune out, as if he were listening to a noise or conversation in the distance. Julia observed these moments of discontent and tried to get Jacob to share his thoughts. He'd abruptly change the subject, insisting there was nothing wrong. But she suspected that he had secrets and felt there was a part of him that she could not reach.

CHAPTER 3

Jacob's mother, Hava, announced Shabbat dinner and ushered everyone to the table. There was no doubt that this moment, the transition between the workweek and the Sabbath, was the most resonant with Jacob. There was something visceral about the moment that divided the everyday from the holy. He could almost touch the calm. The children were clean and combed. The table welcomed them with fine china and fresh-cut red roses. The smell of the Sabbath meal filled the house. For twenty-four hours he could suspend the real world and refuel. It was a time to be grateful and to connect with his wife and family.

As Jacob took his place at the head of the table, an air of reverent expectancy descended on the room. Julia covered her head with a lace shawl and lit the Sabbath candles. She circled the two flames with her hands, pulling the energy toward her face as she covered her eyes and murmured the blessing. Generations of tradition engulfed them. There are Hebrew blessings for everything: wine, bread, fruit, the first time you see the ocean or mountains, for lightening and thunder, and even a rainbow after a storm. A Jew is obligated to thank God for any connection to life.

Jacob absorbed the faces around the table—wife, children, and mother. His mother covered her eyes and murmured her own prayer. She was a handsome woman, her inner strength reflected in her face and direct smile. She had been a young widow. Ten years ago, on an innocuous Thursday morning, Jacob's fifty-three-year-old father put his hand to his chest, sat down, and died quietly on their neighbor's front stoop. Jacob knew that his mother filled her days attending to her growing brood of grandchildren, but still, her face flickered with loneliness.

Jacob's three children stood in front of him, and he lightly placed his hands on their heads and blessed them, first in Hebrew, then in English.

May God bless you and watch over you.
May God shine His face toward you and show you favor.
May God be favorably disposed toward you and grant you
    peace.

The children, infused with pride, returned to their seats and Jacob turned to Julia. He offered the prayer that Jewish husbands voice each week at the beginning of the Sabbath.

An accomplished woman, who can find? Her value is far
    beyond pearls.
Her husband's heart relies on her and he shall lack no
    fortune....
Her children rise and praise her, her husband lauds her.

Hava was moved as she watched her son bless his family. Everyone always said Jacob resembled her, but as he'd grown older, he looked so much like his father. Jacob had a good *neshama*—in Hebrew that meant soul. Like his father, he had a smile so genuine that when he laughed you could see inside him.

Jacob was an improved version of his father. Her husband had a short temper, but she had never seen Jacob, with all his proclivities and weaknesses, express anger.

She knew Jacob believed Julia was his equal. Hava, though a strong woman in her own right, felt that a wife should defer to her husband. It upset her that Jacob and Julia resolved conflicts by consensus. One side of her appreciated that her son viewed his wife as a partner; the other felt that this stranger was emasculating her son by having equal sway in their lives.

Hava regretted that the universe had not granted her more than two children. Judaism's commandment to be fruitful and multiply was taken seriously in her community. Families had at least five children. She had not been so lucky. God had given her Jacob, two miscarriages, followed by her daughter, Naomi. She never conceived again. She had fulfilled her obligation and re-placed herself, but a tiny bit of ego ruled. If she and her husband had made two such fine children, what would have been the harm in several more? Hava was a woman of faith, and she believed that God had his reasons.

———◆◆———

Blessings and special Shabbat songs concluded the festive meal. Jacob loved his children's raucous energy at the table. Before the singing died down, Julia was back in the kitchen. She often com-plained that she was permanently fastened to the sink. There were certain chores that always reappeared like repetitive insanity: pre-paring meals, dirty dishes, sticky counters. Hava and the children paraded the dishes into the kitchen, and Julia washed.

Jacob brought in the last remnants of the dinner and came up behind her. His hands slipped around her waist as he nuzzled her neck. "I love the way you smell."

Julia continued rinsing the dishes and quietly admonished him. "Shhh, the children...lower your voice."

Like an old-time comic, Jacob dropped his voice an octave. "I love the way you smell." It was the dumbest of jokes, and yet she smiled.

His hands still around her waist, he moved her out of the way, "Get out of here. You cooked. I clean."

Julia, with soap on her hands, turned to him, held his bearded face, and gently kissed his eyes. Unaware of the bubbles on his chin, Jacob looked slightly foolish and wholly in love.

CHAPTER 4

The shades were drawn inside room 187 of the Weatherly, a decaying welfare hotel on the seedy side of Williamsburg, Brooklyn. Darnell Walker stood naked in front of a chipped wall mirror that reflected him and the surrounding room. The room was barren but for the mattress on the floor and a chrome desk lamp, which cast an unnerving shadow on the wall. Darnell Walker looked ten feet tall.

The mattress was perfectly made. On it was a copy of the Bible, a pair of jeans, a worn Batman backpack, and a blue plaid shirt. The only decoration in the room was a large poster that had been taped on the wall, a boldly colored picture of Satan and Jesus arm wrestling. Jesus was winning.

The naked man dipped a washcloth into the bowl of soapy water at his feet, wrung it out, and methodically washed his tattooed body. He cleansed every inch of himself, even using the wet cloth to flay the scars of intertwining circles on his back.

As he cleansed, he prayed, "It is for you, God, that I prepare myself. I am your holy messenger now."

Once Walker had finished washing, he anointed himself with oil, taking care to stroke himself to a full state of arousal but not beyond.

Jacob walked with his family to the bus. It was a fine day in Brooklyn, the first such day in many months—the humidity had lifted, and a crisp breeze carried the promise of fall. They should have been contented, but he could tell that Julia was annoyed. He wasn't joining the family outing until after the Knicks game. He pretended not to notice her irritation. If he brought it up at all, they would get swept into cyclical arguing. She would allude to his selfishness, reminding him that she had changed her life to comply with his. He would say that she was conflating two separate points to substantiate her viewpoint. She would accuse him of self-centered opportunistic reasoning. He would flare. She would sulk. Nothing would be resolved, and they would both be angry.

Julia was taking the children to see their cousins, and Jacob would meet them after lunch for a long-awaited trip to the Central Park Zoo. The street was crowded with couples and families on Sunday outings. Yossi bounced a basketball as he jogged down the street, and occasionally he'd pass it to his father.

Jacob's passion for basketball began as an activity for yeshiva boys to burn some energy, so they could focus their minds on Talmud study. Jacob had played on his yeshiva's team and excelled as a point guard. He still enjoyed shooting around with his students after school, and sometimes he played a spontaneous pickup game. The physicality of basketball had been a saving point for him when he went through rehab years ago. He'd play to exhaustion. Anything to keep his mind from obsessing. He couldn't explain to Julia why he loved the game. She had no idea that the rehab chapter of his life even existed.

Jacob held Sarah's hand. Julia walked ahead with Miriam, the six-year-old, who pushed a toy stroller with a baby doll inside. The children vied for Jacob's attention, but he was distracted. He was eager to have them on their way so he could watch the game.

"Dad, you said you'd teach me to do a layup later," Yossi

reminded him.

"After the zoo," Jacob said. "Dribble with your left hand. You have to be able to go to the left."

At eight years old, Yossi was uncoordinated, not a natural athlete as Jacob had been. He awkwardly switched to his left hand, and they continued walking.

Sarah pulled Jacob toward her, her four-year-old voice barely audible. "Daddy, when we get to the zoo, can we look at the penguins for a long time?"

"As long as you want, sweetie," Jacob responded. How could he say no to that face?

——◆——

In the endless days and nights of federal prison, Darnell Walker had found God. Not the storefront deity of his youth, but the all-powerful Jesus Christ of fanaticism. He had always heard voices, but he didn't know that God was talking to him until he was born again. Then the voice made sense.

Walker was dressed and ready. He had never before been this handsome. When he accepted Christ as his savior, he forgave the long-dead crack-whore mother who had seared concentric circles across his back with her cigarettes. Burning flesh leaves a memory on body and soul. Now he owed a debt to Jesus for his peace of mind.

He took his state ID and his parole card and put them in the wastebasket. He added a few photos and personal documents and lit the trash on fire. A trace of a satisfied smile crossed his face as he watched his identity disintegrate. He closed the top button of his shirt, placed the Bible in a small brown paper bag, put on the weighty backpack, and shut the door to his room.

——◆——

Jacob turned back to Yossi. "How're you doing with your free throws?"

"Nothing but net," Yossi boasted. Julia turned around and gave him a withering look.

"...most of the time."

Miriam piped in, "I can make free throws."

"She grannies," Yossi teased. He bent at the waist with the ball between his legs, mimicking an underhanded free throw.

"Big deal! They go in more than yours do," Miriam answered defiantly.

Before the fight could escalate, a bus approached. Sarah tugged on Jacob's hand.

"Can we see the monkeys and the seals too, Daddy?"

"The monkeys are my favorite," Jacob confided.

Miriam noticed a liquor store, "Daddy, buy me some gum. You promised to teach me how to blow bubbles," she whined.

Jacob looked up and saw the bus approaching. "Not now, honey. The bus is here."

The bus's brakes squealed as it came to a stop. Miriam and Yossi arrived at the steps at the same time as a man with a Batman backpack. Yossi accidentally bumped into him, and the man dropped his brown paper bag.

Miriam shoved her brother, "Look what you did. Say you're sorry."

"No problem," the man answered as he picked up the bag. Carefully adjusting the backpack, he noted the rest of the family. "After you," he muttered. Then he waited for them to board.

"We'll see you after the game," Julia said as she climbed the bus steps, with Yossi and Miriam ahead of her.

"The back is empty. I call it!" Yossi yelled as he charged to the rear.

"I called it first," said Miriam.

"No, you didn't!"

"Yes, I did. I whispered it."

"Will the two of you stop it? You're embarrassing me," Julia said as she waited for Jacob to lift Sarah up the steps.

Sarah tugged Jacob's hand and said in her tiny voice. "I'm going to go to the back of the bus, and I'm going to wave to you."

Jacob bent down so she could hear him over the noise of the boulevard. "Okay. I'll wave back."

"Until you can't see me anymore?" she said softly.

"Until you disappear," he replied, kissing the top of her head.

With Jacob's help, Sarah boarded the bus and took her mother's hand, followed by the man with the Batman backpack. The doors closed. Jacob stood on the sidewalk and watched his family work their way back on the bus as it pulled away from the stop. He was immediately relieved that he had some time to himself to watch the game. The cacophony of three children was relentless. He saw Julia, Miriam, and Yossi take their seats in the back row. Sarah climbed on her mother's lap, pressed her face against the window, and waved to her father. They fixed on each other as Jacob waved back. Jacob continued to wave as the bus maneuvered into the busy intersection.

And then—the unthinkable.

An ear-piercing blast assaulted him. The bus exploded, igniting in a ball of flame.

Wounded pedestrians covered their faces and recoiled with terror. Drivers of nearby vehicles got out of their cars, examining themselves for damage. Everywhere was evidence of fire, shrapnel, and bloody body parts. The air smelled of charred flesh and burnt rubber. The bus was a smoldering skeleton. Complete annihilation.

Jacob's face was a mixture of horror and disbelief. He opened his mouth to scream, but no sound came out. Nobody on that bus could have survived. He fell to his knees. He did not hear the high-pitched sirens of the ambulances and police cars or the cries

of the wounded witnesses.
Jacob's world went silent.

CHAPTER 5

Rosie wasn't surprised by the message on her cellphone from the after-school daycare. Robert hadn't arrived to pick up Langston—again. Rosie felt a hot flush, not sure if it was the weather or her anger. Birmingham was miserable in the summer. She cranked up the air conditioning in her ten-year-old Toyota. Between the 95-degree temperature outside and the aggravation from dealing with her ex-husband, she thought she'd go mad.

Rosie lost count of the times she had driven across town to pick up her sad-faced little boy. There he stood, lunch box in hand, impatient teacher's aide by his side, relieved to see her but disappointed that his dad hadn't been in her place. Rosie often wondered how she could have chosen Robert to father her son. She remembered reading in some banal fashion magazine that a woman in her twenties subliminally chooses a man for his genes and his parenting potential. Robert's genes had proved an excellent choice: Langston was good-looking and bright. Robert's parenting, however, left much to be desired. He meant well, but he always put himself first. How could her judgment have been so off?

Two years after their divorce, Rosie was feeling overwhelmed. Being a single mother was hard work. She was always on the run, dragging stacks of papers to grade to Langston's T-ball practices. Her mood cycled from angry to despondent. Robert's failed promises to Langston didn't ease her burden. Langston's relationship with his father—or lack thereof—was making her son a guarded little boy.

Rosie yearned for a simpler life, a place where Langston could grow up with time to roam and discover the world for himself— as she had in her childhood. So she'd decided to move back home. Her late parents' old house wasn't a palace, but it was paid for, and Uncle Mo could help her raise Langston. There was plenty of time for her son to have a city in his life. She felt that he needed the safety and familiarity of a small town.

<hr>

Rosie had told herself that she was moving for Langston, but she knew she was doing it for her own sanity as well. She'd moved back to Brent so she could remember who she was before she'd ever met Robert. The decade in Birmingham had depleted her reserves, both financial and emotional. Enough of Birmingham, its traffic, its strip centers and shopping malls, enough of the rushing and fast food for dinner. She had yearned for the quiet of Brent, where she could spend a Saturday on the porch with a book, or sing in the church choir, or bake a pie.

She was young and vital. She wasn't defeated—she just needed a change.

That's what she kept telling herself as she sat in the teachers' lounge between classes. Rosie found her new job at Brent High challenging. Most of her students came from undereducated families who worked all day and let the television blare all night. The parents were so consumed by daily survival that they couldn't monitor their children's development. Rosie had to reduce her expectations, but she was more determined than ever to reach these kids.

In Birmingham, Rosie had been the hip teacher—the one who heard the girls' confessions of first loves or heartbreaks, the one whose classroom was always open during lunch. She demanded a lot from her English students—novels by Jane Austen and Ralph Ellison, poems by Emily Dickinson and her favorite, Langston Hughes. Rosie was a kind but diligent taskmaster. She knew that most students rose to the expectations of their teachers. The zone for real learning existed in the balance between demanding excellence and understanding limitations.

Or at least that's the way it had been in Birmingham. Rosie wasn't confident in this new environment. She made a point to keep to herself in the teachers' room during nutrition and lunch, purposefully placing stacks of student assignments in front of her to stifle other teachers' attempts at conversation.

Most of the teachers seemed settled into mediocrity. If the district was going to crowd forty-plus students in a classroom and not pay teachers adequately, then they'd do the bare minimum to keep their jobs—and they weren't ashamed to admit it. Afraid that their apathy would infect her, Rosie kept her distance.

Sometime in the second week of school, she noticed a fellow teacher in his forties. His head was buzzed to the skin, the badge of a man who was losing his hair and claimed it. He was broad shouldered, and even though he was lean, his shorter than average stature and wide shoulders made him look stocky. His pale green eyes indicated a mixed-race heritage. His face was open, intelligent, and kind. He, too, kept to himself, grading math tests and listening to music on his phone. It didn't take much snooping to find out that his name was Edmond Scott, and that he was also a recent arrival to Brent High. They smiled politely at each other when they met at the coffee pot, and Rosie noticed he wasn't wearing a wedding band. She wondered if he was divorced, or never married, or if he just didn't like jewelry. That she was thinking about the marital status of a man, any man, caught her off guard.

Rosie waved at Kala Patel, the school counselor, when she entered the teachers' lounge. Although Rosie had been working at Brent High for only a short time, she already felt a connection to the diminutive, coffee-colored spitfire. Kala represented all the good that Rosie saw in America, a fascinating amalgamation of cultures and backgrounds.

Kala was married to Dr. Patel, the town pediatrician. He'd been assigned as a resident to a large hospital in Birmingham, and when a practice became available in Brent, he bought it and set up shop. The locals were wary at first, but now Aadit Patel was simply called Doc. From the moment Rosie met Kala, she identified her as a potential friend. Rosie delighted in Kala's willingness to explain Hinduism, her humorous stories of her family in India, and her knowledge of an exotic world wildly different from Alabama. Kala headed over to talk to Rosie.

Edmond gathered his papers, put his phone away, and approached Rosie. Kala, noticing his intent, veered away, leaving him room to make a move.

Edmond stood in front of Rosie's table. "Don't I know you from church?"

"First Baptist?"

"Right. You're in the choir."

"Yes. I sing soprano."

"You know, I'm a baritone. Pretty good too."

Rosie sensed that he was waiting for an invitation. "We always welcome another voice in praise. Tuesday evenings, seven o'clock."

Rosie wanted to sink into the ground. She sounded like some old auntie: "another voice in praise." What was she doing?

There was an uncomfortable silence. Rosie straightened the piles of papers in front of her.

Edmond shifted his weight from one foot to the other and continued, "So...do you like teaching English?"

"I love teaching English. The problem is reading all these assignments. I want my students to write so they'll improve. But I can never keep up with all the grading."

"That's the beauty of mathematics. It's either right or wrong."

Rosie rushed to fill the air between them. "And there's lesson plans and rereading the texts and..." Her voice trailed off, implying a never-ending to-do list.

Edmond smiled. "Almost forgot what I was doing. Coffee."

He poured and took a sip. "This may be the worst cup of coffee I've ever had."

Rosie kept her head down and continued to fuss with her papers. He spoke quickly, "You know, we're close to last bell. I think I'll grab a cup at the bakery on the corner. Might get a doughnut while I'm at it. Would you like to join me?"

Rosie looked up, connecting with Kala, who stood nearby pretending to make a cup of tea. Kala flashed her a thumbs-up.

Rosie fidgeted, unsure how to respond. She didn't want to appear eager, but she didn't want to discourage him either.

"Thank you, but I've got to get home. My son...I have a son." She fumbled as she went back to her essays.

After a long, uncomfortable moment, Edmond asked, "And a husband?"

Rosie kept her attention on her papers. "No. No husband."

"Well then, maybe another day?"

"That would be nice." She smiled. The bell rang and the madness of a school day's end filled the hallway. She put on her cardigan and threw her purse over her shoulder. Edmond held the door open for her.

Rosie was embarrassed. What was wrong with her? Had she forgotten how to flirt?

<hr />

When Rosie got home from school, Langston was busy digging for worms in the front yard. The door was open, and she could see Mo puttering around the kitchen.

Langston looked up. "Uncle Mo said he'd take me fishing,

just like he used to take you."

Rosie had always drawn on her childhood memories as bedtime stories for Langston. He loved the tales about Nosy Rosie. Uncle Mo had been the first one to call her that. As a child she had always wanted to know why something happened, or what the people said, or where everyone was going. Her questions had been so persistent that Mo had made up a series of bedtime stories that he called "Nosy Rosie." They were long, meandering yarns about a girl detective and her bumbling sleuthing abilities. Each story ended with Nosy Rosie getting herself in a fix and having to be rescued by her "there-in-the-nick-of-time" uncle.

Langston loved the true stories best. He particularly loved to hear the account of his mother digging up worms for bait the first time she went fishing with Uncle Mo. Tunneling through the sandy soil, she'd searched for the right worm; the engorged ones were perfect. She'd put each harvested worm, still alive, in an old coffee can filled with dirt and guarded that can on her lap. As Uncle Mo drove over rough roads to his favorite fishing spot by the Cahaba River, she'd lifted the lid to check on her squirming hostages. Each time she'd get a whiff of the fresh dirt and count the worms to make sure none had escaped their Maxwell House prison. By the end of the ride, they were no longer anonymous worms but named and cooed-over pets. The only problem with this idyllic expedition was that Rosie couldn't stand to thread her new friends on the hook. It was more than unfair—it was cruel. That was when Uncle Mo had taught her the expression "a means to an end."

He'd deftly threaded the condemned worm as he explained, "If you're hungry, you want to catch a fish to eat, don't you? How you fixin' to do that if you don't use a wigglin' worm?"

Rosie had tried to slide the worm onto the hook. Impossible. All she did was prick her finger. This whole fishing thing didn't make sense to her. Why did she have to sacrifice one life for another? Without a second thought, she'd dumped the whole can out in the mud and watched each of her potential worm victims break free and burrow back into the earth. Mo had stood next to her sucking his back tooth.

When the last night crawler had disappeared he'd put his hand on her shoulder and announced: " I don't know about you, but I'm starving."

Rosie nodded her head. She was famished. Mo rummaged through his fishing bag. "How about some peanut butter and jelly sandwiches? That's also a means to an end."

They ate the sandwiches in silence and watched the sun shimmer on the river. That memory meant a lot to her. Rosie loved her Uncle Mo.

As she watched Langston hunt for worms, she realized that the story must have stuck with him, too. He'd been digging for some time, and still no success. Instead, he found a perfectly smooth slate rock, about the size of his thumb. He washed the rock with the hose and dried it on his shirt. The slate was black and shiny, with veins of white.

"This is gonna be my lucky rock," he announced as Mo joined them in the front yard.

"Don't see why not," Mo replied.

"Can we go now, Uncle Mo?"

Mo mopped his brow with a well-worn handkerchief. "It's too damn hot. Fish don't bite when the weather's like this."

Langston piped up. "Damn is a bad word."

Rosie hid her amusement. She must be doing something right.

"I promise we'll go on Saturday, real early." Mo crossed his heart.

"I think we all need a break from this heat. Let's get some dinner," Rosie said. "Leave everything where it is."

Langston and Mo followed her to the car. Minutes later, they turned into the parking lot of the McDonald's on the interstate. Langston wiggled with anticipation.

"I thought you don't like these places," Mo questioned. "I recall 'no fast food' as one of your highfalutin child-rearing rules."

"Yeah, well I break that rule too often," Rosie said with a sigh as they got in line.

They approached the counter, and Rosie waited for her son to place his order. Langston stared at the young man working behind the counter. The boy had the worst case of acne that Rosie had ever seen—giant, angry blemishes covered his face and neck. She recognized him as the sulky, quiet boy who sat in the back row of her World Literature class.

"Hansom—it is Hansom, right?" she asked tentatively. The boy nodded. "Nice to see you working."

The boy mumbled an embarrassed "Hello, Mrs. Yarber" and then looked down. Langston was tongue-tied, gaping at the boy's disfigured face.

"Langston, place your order," Rosie said in her schoolteacher voice.

Mo admonished Langston under his breath. "Stop staring."

They got their food and brought their trays to a table.

"What's wrong with him?" Langston asked.

"It's acne. It happens to some people when they're teenagers," Rosie said.

"Will I get it?"

"It goes away," Mo chimed in. "Eventually."

Rosie could see that Langston was anxious, stealing glimpses of the boy behind the counter. "No, you won't get it. Eat your fries."

CHAPTER 6

Hava had a pounding headache. Even the act of walking made her brain bang around in her skull. She needed a cup of coffee, but the thought of it made her queasy. The past twenty-four hours were a blur. Yesterday she was a defined entity, a grandmother and mother-in-law. Today, a pitiful afterthought. Jacob had to be her only concern. She was his mother and once-removed from the horror. Her job was to be strong for her son, no matter the open wounds she had herself sustained.

By the second day of *shiva,* the Jewish mourning period of seven days following the death of a loved one, the living room of Hava's Brooklyn apartment had been transformed. Furniture was moved to one side and replaced by low stools and cushions for the mourners and guests. This was an outward sign of being struck down by grief, humbled by pain and the finality of death. The gilded mirror that hung over the dining room table was covered with a sheet, a custom designed to discourage vanity and encourage inner reflection during the first week of intense sorrow.

Guests entered the apartment without knocking, the unlocked door another sign of mourning—so that the grieving family was not disturbed. Most callers brought food: a bag from the bakery, a casserole, a pot of soup. Feeding the grieving family was a community obligation. The women organized meals and made sure the family wanted for nothing during *shiva.* They came together to nourish the family and to acknowledge that life can and will go on.

Jacob sat on a low stool. He had not changed clothes since the funeral—his jacket was torn at the lapel as a physical representation of his grief. He was disheveled, his beard uncombed, with dark circles under his bewildered eyes. As the relatives and friends came in, they approached him to shake hands or offer a hug, but Jacob could not respond. When he was out of earshot, they whispered among themselves.

"I came to show respect, but frankly I'm terrified to leave my own house. I'm afraid of everything."

"And who isn't?" murmured another voice. "I won't let my kids ride the bus."

A group of men picked up the conversation. "In Israel, things explode all the time—not only buses but cafés and markets—and everybody goes about their business."

"This is Brooklyn, not Tel Aviv," said Rabbi Weiss. He was in his fifties, tall and thin. His salt-and-pepper beard reached past his neck.

"They *want* to make you afraid. That's the whole point."

"It will pass. I never thought we'd go back to normal after 9/11, but we did."

"What good does that do Jacob?" That voice belonged to David.

David and Jacob had been friends since they were boys. They had always been such an odd pair—where Jacob was tall and good-looking, David was doughy and plain. The families' friendship had even extended to the next generation, with Yossi and Jonathan, David's youngest, in the same class at the yeshiva. Hava could tell by his solemn face that David felt the loss of Julia and the children acutely. How would he explain Yossi's death to his own child? How could he promise to keep the midnight monsters at bay if Jacob hadn't protected his own son? Jacob's tragedy rendered them all vulnerable.

David continued speaking quietly, afraid that Jacob would hear him. "He just sits. Doesn't talk. Doesn't move. I don't know what to do."

"There's nothing you can do," said Rabbi Weiss. "Stay near him. I don't want him to do anything foolish."

Many people talked to Jacob, but he appeared not to follow the conversations, as if he couldn't make sense of the words. When a few of his students arrived, he looked at them without any sign of recognition. He was simply blank, stunned to his core, so deeply submerged in loss and grief that the outside world no longer existed.

Hava was aware that Julia's parents, Barbara and Steve, were huddling in a corner. Propriety dictated that she stand with them, but each time she approached she could hear Barbara reliving the moment she found out about her daughter's death to whomever was offering condolences. Then Steve would counter by launching into a story about Julia's resourcefulness. Each time, the same nonsensical story with no deviation, as if they were working from a memorized script.

"After college, Julia lived with friends in a fifth-floor walkup in the East Village," Steve would say. "Barbara thought the apartment was a hellhole, but the girls were delighted to be on their own and playing house." At this point, Barbara would smile, and he'd continue, "The tiny living room was barely wide enough to accommodate the faded orange corduroy loveseat they'd rescued from Goodwill. The plates and kitchen supplies were leftovers from recently departed grandparents, and their stemware was a mismatched assortment of drinking glasses and old jelly jars."

Hava had no patience left. She wanted to scream. "Tell them something else about your daughter. What of her essence, her soul?"

The relentless headache was making her unkind. Naomi,

Jacob's very pregnant sister, offered her mother a plate of food. Hava declined. She could feel the bile rising in her throat. She nodded toward Jacob.

"See if your brother will eat something."

Naomi, dutiful, maneuvered through the crowded apartment toward her brother, squeezing her belly between a dozen or so of the guests.

She passed by Rabbi Weiss. "Excuse me, Rabbi. Jacob needs to eat something."

"Let me have that," the Rabbi said, taking the plate from her hands.

Rabbi Weiss approached Jacob and handed him the food. Jacob put the plate down on the floor and looked away.

The rabbi leaned in. "I know what you're thinking. You want to know why this happened. I have no answers. But tragic events—like this—belong to a higher divine order that we cannot comprehend."

Weiss placed his hand on Jacob's shoulder. "As you mourn, you need to remember that to God, there are no arbitrary happenings."

He offered his hand to help Jacob stand. "Come, Ya'akov, it is time to pray."

Daily prayers were conducted in the home of the bereaved family so they wouldn't have to go out in public during *shiva*. The guests naturally segregated themselves, the women moving toward the kitchen, the men on the other side of the room. Even outside the synagogue setting, Orthodox Jews pray separately. Julia's parents reluctantly followed orders, splitting up because they were too worn down by their grief to object. Barbara stood on Hava's left and Naomi on her right. Without prompting, Barbara and Hava reached for each other's hand.

The men prayed, their eyes closed, their bodies bobbing and swaying, as they mumbled the ancient words of Hebrew text.

Julia's father opened a prayer book and tried to follow along. Hava noticed his unease. Most likely, Steve hadn't held a prayer book since his own bar mitzvah.

Jacob could not go through the motions of prayer. The rabbi's words echoed in his mind. Even in his dazed state, he was deeply offended by the rabbi's reasoning: God had sanctioned his family's death? His beautiful wife, his innocent children—all part of some "divine plan"?

He couldn't concentrate. The last time his family sat *shiva* was when his father died. Jacob had been absent. Now he was confused. Was he mourning his wife and children? His father? All of them?

His strongest memories of his father were the contentious Friday-night discussions. After Shabbat dinner, his father would propose a topic for the week. Usually the discussion was based on that particular week's chapter from the Old Testament. Every Friday-night meal ended the same way. His father would settle in with a cup of tea and begin the weekly debate on an ethical dilemma. Using his finger as a flesh-and-bone exclamation point, he'd stab at the air and offer his opinion. Jacob would have loved engaging in philosophical gymnastics, but his father was a bully. If you didn't agree with his way of thinking, then you were wrong. Not different, not insightful—wrong.

One week, the discussion was about the *mehitza*, the wall that divided the men's and women's sections in the synagogue. The partition, present in Orthodox synagogues for centuries, had been constructed so that women would not distract the men from prayer. In some synagogues, women were relegated to a balcony; in others, they sat behind a wall at the back of the sanctuary. In Jacob's synagogue, a five-foot latticed wall divided the room. The younger women had requested that it be lowered by eight inches so that they could participate more in the service. They knew that the *mehitza* kept them isolated, gossiping, and chasing children, when they wished for spiritual equality. Jacob thought lowering the partition was a reasonable request

His father balked. Any modification was heretical. "Unacceptable! Feminist nonsense! The outside world will change, but our laws protect us. God ordained it this way."

Jacob argued, "Women have equal rights in the rest of the Western world. If we don't modernize our traditions, we'll alienate women."

Again, his father scoffed. "Soon these women will be asking to study the Torah with men. We cannot bend to the cultural winds of the day. Impossible!"

Jacob kept his cool. "We're strong enough to pray together without compromising our core values. We must allow women to participate..."

"Nonsense!" his father bellowed.

Jacob tried another tactic. "How are we different from fundamentalist Muslims who keep their women in burkas? They don't allow women to pray with the men at the mosque."

Aaron Fisher slammed his hand on the table. "Enough! How dare you compare us to Arabs! Your views are idiotic and destructive."

Jacob gestured to his mother and sister. "Why don't you ask *them* how they feel? They're not invisible."

When Jacob saw his mother and sister exchange looks, he knew that they'd chosen not to rock the boat.

"Jewish men and women have prayed separately for more than three thousand years. I don't see why we need to change now," Aaron declared.

The women got up to clear the table. They knew where the discussion was going. Aaron would berate Jacob until he either backed off or quieted down. The warmth of the Shabbat table would plunge to icy hostility as father and son locked horns.

His mother had opposed his father in many ways, but years

after his death, when she spoke of him, he was the perfect man, the most loving of husbands, the most gentle of fathers.

Suddenly Jacob couldn't breath. The reality of *shiva* was extracting the life from him. He stood and went to the bathroom. Although David followed discreetly, Jacob ignored him and closed the door.

His legs wouldn't hold him. He leaned against the bathroom door. Julia was dead. *Julia was dead and the children never existed.* All of them were figments of his imagination. Even he was a fabrication. Nothing was real. It couldn't be.

The bathroom had two doors: one to the hallway and one to the bedroom. Driven by some unseen force, Jacob quietly exited to the bedroom. From the bedroom window, he looked at the city below. Jacob opened the window. All those hovering people in the living room suffocated him. They meant well, but he couldn't stand the chattering and was nauseated by the smell of all the food. He gulped the air from the open window, but it wasn't enough. Taking only some cash and leaving his wallet and phone behind, he stepped through the window onto the external fire escape. There were only four flights to the street, where he could breathe.

With a mix of remorse and reprieve, Jacob noticed that the early evening air felt good on his skin. Inside, a grieving house was stultifying. He told himself that all he wanted was a moment alone, but the brutal truth surfaced immediately. Jacob needed to get high. It had been years since he'd gotten clean, but that didn't matter now. Obliteration was the surest way out of pain.

Inside the apartment, David rapped softly on the bathroom door, "Jacob, you all right?"

When there was no response, he knocked more insistently. "Ya'akov?"

He jiggled the doorknob. The bathroom door was unlocked, and he cautiously entered; Jacob was nowhere in sight. He went into the bedroom—maybe Jacob was resting. But the room stood empty, the window fully open, and Jacob's cellphone and wallet lay on the dresser. David looked out the fire escape to the street below. No one was there.

David returned to the living room as the prayer service broke up. He approached Rabbi Weiss and whispered in his ear. They pulled Hava aside.

"Gone?" she said with an edge of hysteria in her voice, "Where could he go?"

"Maybe he went for a walk. He'll be back," the rabbi said reassuringly, sensing Hava's fragility.

Her brave face collapsed.

Naomi came to her side. "Don't worry, Mommy. Jacob needed to be by himself for a while. He probably went to get some fresh air. He'll come back soon."

David prayed she was right.

Within minutes Jacob found himself at the crosswalk where he'd last seen Trench McGinnis. Although he'd tried to mind his own business that day, he'd seen when Trench disappeared into the apartment building next to the cleaners. Maybe he lived there. Maybe he could score off him.

The front door opened to a tiny vestibule with a buzzer security system.

There it was—McGinnis—in a hand scratched add-on next to 309. He pressed the buzzer and waited. No answer. Trench wasn't home, and the possibility of throwing away years of sobriety held its breath. He pressed the buzzer again, this time for an insistent ten seconds. The building's front door swung open as a young woman, laden with groceries, made her way into the vestibule and juggled bags to get her keys.

"Oh don't bother," she said in a heavy Brooklyn accent. "That intercom doesn't work. I'll let you in. Bang on the apartment door." She turned her key in the lock and Jacob held the door for her, grateful for access.

Each step of the three flights, Jacob silently repeated *turn around*. But he never did. Getting wasted felt inevitable. He stood in front of apartment 309 and knocked on the door. He could tell that someone was appraising him through the peephole.

Within seconds, the door whooshed open. "Holy shit motherfucker." Trench bear-hugged him in a cloud of yesterday's garlic and stale cigarettes.

Jacob stood rigidly, his arms at his side.

"How the hell have you been?"

After a strained silence, Jacob replied with a staccato, robotic summary: "Clean, wife, three kids. They all died in that bus explosion the other day."

Trench started to laugh. "Man, you always had a weird sense of humor."

His laugh dangled in the air half-formed. Trench watched Jacob rub his sweaty palms on his pants. He was telling the truth.

"Jesus...I'm so sorry, dude. Come on in. Get out of the fuckin' hallway."

Jacob stayed rooted. Trench gently guided him inside the apartment and closed the door.

Jacob's lower lip twitched before he spoke. "It's bad, Trench, I need to get high. Can you help me?"

Jacob wasn't sure what he expected Trench to do—fill a bowl, whip out a needle, pop open a cap of oxy, but whatever form it took, he wanted the relief.

"I got nothin' that'll help you."

Jacob stared at him, and then begged. "Please."

"I've been clean for four years. Besides, with everything that happened, you don't want to do that."

Jacob could feel vitriol surge from the bottom of his feet. Trench owed him a fix. If Trench hadn't saved him, he wouldn't have gone to rehab, wouldn't have returned to his community, wouldn't have met Julia or fathered his children. If Trench hadn't made that phone call, Jacob wouldn't be alive. He wouldn't be condemned to this agonizing reality.

Trench crossed the room to his small kitchen and opened up the mini-refrigerator. "I got a ginger ale, and I can make you a turkey sandwich."

"Fuck you, Trench. Fuck you." Jacob spit out through tightly pulled lips. He walked out the door. If Trench wasn't going to help him, he knew where he could get what he needed.

Trench's voice faded in the background. "Jake, bro, you don't want to do this."

CHAPTER 7

After school that day, Rosie sipped a restorative cup of tea and ruminated about her day. Hansom, the boy from McDonald's, the one with the terrible acne, was in her last class. She made a point of approaching him during discussions, but he didn't engage. When she greeted him by name during lunch or passing period, he pretended not to see her. His body language told her that he was anxious, maybe even depressed. She made a mental note to talk to Kala.

She gazed out her kitchen window at the street and the church beyond. The houses looked worn and poorly kept: weedy yards, junked cars, cracked driveways. Rosie felt self-doubt rising in her chest. Is this why she left Birmingham? Only Mo's house and the church across the street still had green lawns.

A few children a little older than Langston were outside tossing a football. Another was riding his bike up and down the block. They'd now been in Brent for months, and Langston had yet to find friends in the neighborhood.

"Why don't you go across the street and play? Those boys are about your age," Rosie suggested.

Langston glanced out the window and sized up the prospects. He shrugged off her advice. "I don't want to."

Rosie didn't give up. "You walk over there and stick out your hand and say, 'My name is Langston, what's yours?' You remember how to shake hands the way we practiced? Firm grip, look people in the eye, and say your name."

"Kids don't shake hands, Mom. And the big kid on the bike looks mean."

Uncle Mo came over to see what Langston was talking about. "He's not mean. That's Tyler. He's got a cat named Bouncer, a fat old thing who used to come over here all the time—uninvited, I might add."

Langston lit up.

"When Bouncer spies me on the porch, he strolls over, kinda sideways and a little zigzag, like he's tryin' to pretend that he's not on his way. Then when he gets here he wraps himself around my legs until I scratch him behind the ear—has to be his left ear. That cat has me trained, I tell you." Mo winked at Rosie.

Rosie heard herself sigh in relief.

"Why don't we go sit on the porch and see what happens?" he continued. Langston was out the door before Mo could take one step.

Rosie could hear Mo's booming voice as he followed the boy outside, "Hey there, Tyler. I want you to meet my nephew. Is your cat around?"

Uncle Mo was a better father than Langston's own father could ever be, Rosie reflected sadly. She hadn't imagined her life going so wrong when she married Robert. He had been a pre-law student and president of Alpha Phi Alpha at Morehouse College. Robert was the magnetic center of a cluster of cool guys. He was a natural leader with a mischievous sense of humor and a generous wallet.

Rosie spent her undergraduate years at Spelman, a historically Black women's college. She was quiet, content with a few close girlfriends and her books. Rosie was the one classmates turned to for lecture notes. Her color-coordinated loose-leaf binder, perfectly organized and totally complete, had proved many a friend's savior during finals.

All the girls in her sorority had a crush on Robert. So when he began lavishing attention on Rosie, she was flattered and willing. For the first time in her life she knew what it felt like to be attracted to someone. She couldn't wait to be alone with Robert. She took pleasure in their drawn out, nothing-to-do-today lovemaking.

Rosie took Robert home to meet her Uncle Mo in Brent. Since her mother died, Mo had been living in her parents' house across the street from the church where Rosie's late father had been pastor for twenty-seven years. Although Robert was a city boy, he knew how to crank up the down-home charm. He complimented Mo's cooking and dutifully lost to him in chess.

Mo pulled Rosie aside as they were leaving, making sure Robert was out of earshot. "Robert is a great guy, honey, but be careful. He's a tomcat."

Mo's opposition was all Rosie needed to cement her feelings. Couldn't Mo see the truth? Robert read like a philanderer because he was a sexual person. Even though she adored Uncle Mo, Rosie rejected his tomcat warning as self-interest. She knew Mo wanted her to come back to Brent after graduation, and being married to Robert would make that unlikely.

By senior year, Rosie and Robert were spending all their free time together. Robert was president of his fraternity, and Rosie was treated like royalty. Rosie graduated summa cum laude with a double major in English and education. Robert squeaked through a pre-law major. Somehow, between studying for exams and attending fraternity events, Robert proposed.

Robert reluctantly agreed to a wedding in Brent. He would have preferred something upscale, an elegant hotel reception. But Rosie insisted on a small wedding at First Baptist. She wanted to honor tradition, right down to jumping the broom, a custom of African origin that was created during slavery. Because slaves could not legally marry, they created their own rituals to honor their unions. Jumping the broom legitimized marriage and the coming together of two families.

Uncle Mo gave the bride away. Rosie and Robert held hands and laughed as they jumped. They looked like the model of success—stylishly dressed, well educated, and filled with love and potential. The church ladies had clucked and cooked for weeks. The spread in the social hall reception was relaxed and sophisticated all at the same time.

The young couple found a spacious apartment in a modern building in Birmingham and set up house. Rosie began teaching at one of the finest high schools in a diverse suburb. The principal recognized a gem when he saw one—a highly qualified, dedicated young teacher was a feather in his cap. Robert worked part-time while he applied to law schools.

Robert struggled through law school. He was a slow reader, and the professors' expectations for several hundred pages a week overwhelmed him. He became short-tempered and withdrawn. Rosie thought that when he finished school, he'd return to his old self. But Robert, who'd always loved to party, began to drink more. He came home late, alcohol on his breath. She never knew which Robert would appear—the sensitive, fun-loving guy she fell in love with or this bitter, belligerent drunk. Soon enough, the bad days overshadowed the good.

Rosie stared out the window. She saw nothing but her past. Mo came into the kitchen, interrupting her thoughts.

"Trees have grown wild since the last time you were here, especially the ones next to the church. Trying my damnedest to keep 'em trimmed. Not enough time to do it all."

"First Baptist looks great," Rosie offered. "I know how hard you work."

Rosie took a long, hard look at Mo and acknowledged the signs of his nearly seventy years. His gray hair had become sparse and unruly. He moved deliberately, seeming to calculate the amount of energy required for each step or task.

"If you want the house to yourself, Rosie, it's yours. I can move back to the church basement."

"No, Uncle Mo, this is your house. Besides, Langston needs to have a cranky old man in his life. Makes things exciting."

Rosie took stock of the house. Other than a flat-screen television that she had brought, nothing had changed. Langston had taken over her childhood bedroom, pinning his superhero posters to the walls and finding a special place in the closet for his Legos.

The day of the move, Langston had asked, "Will Daddy know how to find us?"

Rosie was confounded. No matter how many times she explained the move, no matter how much love she gave her son, and no matter how many times his father had disappointed him, Langston still craved Robert's attention.

"Of course—he knows where we are," she assured. "You want to call him?"

Langston ignored her.

She remembered being in the house when she was a child, interrupting her father when he was composing a sermon, reading on her bed for hours. She had loved watching her mother apply cherry-red lipstick, check her image in the mirror, then fasten her broad-brimmed Sunday hat to cross the street for church. Just the other day, she caught herself looking at that same mirror.

During her marriage, Rosie hadn't joined a congregation. She'd forgotten how much she loved to be in church. Returning to First Baptist had renewed her spirituality.

On Tuesday nights, she crossed the street for choir rehearsal. As a girl, she'd joined her mother in the First Baptist Choir. In high school, she was a regular soloist. Since her return to Brent, she hadn't missed a rehearsal or a Sunday service. The rhythms, the lyrics, and the moving melodies all came back to her. The choir director, Mr. Day, was thrilled to have Rosie's voice and enthusiasm.

As promised, Edmond the math teacher showed up at rehearsal. He acknowledged her with momentary eye contact and a nod of his head. She took this as a sign of his interest, but she wasn't sure. He didn't look at her again, keeping his eyes on his sheet music or Mr. Day instead. She thought momentarily of inviting him over for coffee after rehearsal but changed her mind. She sent up a silent wish that Edmond would ask her for a date. That's all she wanted—a date.

CHAPTER 8

Jacob wandered Brooklyn, searching for the few street corners in Bensonhurst where heroin was sold years ago. Trench had taught him that only beginners score on the street. Jacob knew better, but he had no choice. He needed that mindless oblivion that comes in the first rush after shooting up. He needed escape from the unceasing pain.

As he walked, his anger was amplified by a memory of the last moments of his family's life. He tried to block the images, but fragments popped into his head like funhouse mannequins on a gruesome, repetitive loop. *Shut it out.*

He tried to bat away the pictures and concentrate on the streets, but the corners all looked the same. Had he been walking in circles? The images of his family overpowered his consciousness. *Shut it out.*

He saw Yossi put the basketball under his arm as he got on the bus. He pictured Julia reaching for Miriam's hand as they walked through the bus to the back row. *Shut it out.*

Sarah waved at him as the bus pulled out of the intersection. He watched the bus explode and vanish. *Shut it out.*

Wake up, damn it! Turn off the pain. Close down the feeling. Jacob squeezed his eyes shut, hard enough to blind his soul. Hard enough to narrow the pain, eliminate the memory, remove the injury. *Shut. It. Out.*

HIs thoughts had no language, only the combative and familiar war between getting high and staying clean. With a ferocious act of will, he released the craving for chemical deliverance. He would not get high but instead give birth to a new self, a blank self. He stopped in the middle of the sidewalk and held his breath. The longer he starved his lungs, the smaller the terrifying images became. He squeezed all memory out of his mind.

Keep walking. Jacob concentrated on his gait, on the rhythmic sound of his feet on the city streets. He walked into the night, across the Brooklyn Bridge. He walked through the vacant Financial District, past the new World Trade Center. The city was quiet at this hour. He turned on Broadway and walked through Greenwich Village, swarming with late-night bar hoppers and college students. His feet carried him farther, past the Flatiron District and the chic stores on Third Avenue. By now, it was early morning, and trucks lined up in front of the restaurants and markets with deliveries. But Jacob didn't notice any of the activity.

Finally, his feet led him into the vast concourse of Penn Station. He entered a restroom and approached a sink, staring at his face. He tugged at his skin, trying to get his vision to connect with his brain. No one recognizable looked back.

A filthy homeless man babbled to himself at the neighboring sink. "You crazy piece of shit. You think you can do that to me? I'll take a bomb and shove it up your ass. I'll blow you up from the inside, motherfucker."

Jacob froze in fear. For a split second, the word "bomb" penetrated his stupor. Over and over, he saw the last moments of his family: Yossi and Miriam clamoring for the backseat, Sarah waving from the window, the deafening blast.

The homeless man took a razor out of his shopping bag and squirted a handful of soap from the dispenser. He gave himself a sponge bath, unbuttoning his soiled shirt to wipe his armpits with a wet paper towel.

Jacob continued to stare at himself in the mirror. He touched his beard. He brought his face to within an inch of the mirror, as if the proximity would bring recognition. He was looking at a stranger.

The homeless man used his disposable razor to shave his stubble. Jacob stared at him, like a child watching his father's daily ritual. The man whistled as he cleaned up the remnants of soap and whiskers in the sink. Then he threw away his razor, gathered his belongings, and left.

Jacob retrieved the razor from the trash can. He removed his jacket, fringed undergarment, and skullcap and deliberately placed them in the trash. He pumped the soap dispenser, lathered his face, and began to shave. Shaving hurt. He had to pull hard on his skin to cut through the thicket on his face. The old razor left his face raw. The skin underneath the beard hadn't seen the light of day in twelve years. It looked almost translucent.

When Jacob left the restroom, he was a different man. His beardless face looked young and innocent. In his white shirt and dark pants, he blended easily with the crowd of travelers arriving in Penn Station. He bore little resemblance to the Orthodox cantor he'd been only hours before.

Jacob descended to the train platforms. Loudspeakers announced the arrival and departure of local and express trains. The PA system crackled, "The Crescent Line will be departing in ten minutes from Platform 19. Stops in New Jersey, Pennsylvania, Virginia, the Carolinas, Georgia, Alabama, Mississippi, and Louisiana."

Jacob boarded a train. He walked through the cars until he found an empty row. He was weary to the bone, nearly catatonic. As the train pulled out, the sound of the wheels on the track quickly lulled him into sleep—his first sleep in days.

The train moved out of the city and into the vast countryside. At the stop in Philadelphia, an elderly woman came down the aisle with a roller suitcase. She was about to sit down next to Jacob, but when he made whimpering noises in his sleep, she continued to the next row. He curled up in a ball like a child and slept deeply.

A conductor patrolled the car checking tickets. He nudged Jacob into wakefulness. "Ticket?"

Jacob didn't respond.

"Where you headin'?"

Jacob shrugged.

The conductor raised his voice as if the louder tone would penetrate this man's daze, "Where you goin'?"

Jacob still didn't respond.

"If you don't know where you're going, I have to charge you for the end of the line."

Jacob stared at him. The conductor's walkie-talkie squawked, "Anybody speak Spanish? I need help in car five."

The conductor unclipped the walkie-talkie from his belt, "*Hablo español.* I'll be right there."

As soon as the conductor stepped away, Jacob turned toward the window and fell asleep again. When the conductor returned, he was unable to wake him. Jacob slept through seven states.

Jacob awoke twenty-two hours later as the train pulled into Tuscaloosa, Alabama. He stumbled off the train, blinking at the bright sun. After all those hours in the air-conditioned train, he began to sweat heavily. The triple-digit temperature and the weighty blanket of humidity overpowered him. He gagged from the stink of a hot dog stand mingling with body odor and rancid perfume. There was no way he'd get back on that train.

He walked across the station to the Trailways bus stop, where a bus sat idling with the doors open. Jacob watched the driver get off the bus and head toward the station office. He used the opportunity to board the bus and take an empty seat.

Thirty-five miles later, Jacob got off in Brent, Alabama. Brent was once a proud and thriving Southern town that had serviced the surrounding agricultural community. Now it was struggling to hold its head up.

As he left the bus station, he walked through downtown and noticed that many of the businesses had been boarded up. The shuttered shops still revealed their faded names: Johnson Hardware, Stardust Cinema, and Beverly's Dress Shop. They had been replaced by the corporate entities he had passed on the interstate: Walmart, a multiplex movie theater, and Sears. Jacob kept walking, going through the affluent section of town, where magnolia trees lined the streets and houses sat back on graceful lawns.

Eventually, he entered the poor part of town. He wandered through a neighborhood made of former company houses—identical, boxy wooden two bedrooms, now dilapidated. He was dizzy from hunger and thirst. He stopped at the steps of an old clapboard church. He sat down, leaned against the building, and put his head back. Once again, he surrendered to a deep sleep.

CHAPTER 9

Rosie used her dishtowel to swat a fly buzzing its final death throe in the corner of her kitchen window. It was a blazing Alabama afternoon—Indian summer—the kind of day that made you think cool would never happen again. The sun heated the earth to the point where the temperature outside a body matched the one on the inside. Rosie splashed cold water on her face for the few minutes of relief that evaporation would grant. Through the window, she noticed a man curled up on the steps of the church. She could clearly see that he was white. Judging by his wrinkled clothes and stubble, he was a derelict of some kind. He looked to be sleeping. The sun was beating down on him, but he appeared unaware. Surely that man would blister.

The phone rang, intruding on her surveillance.

"Hello?"

"Yes, this is Rose Yarber, but I don't have an account at Bank of the South."

She sighed. She knew what was coming.

"I don't know where Robert Yarber is right now. We've been divorced for a long time."

Rosie cut the voice off. "Welcome to my world. He doesn't return my phone calls, and he owes me money, too." Exasperated, she slammed down the receiver.

"Not my drama," she said to herself. "Son of a bitch."

Rosie remembered when her marriage began to crumble. After Robert's admission of "meaningless infidelity," they had worked diligently on their relationship. He tried to engage with Langston when he was home and be more helpful with household chores. When Langston was in kindergarten and had a terrible bout with flu, Robert stayed home to care for him. As soon as Langston was well enough to go back to school, Rosie got sick. When she woke at three in the morning drenched in sweat, Robert was just coming in. He claimed he'd been at the office, but even in her delirious state, she knew something was very wrong.

The wrong came in the form of another woman. One of the partners in the firm, a woman eight years Robert's senior, had started to invite him for drinks after work. She was sexy in her high heels and Chanel suits. Having a mentor protected him from the other lawyers in the firm. His inefficiencies and lack of drive were safe from criticism as long as he hid behind a senior partner's metaphoric skirt. Robert didn't object to her six-figure income or her vacation home on the beach, either.

Not long after Langston's sixth birthday, Robert moved out. Rosie and Langston stayed in the apartment. Rosie did what she could to limit the damage of the separation, but Langston whined and clung and had difficulty falling asleep. She assured him of her love constantly. She planned weekend activities, made play dates for him, and, despite her own hurt, encouraged Robert's visits.

In their Sunday phone calls, Mo could hear his niece was in pain. He resisted the urge to lecture or berate, instead reminding her that staying busy was the best antidote to self-pity. Rosie threw herself into work. She became chair of the English department at her school. When Langston began playing T-ball, she became the team parent. Although there were men who'd expressed interest in her, men she met through mutual friends or at the gym, she used Langston as an excuse not to date.

Rosie was never one to whine. The months passed, and there

was no hope of reconciliation. They used a mediator for the divorce. He gave her primary custody, as long as he could stay in Langston's life. He'd pick up Langston from school one afternoon a week and spend a weekend with him once a month.

Soon enough, Robert and his new lover began to quarrel—at first over restaurant choices and golf dates, but eventually over Robert's spending habits and poor performance at work. Losing his job was inevitable, as was falling behind in child support, defaulting on his student loans, and maxing out his credit cards. He drank heavily, convincing himself that if he drank only when he went out, he was not an alcoholic. But there was always a reason to go out, like there was always an excuse for not spending the afternoon or the weekend with Langston. He often made promises to his son, promises as empty as his bank account.

Rosie distracted herself. She wiped down the kitchen counter even though it was spotless, opened the tap again, and filled a glass with water. As she drank, she once again focused on the man asleep on the church steps. The sun had moved off his face, so his body was partially in shadow.

Rosie double-bolted the front door. She'd never seen an unfamiliar drifter in this part of Brent. She'd seen locals who were crazy, drunk, or high, but not a stranger. She observed the man three more times that night, once again from the kitchen, once when she turned the TV off before she went upstairs, and once more from her bathroom window before she went to sleep. He was out cold. She would have thought him dead, but his body had rearranged itself ever so slightly between her check-ins.

The next morning, as Rosie rushed around the kitchen, Langston sat at the breakfast table, one leg tucked under him, the other swinging gently back and forth. He took leisurely spoonfuls of cornflakes.

"Mom, listen to this," he said, reading the back of the cereal box. "What building has the most stories?"

"I don't know. I give up."

"The library!" he said proudly.

"Good one," Rosie said, smiling. "That reminds me—did you pack your reading book?"

"Yeah."

Rosie shot him a stern look, and he instantly corrected himself. "Yes, ma'am."

She nodded approvingly, "What about lunch—take or buy?"

He returned to the cereal box and ignored his mother.

"Langston Yarber, do you hear me? I've got enough to do this morning without having to repeat myself."

"Buy." Instantly, Rosie felt tension in the air. She felt insulted whenever he gave curt answers. She believed that a fresh attitude was a sign of disrespect. He corrected the moment, softening his abruptness by offering more information. "We have corn dogs on Tuesday."

Rosie went to her wallet and took out a few bills. As Langston cleared his dishes, she tucked the money into his pocket. It was an excuse to get close to her son. He was a full-blown boy now, but he still made her melt like he did when he was a baby.

"Don't forget to turn in your homework."

"Yes, ma'am."

His response was satisfying. She believed in discipline and manners and children who respected authority.

"Uncle Mo will walk you to school. Now go brush your teeth."

Rosie headed to the back of the house and knocked on Mo's bedroom door. "Mo? I'm leaving."

There was no response.

"I have a faculty meeting this morning."

Still no response.

"Langston's ready."

Mo grumpily opened the door. She heard the television news in the background.

"Don't worry. I got it covered." Mo walked over to his TV and turned it off. "The world's on a short fuse and I gotta get a boy to school," he muttered as he made his way to the kitchen.

Rosie threw her school bag in the back of her car. She was about to start the engine when she saw the vagrant still lying on the church steps. She quickly got out of the car and walked back into the house.

Mo was pouring a cup of coffee as she entered. "Forget your keys again?"

"No. I wanted to tell you to watch out for that drunk on the church steps. He's been there since last night. Make him leave. He gives me the creeps."

Mo crossed to the window, assessed the man on the steps and took a thoughtful gulp of his coffee. "Yeah, I'll give him his walkin' papers...if he's alive."

Rosie looked out the door and across the street. "Well, he's moved around since I first saw him, so he's not dead."

Langston crossed to his mother's side to see what everyone was staring at.

"Mind your own business," Rosie said, turning him away from the window.

She shot Mo a do-something-about-this look and left for work.

Langston hefted his backpack on his shoulder and waited while Mo locked the front door. They passed the sleeping body on the church steps.

"What's wrong with him?" Langston asked.

"Looks like he's pretty damn tired," Mo answered as he took Langston's hand protectively.

———◆———

Rosie stood in front of the blackboard. It was last period, World Literature, her favorite class. Unlike her other classes, this one was an elective, so all the students actually wanted to be there. They even *liked* to read.

Although there was some bantering in the room, the students participated and stayed on topic. Rosie was animated. She challenged the kids to analyze their personal experience to fill in the chart she'd written on the board. She needed to excite them about the next reading selection.

Across the top of the blackboard was a heading: *CONFLICTS IN LITERATURE*. Underneath were subdivisions: *Man vs. Man, Man vs. Nature*.

She sat on the corner of her desk, "Come on, folks, what else have you been seeing in these short stories? Any ideas?"

The class was silent. Rosie pointed to the board.

"These are all *external* conflicts. Think, people." She again gave the class a moment. "Think about your own life. What's *your* biggest obstacle?"

A lanky boy from the back of the class responded. "I get in my own way."

Rosie slid off the desk and picked up the chalk. "Right!"

Janine, the heavyset girl in the front row, agreed. "Like feeling too lazy to work out even though I know it's good for me?"

A male voice threw out a biting insult. "Yeah, like you ever exercise."

Janine flushed bright red, and Rosie snapped her head in the general direction of the taunt. "Enough," she ordered. Then she stood next to Janine and acknowledged her by resting her hand lightly on her shoulder.

Rosie continued, "Some of our toughest moments in life are when we're in conflict with ourselves. Let's think of some other examples." As hands shot up across the room, Rosie turned and added to the board: *Man vs. Self.*

When the bell rang, Hansom, the acned boy who sat at the back of the class, waited for the others to leave before he approached Rosie's desk. He was small and slender, with fine bone structure and delicate eyebrows.

Alarming cystic blemishes disfigured his face. One angry flare-up sat in the middle of his forehead, making him look like some Cyclops. The spots on his cheeks and neck were red and inflamed. She pretended not to notice. He stood stiffly in front of the desk. Rosie waited for him to state his query.

He finally spoke, offering an uncomfortable smile. "I like this class, Miss Yarber."

"And I like having you in class."

"Here," Hansom said, reaching into his backpack for a small homemade wooden bird. "I made this for you."

Rosie was impressed by the detail and proportion. "It's lovely. I'm going to keep it on my desk."

She carefully placed the whittled bird on a stack of papers. "Thank you so much, Hansom."

Hansom lowered his head, embarrassed by the compliment, and walked away.

Rosie was moved by the gift. She knew from talking to Kala that his home life was loaded with trouble. His mother had abandoned him, and he lived with a grandmother who was too old and disabled to do a proper job of raising him. Adding insult to injury was that name—Hansom. He was an obvious target for adolescent bullying.

Reaching a kid like Hansom—befriending him, motivating him to read and write, taking him away from his beleaguered life—was utterly satisfying. Interactions like these reminded her why she loved teaching.

Janine, the girl from class, waited for Hansom by the door. She was one of the eight percent of the student body who was white. She and Hansom made the oddest pair: one slight and timid, one thick and bold. Hansom wore tight-fitting T-shirts and skinny jeans. Janine had heavy eyeliner, dressed only in somber colors, and wore her hair down to her shoulders on one side and shaved on the other. Rosie had seen mismatched pairs like this in every school. They had little in common, yet they stuck together. Hansom and Janine rebelled against the mainstream because they couldn't find a place in any of the social groupings. Rosie was glad that Hansom had at least one friend.

A commotion in the hallway changed Rosie's quiet musings to alarm. There was the sound of scuffling, and a female voice screamed a string of curse words. "Fuck-you-you-turd-piece-of-shit." The girl's voice went up an octave, "Your-mama's-a-whore- and-your-daddy's-a-dickwad."

Rosie opened her door to witness Janine shove the student who'd insulted her in class against the wall. Hansom covered his mouth to hide his delight at the kid's comeuppance, and the kid instantly turned the full force of his aggression on Hansom. The kid was enraged. He propelled himself off the wall and slammed his body into Hansom, knocking them both down. Then he stood up and started kicking Hansom's body anywhere he could. Hansom balled up and tried to cover his head, but the barrage kept coming. Janine tried to pull the attacker away. He punched hard into her soft middle, and the breath went out of her.

Rosie yelled "Stop!" as loudly as she could, but the aggressor was deaf with rage. Janine started to dry heave, and the attacker kept kicking Hansom. Magically, Edmond appeared. He lifted the kicker off his feet by the back of his neck and threw him five feet down the hallway. Rosie went to Janine while Edmond helped the terrified Hansom to his feet.

Edmond thundered at the kicker. "FRONT OFFICE... NOW!"

Before Edmond followed the aggressor down the hall, his eyes connected with Rosie. She momentarily wondered what it would be like to have Edmond's arms around her.

CHAPTER 10

Jacob, still lying on his back on the steps of the church, saw the cloudless sky, the sugar maples, the contours of the roof. He watched a few crows dart through the trees, their raucous cawing demanding attention. He understood what he saw—sky, trees, building, birds—all familiar even if he couldn't place them. But when he sat up to look around, he couldn't make sense of the whole. He had no idea where he was or how he got there. A nearby wooden sign read *First Baptist Church.*

An older African American man stepped into view. He was tall and gangly, like his arms and legs were too long for his body. What was left of his hair was gray, and his front teeth overlapped. The man offered Jacob a sandwich in a plastic bag and coffee in a ceramic mug. "Here. You look like you could use this."

Jacob gratefully accepted the offering. He didn't reply.

He knew he should say something to the man, but the words would not come. He nodded his head as he unwrapped the sandwich. Without examining the contents, he tore into the food. His empty stomach had been rumbling for hours, but he hadn't made the connection from belly to brain. He took huge bites, barely taking the time to chew between mouthfuls.

"Where you from?"

Jacob understood the question, looked at the man and shrugged. He took a slurp of the coffee and unexpectedly remembered drinking coffee with Julia. Her eyes crinkled as she laughed loudly at something or someone he couldn't see. Before he could examine the image, he pushed the thought of her from his mind.

"You need help? You have family in these parts?" The old man waited for his response.

Jacob silently finished the sandwich and looked down at the ground, embarrassed by his inability to answer.

"Listen, buddy, I don't know what your story is, but people will be wondering why you're hanging around here. You're going to have to move on," the man ordered.

Jacob didn't move.

"You speak English?"

Jacob did the best he could—he nodded.

"I take it your mama didn't teach you any manners," the man said. There was a long, uncomfortable moment of silence.

The man shooed him like a stray dog. "Move! You can't stay here. Go home."

Jacob rubbed his chin. The stubble was coarse, uncomfortable to the touch. His face was unfamiliar to him. He couldn't bring himself to speak. He didn't care about this man, he didn't care about this town, he didn't care about his own exhausted and reeking body. No emotion registered other than his loathing for being alive. He got up slowly and walked away from the church.

Mo watched the drifter move down the street. He was rumpled, greasy, uncombed, maybe not in his right mind. He didn't carry a suitcase or even a few plastic market bags. Usually the homeless cart their lives on their backs. And the man didn't smell like alcohol.

Mo took out his keys and unlocked the church doors. After forty-five years, he had his routine down pat. He made his way through the pews, picking up hymnals and pamphlets and stacking them at the entrance table. He did his second walk-through with a dust rag and furniture polish. Then he turned his attention to the pulpit and cleaned Pastor Johnson's lectern. He straightened up the choir's folding chairs and wiped down the organ.

In the social hall, he readied the coffee maker for choir practice, tucked in the chairs, and sponged down the tables. Through the small window he saw the homeless man asleep again, this time under a poplar in the parking lot. Mo shook his head and continued his routine. He'd make the guy move on when he finished.

He worked up a light sweat mopping the social hall and entry. Finally, he gathered the trash and went out to the dumpster in the parking lot. He loudly dumped the garbage. When that didn't rouse the sleeping man, he went over and kicked the man's foot. The drifter opened his eyes.

"Didn't I tell you to leave? Don't come back," Mo said gruffly as he pointed down the road, "or I'll have to call the police."

———◆———

Mo drove his ancient Ford Ranger toward the interstate, passing the American flag that flapped in the wind over Brent High School. He'd learned the protocol to raise, lower, and fold the flag when he was a Marine.

Serving in Vietnam had been the central event of his life. He was patriotic, and he'd believed in the Domino Theory. If the US didn't stop the Communists in Vietnam, they'd have continued to the Philippines and marched across the Pacific to Hawaii, and then onto the shores of California. Although Mo had had a job as a machinist lined up at the textile plant, he'd enlisted in the Marines right out of high school. His father had been in Europe during World War II, driving a fuel truck in and out of battle zones for Patton's tanks. Even though Black soldiers were often given the worst jobs, his father believed in the promise of the military: service, brotherhood, and honor above all.

Mo served his time in the military doing what he was told.

One day he'd be guarding a base, another day, he'd be on a helicopter going deep into the jungle. He endured daylong marches, watched villages burn to the ground, and saw barely adolescent girls sell their bodies for rations. His platoon would fight for a hill all day, spend two nights there, and then abandon the ground. Two or three months later, they'd fight for the same hill again.

Although he never openly disobeyed an order, he began to question the sanity of their mission in Vietnam. Watching his friends die or get maimed prompted deeper thoughts: about good and evil, man's cruelty, and God's role in the universe—if there was a God. He poured out his philosophical ramblings in long letters to his sister back in Brent. She responded by sending him a Bible. He read it from cover to cover, but he never found answers.

Whatever ambition Mo had had before the war, he lost in Vietnam. His sister had married the minister of First Baptist Church in Brent, and his new brother-in-law offered him the job of caretaker. It was a decent job that allowed him to live quietly in the basement of the church. In those first years back, he dreamt of choppers flying over his bed, coming to take him to a firefight. When demons from the war interfered with sleep, he kept reading his Bible.

As he passed the neighborhood park, he saw the figure of the man from the church steps curled in a fetal position on a bench.

"That man sure likes to sleep," he mumbled.

As he waited to pay at the Safeway, he double-checked his list and divided his purchases into two piles—one for home, one for the church. The overweight, middle-age cashier smiled broadly when she saw Mo in her line.

"Hey Maurice. How you doin' today?"

"Can't complain."

The yellow ribbon and American flag on her apron reminded Mo that the cashier's son was a Marine.

"How's your boy?"

"He'll be back from deployment in thirty-two days. Prayin' that he comes home safe."

"I'll put in a good word for him on Sunday."

On his way home, he made a point of driving past the park. The homeless man was no longer on the bench. To make sure he was gone, he drove around the perimeter of the park. No sign of him.

———✦———

After walking Langston to school the next day, Mo was standing at the kitchen sink, washing the breakfast dishes. He saw from the window that the drifter was back where he'd been when Rosie first spotted him—on the church steps. He wasn't sleeping, just sitting and staring into space.

"Like a damn lost dog," Mo said to himself.

He crossed the street and sat down next to the man. "You got nowhere to go?"

Although he looked troubled, the man held Mo's gaze. Mo figured a man who had problems with the law wouldn't look him directly in the eye. But he was still suspicious.

"You got a wallet? Some kinda ID?" Mo stood up, reached into his own pocket, pulled out his wallet, and pointed to his driver's license. "See here. My name is Maurice. But people call me Mo. You got somethin' like this?"

The drifter stood up, his eyes darting back and forth in fear. He simply shook his head.

Mo leaned toward him. "I'm not gonna hurt you now. I'm gonna touch your pockets to see if you got somethin' in there that's gonna tell me who you are."

Mo reached over to pat the drifter's pockets, and the man recoiled. Mo quickly pulled his hands back to neutral.

"Okay, buddy, you don't have to be afraid."

The man looked like an animal that had been abused,

cowering and afraid of the next blow. Mo felt bad for wanting to run him out of town.

"You don't seem dangerous to me, maybe down on your luck. And you smell pretty ripe. Could use some soap and water. Come with me." Mo walked toward the church entrance, but the man stayed rooted on the steps.

Mo turned. "Are you gonna stand there all day? Nothin' bad's gonna happen. We don't do that 'round here."

Mo led him into the church, down the basement steps, and into a small caretaker's room: a cot, a chair, a corner partition that screened a sink, shower, and toilet. The bed was tightly tucked, military style.

Mo kept up a steady banter. "I used to live here. When I came back from the war, I needed solitude. Couldn't handle any noise. Didn't much feel like working in the factory. My sister was married to the pastor, Rosie's father. He told me I could be the caretaker for the church and live here for as long as I needed. I stayed till I married Elsie. By then I was feeling more sociable." Mo smiled at the memory.

He'd met Elsie standing on line at the bank in Brent. They were both in their fifties. She was a kindergarten teacher and a widow with a grown son. Mo was lonely. They had ten wonderful years together, until cancer took her away. Mo kept in touch with her son, a history professor at some fancy university in Boston, but he hadn't seen him in years.

As Mo puttered around the room, pulling a fresh bar of soap and a clean towel from a box under the bed, he prattled on. "After Rosie's mother—that's my sister—passed, Rosie wanted me to live in the house. Keep it nice. Now that she's back in town, she wants help with the boy. I'm pretty good with kids. Never had any of my own."

Mo handed the drifter the toiletries. He mouthed his directions slowly, loudly, hoping that he'd be understood.

"You get yourself cleaned up, have a decent night's sleep. I'll get you something to eat. But tomorrow, you gotta move on. Go home."

The man nodded. He tried a smile, but his mouth did not cooperate. To Mo, it looked like his face was contorted in pain. The simplest form of courtesy—a smile—seemed toxic to this man's very being.

"You need anything else?"

The man stood silently.

"You can't stay here after tonight. This is only for one night," he repeated, holding up his finger.

As Mo closed the door of the caretaker's room, he wondered why the man didn't respond. He wasn't deaf—he reacted to commands. Perhaps he was mute.

Whatever the reason, Mo figured he was genuinely troubled.

CHAPTER 11

The next morning Mo was up before Rosie, preparing a large breakfast. Rosie came into the kitchen and poured herself a cup of coffee. Langston was engrossed in the back of his cereal box. Rosie wondered what new delight he could find in the back of the same cereal box day after day. He should have had it memorized by now, right down to the ingredients.

"I won't be home till nine. Back-to-school night. You two can fend for yourselves," Rosie said.

She noticed that Mo was cooking eggs sunny-side up.

"You eating eggs with the yolks?"

"I'm making eggs with some yellow in 'em."

"The doctor said that's not good for you."

"Yes, he did. I guess we won't tell him." Mo winked at Langston. He continued to put the plate together without comment. Rosie sipped her coffee and watched Mo put butter and jelly on the toast. She turned to Langston.

"Stop messing around and eat your breakfast."

"I'll think I'll eat mine while I fix that shaky pew down front," Mo said.

He took an extra shirt from the back of the chair, put it on over his T-shirt, and left with the plate.

Rosie watched him cross the street to the church, not sure what to make of Mo's strange behavior this morning.

"Langston, you about ready to go? I can't be late."

———◆◆———

Jacob made the cot in the caretaker's room and hung his wet towel on a hook on the wall. His hair was damp and his face was clean, but he wore the same grimy shirt and pants. He sat on the cot, staring at a crack in the wall. The minuscule fault started in the corner of the room and traveled toward the floor, dissipating halfway through its journey. Jacob wondered whether the crack would eventually go in a different direction than what was obvious. He kept tracing the crack's route.

There was a soft knock and Mo entered.

"Not a bad bed, huh?" Mo paused hopefully, waiting for a reply. "I brought you something to eat."

Jacob took the plate.

"I brought you a clean shirt, too."

Mo peeled off his outer shirt and gave it to Jacob.

"You can eat, change, and head back to wherever you came from. Is that clear?"

He mimed eating. "You eat." He pointed to the shirt. "You change." Then he pointed to the door. "And then you go. I've got chores to do," he said as he left the room.

Jacob ate the eggs in silence. He tried to keep his mind blank, but the sound of an engine backfiring somewhere in the neighborhood startled him. He saw another image—this one of a wall of black smoke moving toward him. His heart raced. He held his hands in front of his face, as if he could protect himself from the images that were sure to follow. Jacob willed himself to throw the switch of blankness. He stopped the flashback. After a few moments, his pulse returned to normal, and he picked up the plate and licked off the lingering yolk.

———◆◆———

Mo's morning was dedicated to garden maintenance. He plucked the spent blossoms off the yellow mums, trimmed the bushes and hedges, and watered the flowerbed in front of the church. Jacob emerged into the bright light with Mo's old button-down hanging on his thin frame. Jacob fingered the shirt and forced a weak smile. Without stubble, his face looked boyish and innocent. Mo turned off the water and picked up a broom.

"Ever notice how some jobs never get done? Like laundry or food shoppin' or this sweepin'? You do 'em, and then you do 'em again. I guess it passes the time."

Mo pointed with the head of the broom. "The bus station is straight through town. Stay on this road."

Mo returned to sweeping the church steps, which were covered with fall leaves. The strange man stood and stared. When Mo leaned the broom against the wall and wiped his face with a well-worn handkerchief, Jacob reached for the broom.

"Okay, buddy. You want to finish here? It ain't my favorite job. I'm happy to hand it off."

Jacob began to sweep. Mo disappeared into the church mumbling about stocking paper in the bathrooms.

Jacob swept methodically from corner to corner, gathering the debris in neat piles. A snapshot injected its way into his mind's eye: Sarah collecting colored leaves to decorate the upright piano in their crowded living room.

Sarah, the youngest, had loved to watch Jacob at the piano. When she appeared at his side, he'd quickly change from blues chords to something childlike and lighthearted. He'd appeal to her inner musician with a simple, repetitive melody. He never tired of looking at her enormous blue eyes, upturned nose, and rosebud mouth. Even at four, she had a delightful sense of humor, and it gave Jacob great pleasure to make her laugh.

She loved *The Itsy Bitsy Spider*. For each note, he'd sing the accompanying syllable:

The it-sy- bit-sy spi-der
went up the wa-ter spout

Then he'd solemnly nod to Sarah who, with great theatricality, would hit the accent note and throw her head back in open-throated celebration.

On the nearby sofa, the older children would be playing a version of *Name That Tune*. Yossi would pound out the rhythm of a familiar song on Miriam's back, and then they'd switch roles. Whoever guessed quickest won. All well and good if the pounding remained gentle, but it seldom did. They were only eleven months apart and in each other's business all the time. Competition was constant. Julia was always pulling them apart or trying to distract them from their manufactured confrontations.

Julia.

The memory pierced him. He bit inside his cheek until he recognized the distinctive taste of blood. The pain allowed him to wipe the vision of his family away and keep sweeping.

———◈———

A half hour later, Mo came out to check on the drifter. He watched him creating neat piles of leaves. Mo rubbed his head, trying to make sense of this bizarre man.

"It occurs to me that you might have missed today's bus. You can stay for a bit downstairs—but you got to stay out of sight."

Mo gestured to the house across the street. "I live over there with my niece and her little boy. If Rosie finds out I let you stay here, she'll chew my head off."

Jacob looked up from the broom. There was kindness in the old man's voice. "There's some cookies in the pantry left over from the senior citizens' meeting. That'll have to do for now."

Mo was puzzled by the stranger's behavior: He knew how to clean himself and shave and sweep things into neat piles, but he grimaced and blinked and scowled like a madman. Mo sucked his back tooth, the one that always snagged food. He waited for the man to look at him. Maybe he was mentally ill.

Mo grew uncomfortable with the silence and jabbered on, "Listen...about Rosie. She's a good egg—kind and funny. A terrific mom, too. But she's got an extra layer of shell on her. I guess you could say she's more like a hard-boiled egg. She married a piece-of-shit husband. I told her he was trouble, but she told me to mind my own business. She kinda built up this wall that makes her come off meanish."

Mo gently reached out to stop the man's sweeping and looked him in the eye. "Remember—stay out of sight."

CHAPTER 12

After Jacob disappeared, Hava tried to resume some kind of routine to fill the long hours between waking and sleeping. She mostly busied herself with Naomi's household, as her daughter was entering the last weeks of an emotional and difficult pregnancy. In the weeks after the explosion, Naomi almost lost the baby. The doctors said stress was a factor. In order to protect her daughter's half-ripened child, Hava held her own raging grief at bay. Now it remained as a constant lump in her throat, as if she had overstuffed a bottle with cotton and couldn't get the cap back on.

Hava shopped and cooked for Naomi and played with the older children. As she had done since she was a young mother, she attended the rebbetzin's *shiur*, a weekly women's lesson on the Torah taught by the rabbi's wife. But she could not keep her mind on the discussion and found her thoughts wandering through the window to the tops of the trees. She kept her phone in her pocket or by her side, hoping to hear from Jacob, fearing she'd hear something terrible from the detective in charge of the investigation.

She nearly jumped out of her skin each time the phone rang. This time it was Barbara, Julia's mother, asking to meet for coffee. They had never developed a relationship beyond family events, although they'd supported each other through that horrific first week of mourning. They were cordial and considerate but nothing more. Barbara had been a career woman, a corporate lawyer, and Hava felt unsophisticated and out of step with the times when Barbara was around. She sensed that Barbara had never felt comfortable with her either.

The two bereaved grandmothers met at a coffee shop near Jacob's house. Hava had arrived early, and Barbara came in, pale, out of breath. They both ordered hot tea. After small talk and tears, Barbara got down to business. Why didn't Jacob answer her calls?

Hava had been hiding Jacob's absence from everyone but Naomi. She told people he came back after *shiva* but wanted to remain in seclusion. Hava thought that would be the best way to handle his disappearance, to protect herself and her son from the judgment of their community. No one needed to know that he'd been missing for two weeks, and that she was out of her mind with worry.

"People handle grief in different ways. He's not ready to talk to anyone."

"We are not 'anyone.' We are family."

Hava felt the heat rise in her cheeks. There was no way to explain his absence unless she embellished the lie.

Barbara shredded a napkin. "Please, Hava, he's all we have. Our entire future."

Hava sensed that Barbara resented her. An act of violence had obliterated Barbara's future. Julia had been her only child, and the grandchildren her only immediate family. Hava still had her daughter and her growing brood. Naomi's pregnancy promised the distraction of new life.

She cut Barbara off. She knew she was being cruel, but the tightening of her throat threatened to release all of her emotions. "Don't take it personally. Jacob will call you when he's ready."

Once again, she found herself hiding the truth and making excuses for her son. She remembered Jacob's difficult time, his final year in yeshiva. He stayed out late, his clothes had a foul, earthy smell, and he was always asking her for money. When he was home—if he came home at all—he seemed depressed, not her curious, energetic son.

She didn't want to share her fears with anyone in the community, so she went to the public library to research his behavior. The librarian pointed out some useful websites. Jacob certainly wasn't the only teenage boy who went through a rough patch. Was this normal teenage rebellion, or could it be something more?

Her meanderings in adolescent psychology led her to a link about drug and alcohol use in teens. The behavior seemed to describe Jacob, but how could that be? He was a good boy, an outstanding student, and a caring human being. She knew from gossip that there were cases of substance abuse among the Orthodox. It was a *shonda*, a disgrace on the family, to have such a child. She didn't dare share her worries with her husband. He'd always been so critical of Jacob—she feared her suspicions would cause a blowup. Hava didn't confront Jacob either, largely because she was afraid of the truth. Whatever the problem was, with love and time and God's help, her son would return to himself.

So here she was again, lying to protect Jacob. If she revealed to Barbara that Jacob was missing, she would have to acknowledge her own fears. If Jacob was dead, then she too would have a different future. If he was alive, he could heal and marry again and make more children.

Hava made an excuse. She looked at her phone. "I'm sorry. I have to go. I have to pick up Naomi's daughter from preschool."

As she reached the door of the coffee shop, Hava had a change of heart. How could she be so unkind? Julia's parents deserved honesty. If she'd learned anything from Jacob's drug abuse, she needed to set aside her guilt and share the truth. She returned to Barbara, her sister in grief, and pulled her chair close.

"Jacob is missing," she confided, "and I have no idea if he's dead or alive."

CHAPTER 13

Rosie buttoned her jacket as she crossed the street to church. The evenings were finally starting to cool off, and night was coming earlier. She smelled the wet gravel after a brief afternoon rain. Choir practice was demanding, but it was also the best part of her week. She felt an air of anticipation as she saw cars pull into the parking lot. Younger folks gave rides to those who didn't have transportation. Some of the old-timers had trouble walking, so they leaned on the more vigorous as they navigated the front steps. Their bodies might be breaking down, but their voices were still strong, and their sense of community, even stronger. They called out to each other in greeting. There was a camaraderie on Tuesday nights that Rosie couldn't find anywhere else. When a song came together in rhythm and harmony, she felt complete.

Mr. Day, the wiry, animated choir director, chatted with his accompanist, an elderly gentleman who softly practiced his chords as they looked over the sheet music for the evening's selections. Rosie took her seat with the sopranos and opened her music folder. She noticed that Edmond had already found a spot among the men. When he tried to catch her eye, she pretended to be preoccupied with the buckle on her watch. With the exception of the wedding band that was now gathering dust in her dresser, that watch was the only piece of jewelry Robert had given her. She kept meaning to get a new one, but Langston called it "Daddy's watch," so she kept wearing it.

All those years in Birmingham, Rosie had suppressed her religious feelings. During her marriage, she'd turned away from tradition. Robert didn't grow up in the church, and he never felt comfortable when she dragged him along. But now, back in her childhood home, she again felt the strong pull of faith, and that faith compelled her toward First Baptist—and the choir. When she sang, serenity washed over her, bringing purpose to her harried life.

Mr. Day began rehearsal, "All right folks, let's stretch our muscles." He blew a pitch pipe, and the group matched the note, starting low then moving slowly up the scale. This was a regular drill. After a few moments of humming, he moved to lip trilling, again starting with a low tone and moving higher.

Mr. Day stopped in front of Edmond. "Relax your lips and control the sound from your diaphragm. Your lips should vibrate as the air passes over them."

Edmond imitated Mr. Day's exaggerated sounds. The effort made him look ridiculous. When the others laughed in good-natured teasing, Rosie laughed too loudly.

⟫•⟪

In those first few days, Jacob acclimated to his new surroundings. First Baptist was a simple structure, and he quickly learned its ways. There was a chapel that held three hundred people, a dais with a podium, a platform with folding chairs for the choir, and three throne-like, velvet-covered seats. There was a social hall with a well-worn upright piano and a small kitchen. If he walked through the social hall, he'd arrive at two small classrooms and the pastor's office. There was an alcove above the chapel for the electrical panel and the organ pipes. The tiny basement held his small caretaker's room and a storage closet. On weekdays the building was quiet, with only the pastor and Mo coming and going. In the afternoons and evenings, there was more activity—meetings, youth group, Bible study.

Jacob was asleep in the caretaker's room. He couldn't shake the exhaustion, nor did he want to. He slept whenever he wasn't doing chores for Mo. Sometimes, he'd wake up with a feeling of calm. More often, his dreams left him in a cold sweat, with his heart racing and weakness in his limbs. Either way, the images from the dreams—the people, the places—were irretrievable when he woke. The only image that was claimable was that of blue eyes— Sarah's innocent, wide eyes, with a fringe of black lashes. The eyes frightened and comforted him at the same time. He wanted to see those eyes when he slept, but also dreaded the vision.

The sounds of rehearsal—piano, vocal warm-up, scales—invaded the room. Jacob was pulled into consciousness by sound. Singing. Music. He strained to hear the voices. Although he didn't recognize the melody, the rhythm and plaintive tones took him back to the Brooklyn basement where Lenny had taught him to appreciate the blues.

Lenny had often functioned as the Shabbos goy, a non-Jew who could perform prohibited tasks on the Sabbath for the religious Jews who rented in the building. The strict rules of Orthodox Judaism dictated that no work could be done on the Sabbath. Flipping a light switch or turning on a heater could be construed as breaking the rules. On occasion, someone would forget to set the automatic timer on the lights before the Sabbath, or the weather would take a cold turn after the day of rest had begun. That's when they'd call on Lenny, who could throw the switch without consequence.

Jacob remembered the exact moment he first heard the blues. One Saturday, his elderly uncle was staying with them, and the temperature inexplicably ratcheted up over one hundred degrees. Jacob's mother sent him down to Lenny; they needed the Shabbos goy to turn on the air conditioning or his uncle would be ill. Jacob went to Lenny's basement apartment with the urgent request.

As he descended the four stories to ask for Lenny's help, he acknowledged the building as a living entity. All of the windows and doors were open in a futile attempt to catch a breeze. Jacob heard toilets flushing, babies shrieking, and snippets of human conflict.

Even before he knocked on Lenny's half-opened door, he was aware of the sound from the record player and the woman singing. The voice wasn't merely singing. She was storytelling and praying all in one.

Over the next year, Jacob visited Lenny with any excuse he could invent, and Lenny, enjoying the company of a fellow music lover, introduced him to the great blues singers. Jacob would sit on the old brown couch, the one Lenny had scavenged from Mrs. Strauss's apartment after she died. No relative had laid claim to the worn upholstery, so Lenny hauled it down to his place. He'd put duct tape over the hole on the arm where her cats had shredded the fabric. Lenny tried to drape an afghan over the silver tape, but the metallic swath always revealed itself. Other than that hole, the couch suited Lenny—comfortable and warm, like the music that came from the old vinyl records.

Jacob loved the way Lenny's face softened when he listened to the blues. Lenny would close his eyes and move his head back and forth. Sometimes he'd pretend that he was drumming and bite his lower lip while he acted out his fantasy.

"You hear that? That rhythm is the heart of the blues. You know what makes it special? The music lives on the two and the four beat. The snare, not the kick. You know what I mean?"

Jacob nodded, not wanting the lesson to be interrupted. He studied piano, but Lenny was talking about a whole different world of sound. Once Lenny felt that Jacob understood the blues, he moved him to the next circle of learning, jazz. The two of them would sit on that old brown couch, eat crackers, and listen to the intricacies of Miles Davis and John Coltrane.

Lenny's music became his own. In his teens, Jacob had expanded his taste to include rock 'n' roll. Listening to the radio late at night, he'd fantasize about wearing jeans and T-shirts and having sex. He longed to be a typical American, and he'd argue with his father about the worth of being observant and living isolated from the mainstream.

His father grumbled that Lenny was poisoning Jacob's mind. Jacob spent too many hours in that basement apartment listening to old records instead of learning. But Jacob *was* learning. Lenny had a small electronic keyboard on which he experimented, modifying his years of classical piano lessons to the rhythms Lenny had taught him to love. Jacob had a natural aptitude for the blues.

After one inspired riff, Lenny pointed at him, wiggled his finger, and declared, "You're an old soul, my friend."

Jacob was elated. He couldn't wait to tell his parents.

His father shattered his pride. "That man doesn't know anything about your soul. You're a pisher. Stay away from that *shvartza* and his immoral music."

Jacob flared. "There's nothing immoral about him. And don't use the word *shvartza*. It's offensive."

His father roared with rage. "Not abiding by my rules is what's offensive!" Jacob braced himself for a physical confrontation, but this time his father was satisfied getting the last word. "There's nothing offensive about *shvartza*. It means black."

There was no winning this argument, or any others in their combative relationship, so Jacob withdrew. He kept his opinions to himself and his mouth shut. He feared that if he didn't, his father would forbid all visits to Lenny's apartment. Not that he would have obeyed. Jacob suspected there was something wrong with Lenny when he didn't eat the crackers anymore. He got so thin that his hands shook when he swept the hallway. The jazz lessons became erratic and soon stopped altogether. When Lenny died, he left a handwritten note giving his turntable and record collection, the only things he truly valued, to Jacob.

The night he received his inheritance, Jacob heard his parents argue over whether or not he'd be able to keep the gift. He sat on his bed and listened through the walls.

"He needs to spread his wings. If we chain him then he will always be drawn to *tref*," his mother argued. She was talking about music, but she used the Yiddish word *tref*, which referred to any food that was not kosher.

His father was less amenable. He barked back, "Stop indulging him. When he wanders, it won't be my fault."

His mother countered. "You don't lose someone from listening to music. You make them more curious about what they're missing. That's why they wander."

Jacob heard his father turn over in the creaky old bed, away from his mother. This signaled that his mother had prevailed. He was relieved that she'd stood up for him—she usually deferred to his father and followed rules strictly.

Jacob's parents let him keep his inheritance from Lenny. He played the records softly whenever he could. His father had been right—listening to *tref* music would never be enough. He needed to get closer to the music. An instinctive drive compelled him to seek out the source of the sound. No longer satisfied by a recorded artifact, he craved the intensity of live performance. For months, he scoured the entertainment section of *The New York Times* for names of familiar jazz musicians. If any of them were scheduled to appear, it was always at some uptown hotel or Lincoln Center. The price of admission presented an obstacle. How could he come up with the sixty-five dollars required for even the worst ticket?

One day, while waiting for the J train, Jacob noticed a small advertisement plastered on the subway wall. A jazz club in the Village was hosting an evening called "Famous Surprises." This was the club that Lenny had always talked about. Coltrane had played there; Miles Davis, too. Maybe one of Jacob's heroes would be playing that night.

It didn't take long for him to make up his mind. He concocted a lie about a late-night study lesson and sleeping at a friend's house. His parents never questioned him.

Jacob's heart raced—he had never been in a nightclub and didn't know what to expect. He must have walked back and forth in front of the club a dozen times before he decided on a course of action. He knew that he'd have to blend in and intentionally wore a Yankees cap instead of his *kipah*. Clearly the cap alone was not going to allow him to mingle unobtrusively. He walked halfway down the block and tucked his fringed undergarment inside his pants, pulling out the tails of his shirt and rolling up his sleeves.

He loitered momentarily under the canopy that read "Village Vanguard." He could go home, tell his parents that the night ended early, and that would be that. No harm, no foul. As he debated, the door to the club swung open and the sound of a jazz combo flooded his senses with longing as surely as fresh baked bread made him hungry. He walked through the door and descended the stairs into a dingy, smoke-filled basement club. He found a seat at a back table. The card on the table said ten-dollar cover, two drink minimum. Jacob figured his thirty dollars would carry him for the cover and two Cokes.

The sounds of that night rooted themselves in his body. The performance changed him. With each measure, beat, and improvisation he became more alive. He sat transfixed through multiple performers until a very specific magic happened.

Two aides led an old African American man to the stage and helped him get seated at the piano. His mobility was compromised, but his playing was superb. As the song settled in, he became a young man, his fingers agile and playful. Jacob found himself, like others in the audience, tapping the table and keeping time with his head. Sitting with people who felt about music the way he did—even if he didn't know them—felt like a religious service without the dogma. He couldn't stop grinning. He belonged here. Jacob studied the club's schedule carefully. He would return as often as time and money allowed.

———•••———

The sound of First Baptist's choir rehearsal seduced Jacob. The gospel music was authentic and powerful, an expression of raw emotion. As it had in Brooklyn, the music pulled him out of hiding. He made his way down the darkened hallway and quietly crept up the stairs that led to an alcove. From here, he could watch unobserved as the choir moved into the first song of the evening. Listening to the passionate vocals, he could forget his emptiness, if only for a few moments.

Mr. Day bounced from the sopranos to the altos to the tenors, persuading them to open their voices. The song was energetic and upbeat, reflecting the joy of the lyrics.

> *You turned my mourning into dancing,*
> *My sadness into gladness;*
> *My glory will sing your praise*
> *Forever*

On the word "forever," the sections of the choir echoed each other in harmony. Mr. Day was not satisfied and made them repeat the phrase several times.

At the end of rehearsal, Mr. Day closed his notebook. "Great work, folks. That'll be it tonight." The choir members came together and joined hands in a circle, bowing their heads. They hummed and swayed in unison.

Mr. Day began. "Jesus—bless these souls who lift their voices in prayer and joy."

The choir responded with a quick "Amen." They continued to sway, all heads down. The rehearsal had been disciplined, but now the prayers were personal, more urgent.

A big woman slowly lifted her head and claimed focus. She asked the community to pray for her nephew who was battling a crack addiction. Then a distinguished gentleman in his sixties, dressed in suspenders and a bow tie, asked them to pray for his granddaughter who was taking her nursing exams.

The group swayed for another moment. When no one else spoke, Mr. Day, obeying the silent conclusion, broke up the circle. "See you all on Sunday morning."

The members of the choir returned to their seats to claim their belongings. As the singers dispersed, Mr. Day climbed the narrow stairs to the alcove where Jacob had been watching. Jacob stepped into the shadow and held his breath. Humming to himself, Mr. Day flipped off the sound system for the sanctuary and left without noticing him.

⊷•⊶

Down below, Rosie gathered her music, oblivious to Edmond standing next to her. As she put her arm through the sleeve of her jacket, she accidentally poked him in the eye. He instinctively flinched and covered his face.

"I'm so sorry. I didn't realize you were that close."

Edmond blinked rapidly. "No problem. A patch will make me look mysterious."

He stood in front of her with one red eye tearing. His grin reminded her of Langston when he had a new joke to tell, an upturned mouth that twitched at the corners with anticipation. She waited for the punch line, but it never came. He just grinned and rubbed his eye. He could be charming.

"Do you remember when you asked me for coffee?" she said, lifting her purse to her shoulder.

Edmond's grin vanished, leaving a serious expression in its place, "No. Why do you ask?"

Rosie stood there, embarrassed. Had she misinterpreted events? There was a quick spark on Edmond's face. He was teasing.

She remembered how to play this game. "You should know that I'm not a big coffee lover, but I do like a glass of wine every now and then." She turned to leave, and as she walked to the door she waved her hips a little more than usual.

"Wine sounds good to me."

Relieved, she looked back as she went through the church door. There was that grin again.

CHAPTER 14

Robert Yarber stood in the dressing room at the Gap trying to find a pair of khakis and a crisp shirt that would read like standard-issue middle-class-guy. The reflection in the mirror wasn't half bad. Twelve years ago he might have been a model. Twelve years ago was a long time. He rubbed his still-square chin and pulled his shoulders back. The mirror reported that he could throw on a blazer and a solid tie and not look like he was trying too hard.

There were too many lawyers in this world. When he got fired from his last firm, he found it difficult to find an opening. His drinking hadn't made job hunting any easier. Tomorrow he had an interview with an old law school friend from a downtown firm who said they were looking for some research help. It was a step down, but he knew if he nailed the research, he could work his way back into a caseload. There was only one other Black lawyer in the firm. They needed the diversity.

Robert was willing to start at the bottom if need be. He was five months sober. His skin was looking healthy again, and his waist had shrunk from bloated to familiar. Tall and long-legged, he could always walk into a store and walk out with a 32-32, no alterations. At least that hadn't changed. Nothing else about his life was even remotely the same as before.

He wasn't sure when his downward spiral first began. Was it

about money? Or was it having to bill out ridiculous hours at the firm? Or his wife's neediness? Or was it fatherhood—the actual act of producing a child—that had flipped the switch?

Most men kicked ass when their families began. He'd done a complete reverse, heading so fast toward irresponsibility that he gave himself whiplash. First, the drinking became an unforgiving habit, and then came the random one-night stands for nothing more than sheer, conquering entertainment. Some of them involved good sex, even memorable sex, the kind he mentally hauled out when the mood hit in the shower. But those hookups were always hollow. He'd tried to explain that to Rosie, but she didn't believe him. Robert had never thought of himself as callous, but Rosie's unforgiving condemnation wore him out. He'd shut down any feelings for her, but he refused to shut down his love for Langston. So he stayed.

One day he came home and Rosie had packed his clothes. A part of him knew the end was coming, and he found himself strangely relieved. He'd tried to make the marriage work, but there was no way around her most annoying personality glitch: The woman was a meddler. At first, her interfering felt like concern, but he came to understand it as her way of controlling the world. Even when they made love, her hand would rest lightly on his, always ready to stop him or to interfere with the natural flow. Rosie used her bossiness to distance herself from passion. That was why he'd stepped out on her. He missed the passion. Damn all her intellectualizing.

Yes, he could live without Rosie, but his son? He didn't realize how much he loved Langston until the threat of not seeing him daily became reality.

Robert's drinking had begun to control his life. Months of his life felt hazed over. Alcohol anesthetized his ability to connect on any level.

At first he wouldn't drink until the end of the workday, but that social boundary quickly expanded. Lunch would include a glass of wine or a beer, and hard liquor began mid-afternoon. He kept a bottle of Jack Daniels in his office and by the end of the day, he'd have nursed two or three drinks. On the weekends, he'd begin as early as 10 a.m. and continue until he fell asleep in front of the television. One weekend in particular was his undoing.

The pressure to deliver on an important case had been all consuming at the office, and he had also begun an intense sexual relationship with one of the female partners. The difficulty in hiding the affair from Rosie was weighing on him. Two fingers of gin downed first thing in the morning would make a long day tolerable. When Rosie would ask him to watch four-year-old Langston on a Saturday afternoon, he wouldn't complain. He'd put on an animated movie, throw back a few, and enjoy himself. This would have been like any other Saturday if he hadn't indulged too much and fallen asleep on the couch. When the movie was over, Langston decided to go outside in front of their apartment building, where Rosie found him sitting on the curb. He wanted to cross the busy street and go to the park, but he knew he wasn't allowed to cross without an adult. Langston never got to the park that day, but he did witness a horrific argument in which Rosie ranted at the inebriated Robert and kicked him out.

Months later, when he lost his job, he knew that it was change or die. His sponsor was an older man, twenty years sober, who steadied Robert, gave him footholds for finding his way back. Step by step: acknowledgment, apology, amends. Each day Robert claimed back a bit more of himself. What he couldn't reclaim was his ruined marriage or his son. He had damaged Rosie and Langston as surely as he had poisoned his body with gin. Livers regenerated, injured cells healed. Souls were another matter altogether.

Robert took out his cellphone and texted Rosie. *Miss the kid. Visit Sunday?*

He stood in the dressing room and waited for a response. Maybe she was in class. Maybe she wasn't and had chosen to ignore him. Seconds later his phone buzzed.

After church, 1pm. RU keeping this promise?

I'll be there.

Last time you bailed. No more excuses.

Robert was about to send back a reassuring text, but her reminder that he hadn't shown up infuriated him.

I forgot I have a phone conference. Another time.

He instantly regretted the decision.

I'll reschedule the call. See you Sunday.

Robert waited for her response, but none came. Suddenly, he missed gin more than he missed Langston.

During lunch period, Rosie patrolled the schoolyard, as was required of all teachers once a month. As she scanned the herd for signs of altercation or discontent, she spotted Hansom and Janine in the farthest corner of the yard. From her vantage point, Rosie watched them interact. Sometimes one friend was all it took to make a difference.

Hansom and Janine had learned through painful experience that this time of day was fraught with danger. Their fellow students were set free from the expectations of classroom order and teacher supervision. At lunch, camouflaged by the hubbub of food and socialization, the student population indulged in its favorite pastime—ferreting out the weak among them and exposing their vulnerabilities. Hansom and Janine had learned to avoid the most adept hunters. They sat far away from the herd, half hidden in shadows.

Hansom seldom brought anything to eat. He said he didn't get hungry during the day, but Janine didn't believe him. She always packed extra, and they'd share. Today, he eagerly accepted her offer of an American cheese sandwich on a hamburger roll and a small bag of corn chips. As they settled into their routine, Janine noticed that Hansom was picking at one of many new facial eruptions.

In her best maternal voice she said, "Don't do that. You're only going to make it worse."

They chewed without further conversation. Hansom started to touch his face again but stopped himself.

"You know, if you wash your face with bleach, it will dry up the bad ones," Janine offered. "Clorox kills bacteria. When someone has a disease they wash everything down in bleach so other people don't get it. Or if you get mildew on your clothes, you bleach them and the stink goes away."

He pointed to her pudding cup. "Are you gonna eat that?" She shook her head and gave it to him.

"You'll have to slurp. I forgot a spoon."

Hansom made an exaggerated slurping sound.

Janine moved a few inches away, "Did anyone ever tell you you're disgusting?"

Hansom repeated the sound. "Only the ladies."

Jeanine snorted in appreciation of his lowbrow comeback, "Yeah, right. Like you're interested in girls."

⸻◆⸻

Sunday afternoon would be Robert's first visit since Rosie and Langston moved to Brent. Their communication had been tense, but she knew Langston needed his father, so she was accommodating. She didn't even bring up the back payments in child support. On Saturday, she checked her emails, texts, and voicemails obsessively, expecting him to cancel or make an excuse. No messages.

On Sunday, Mo helped Langston put his tie in place for church. The boy couldn't stand still and kept up a steady stream of questions.

"What time is Daddy coming? Will we have lunch together? You think he'll bring me a present?"

Rosie shot Mo a look and mouthed "help."

Mo took the boy's hand as they crossed the street to First Baptist. He tried small talk to draw Langston away from his anxiety about his father's visit. Langston wouldn't give more than one-word answers. But when Mo suggested they play I Spy, all of a sudden, he became animated. Sometimes, Mo figured, the best way to talk about something was not to talk about it at all.

The congregants shook hands, kissed cheeks, complimented one another, and caught up on the week's gossip. As they settled into their seats, the deacons, identified by their burgundy ties, and the deaconesses, in identical white dresses and hats, passed out prayer books. Mo and Langston took their seats in the front row.

Rosie buttoned her robe over her dress and took her seat with the other choir members on the pulpit. For the next two hours, she'd block out thoughts of Robert, school, and money, and concentrate on her relationship to God.

Pastor Johnson, First Baptist's spiritual leader, entered the sanctuary in a shimmery cream robe with a colorful hand-embroidered surplice. The garment conferred a regal bearing on his portly figure. He smiled broadly, shaking hands and nodding to congregants as he worked his way up to the pulpit. As he ascended the steps to his throne-like seat, the worshippers quieted down. Pastor Johnson signaled for the congregation to rise, and Mr. Day led the choir in the opening hymn. This was the moment Rosie waited for all week. The organ played a few introductory bars, and the choir joined in song.

As the music died down, Pastor Johnson stood, his arms raised. Then he opened Scripture. He was ready to preach. The pastor's words brought comfort to lives battered by the corrosive force of a struggling economy. Brent had suffered in recent years from high unemployment, poorly funded schools, and the devastation of drugs and alcohol. As he spoke, there could be heard the occasional "Amen."

When the service ended, Rosie and Langston left the church, hoping to find Robert waiting in his car by the curb as agreed. No luck.

As they entered the house, Rosie suggested, "Why don't you change out of your church clothes before your father gets here?"

"I want him to see my new suit. Are you sure he said this Sunday?"

Rosie took out her phone. "Yes, he texted me."

She showed Langston the text in which Robert asked if he could visit. She didn't scroll through their sniping.

While she fixed Mo and Langston some lunch, she kept monitoring the street, hoping to see Robert pull up. Langston posted himself in the front window, his enthusiasm waning by the minute. He maintained a sullen silence during lunch. Rosie did not offer any excuses. Finally, Langston pulled off his tie and jacket and turned on the TV. His father had forgotten.

⸺⸎⸺

A few days later, Mo went to meet Langston after school on their designated corner, and when Langston didn't show up, he immediately called Rosie. Perhaps she'd picked him up early and didn't tell him? Neither Langston's teacher nor the school office had noticed anything unusual. Maybe he'd gone to a friend's house and didn't tell his mother? Mo returned home to wait.

Rosie found Mo pacing the living room. She called every parent in Langston's class, but no one knew where he was, and their children had been home for hours. Her mouth went dry, and her palms began to sweat. She forced herself to think rationally, pushing the worst-case scenarios out of her head. Child abductions seldom happened in small towns, but she wasn't going to wait another minute. She would call the police.

As she dialed, there was a knock on the door. Mo raced to open it. Robert stood there with an exultant Langston riding high on his shoulders.

Rosie forced herself to sound calm and pleasant. "Mo, why don't you take Langston in the kitchen for a snack so his father and I can talk?"

She saw Robert's shoulders tense as he braced himself for the inevitable scolding. The excuses started flowing, "I had a free afternoon, and I thought it would be fun. Langston was so happy to see me. He forgot to tell me he was supposed to meet Uncle Mo."

She cut him off. "Why didn't you call on Sunday? Why didn't you call today?"

"I lost my cell," Robert shrugged. "Didn't mean to put you out."

"Have you been drinking again?"

"One hundred eighty-one days sober." Robert continued proudly, "We went for a picnic and played at the park. I am truly sorry if I made you worry."

Rosie was silent. At that moment, she hated him. She couldn't see the man she once loved. She would be perfectly happy never to see his face again. But that was impossible. He was the father of her child. She felt trapped.

Robert tried to ease the tension by blathering about hanging out with their old friends from college. She stood up and walked to the door. "Go. I don't want to talk to you anymore."

He stopped and gave her one of his soulful looks, the look that used to make her knees weak and now made her stomach turn. "I told you I was sorry. I should have called, you're right." He tried to mollify Rosie by admitting his culpability.

She wasn't buying. She snapped. "I will not allow you to hurt my son. It's one thing that you've hurt me, but you cannot hurt my son. You ever want to see him again, you go through me."

Robert opened his mouth to protest, but Rosie hustled him out the door. "I know I said you could have him on Thanksgiving, but I've changed my mind."

As she closed the door, she had a flash of guilt. Kicking him out was harsh. He might stay away indefinitely—and Langston would suffer. It was a no-win situation—given the choice between an absent father and an irresponsible one, what was best for Langston?

Mo sucked his tooth as he stood in the doorway. He had witnessed the entire scene.

"That man gives new meaning to the word 'fuckup,' " Mo muttered.

CHAPTER 15

Jacob found solace in making order out of chaos, in working his body until he sweat. He cleaned the storage closet in the basement of First Baptist. It was one of those closets where people shoved things they didn't have the heart to throw away.

The confines of the closet reminded him of his windowless office in the yeshiva. There he would immerse himself in study and preparation for teaching. He taught the fourteen-year-old boys, a challenging age, some almost full grown and shaving, others with squeaky voices and scrawny bodies.

The curriculum was an intense study of the Talmud, the long tractates of Jewish law, analyzed in small student groups. He delivered a daily lecture emphasizing the teachings of the rabbis—lessons that helped the students find the necessary soulfulness and joy of Jewish observance.

He could see himself at the classroom podium, busying himself with notes and marking a page in his heavy Hebrew textbook. The students wandered in, dressed like Jacob in the dark suits of Orthodoxy. As each boy entered the classroom, he took off his fedora and centered his *kipah*. They joked and roughhoused on the way to their seats.

Jacob hummed a wordless tune, the traditional method for bringing a classroom to order and to prepare for the serious study ahead. The tune began softly, but as the boys settled into their seats, they joined in. The humming grew more ecstatic. Although the tune still had no lyrics, they added a syllable, a *ya-ya-ya*. The room buzzed with energy. Finally, he gestured for the boys to stop singing and listen.

"Kol Ha'olam kulo gesher tzar me'od, ve'haikar lo lefached," he chanted. As he sang the verse, Jacob closed his eyes and entered a spiritual trance. Many of the students were also absorbed by the music. The singing came to an end, and Jacob began to teach.

"What do these words mean?"

He pointed to a boy in the front row. "The whole world is a narrow bridge, and we must not be afraid."

Jacob held out his arms as if balancing on a thin beam. He treaded carefully, one foot in front of the other, peering at the imagined dangers below. The boys were absorbed in his performance.

"A narrow bridge," he said as he feigned a fall and caught his balance, "but what's down there? Rushing water? Jagged rocks? Animals with sharp teeth?"

The boys were hooked.

"Pretty unlikely in Brooklyn. So what's down there? What are we so afraid of?"

Hands shot up around the room, but he knew to give the boys some time to think. He pointed to a small boy in the back of the classroom.

"I'm afraid of pain."

"That's because you're a pain in the ass," said the boy next to him. The room erupted in laughter.

"This is not an anatomy lesson, gentlemen," Jacob responded.

He pulled out the heavy Hebrew book. "Let's open our texts and see what the rabbis have to say."

⸻◆⸻

Jacob's memory of teaching felt like it belonged to someone else. He no longer cared what the rabbis said. Their words were useless, like the jumble of castoffs in the church storage closet he was cleaning out. He sorted the junk into neat piles: leftovers from rummage sales, faded choir robes, membership records, and boxes of old cooking utensils. Within minutes, his hands were grimy, and his hair had a layer of dust. He caught sight of his barely recognizable self in the blade of an old kitchen knife. The image undulated, as if distorted by heat waves rising off a summer street.

Thoughts of Brooklyn assaulted him. What if his family was alive? Maybe they were waiting at home for him, and he was the one missing. He would go to the front door as usual. The children would run to him with kisses and complaints, and all would be normal again. Jacob kissed the air. The weight of his imaginings pulled him to the floor. They were gone. If only the knife in his hand could perform grief surgery.

Furious at the universe for allowing him to pretend, for sanctioning one moment of fantasy, Jacob thought how simple it would be to use the knife to end his life. He could slowly bleed to death as an unnamed stranger on the floor of a church's supply room and the pain would be over.

He stayed on his knees for a long time, until he felt nothing. He rose slowly and put the knife in a box marked "Utensils." He washed the walls and floor of the closet and put the contents back in neat, orderly piles. Once again, his mind was occupied with only the task at hand.

Mo found him engrossed in his work. "Well, I'll be damned! Nobody's touched this room in years...except to throw in something that don't have a proper place."

Mo examined the well-organized shelves and slapped Jacob on the back. Jacob attempted a smile. He was pleased that Mo liked his work.

"You remind me of my old friend Sam. We were in the service together. He's been dead now about forty years. Boy, was that guy a stickler for order. Even lined up his shoes by color."

Mo took a step back. "That's what I'm gonna call you—Sam."

Mo showed him the reason for his visit: Chinese takeout. "Come on, Sam. Let's eat."

⊰•⊱

Spending time with her daughter and helping with the grandchildren was Hava's reason for getting up in the morning. She especially enjoyed taking the toddler out in a stroller. This way Hava had a captive audience. She could introduce him to the world: "Look, I see a boy on a bicycle!"

"What does a doggie say?"

"The taxi is yellow!"

She kept up a steady patter, pointing out all the little things of interest at the child's eye level. The new stroller was cumbersome. Up the curb, down the curb, straining her back. Talk, feed, clean, comfort. The routine kept her occupied. She was offering the baby a cracker when, out of the corner of her eye, she noticed a man. In the sea of black suits, she recognized his profile. The familiarity took her breath away; he was only ten feet ahead of her.

"Jacob...Jacob." She could barely get the words out. Why was he walking so fast?

Twenty feet away.

She couldn't leave the baby and run after him. Jacob didn't hear her.

"Jacob!" her voice sounded shrill. Other people turned to look at her, but not Jacob. She pushed the stroller past the other pedestrians, as fast as she could.

Thirty feet away. Soon he would be out of sight.

Hava wanted to scream for somebody to stop Jacob. But miraculously, he turned toward her. Her heart was beating triple time. It was in her throat, her arms, her hands.

"Thank you God, thank you G..."

It took a moment to compute the reality. He didn't look

anything like Jacob. Had she lost her mind? The only trait similar to her son was his height and coloring. She stood frozen in the middle of the sidewalk, trying to absorb the crushing disappointment. She had dared to hope. Abruptly, she needed to sit down. She maneuvered the stroller to a bench at the closest bus stop.

Why couldn't she get her heart to slow down? Her head felt like it had come loose. As Hava lowered her body onto the bench, she reminded herself to breathe, and she heard her body respond with one ragged intake of air after another. Slowly, her rhythm returned to normal, but each time she exhaled, she heard a high-pitched wail. Someone was crying. It was only when she noticed the baby staring at her that she realized the sound was coming from within.

A cold autumn rain battered Brent, but inside, First Baptist was warm and inviting. It was Tuesday evening, and the choir had been rehearsing for two hours. The pianist stood, stretched his back, and rubbed his hands. Mr. Day was sweaty and disheveled from the exertion of conducting the choir.

Mr. Day concluded his announcements. "I want everyone here at eight forty-five on Sunday. No more stragglers."

The members grumbled an acknowledgment.

"One more thing," Mr. Day continued over the din. "People, are you listening?"

They begrudgingly gave him their attention.

"Plan to work on the songs for Gospel Sunday at next week's rehearsal. Unless you're dead or dying, I expect you to be here for rehearsal every Tuesday. No exceptions."

The prospect of Gospel Sunday sent a spark through the group. Each year the gospel radio station sponsored a spring festival for the regional churches. Local music celebrities judged the performances. The winner got a donation to their church fund and bragging rights for the year. After the competition, there was a huge picnic in the park, with barbecue cook-offs and pie-making contests. The hospitality was the South at its best.

Rosie appreciated that Gospel Sunday still stirred such enthusiasm. It's not like the winners would be featured on some slick televised talent competition. At the most, there might be a thirty-second sound bite on the local news and some poorly filmed YouTube clips on the singers' Facebook pages. Nonetheless, the competition was genuinely heated and the tradition sincerely honored. The whole county came together to celebrate this throwback to a simpler time. Gospel Sunday was human, real, and spiritual. She loved it.

Mr. Day approached Rosie. "Will you lock up tonight? My wife's neck is out of whack, and she needs help with the kids." He turned to go and added, "Don't forget the lights in the balcony."

She began the rounds of locking up, a routine she remembered from following her father around after services. She first turned out the lights in the small office wing off the chapel, then on the pulpit. She passed the basement and checked that it was dark and quiet. She climbed the stairs to the organ alcove and utility room and stepped into the closet to shut off the sound system. Her instincts told her something was off. She noticed the unmistakable smell of a living creature. The hairs on the back of her neck stood up. Damn raccoons. They must be nesting again.

Needing to confirm her suspicion, she pulled the string that controlled the bare light bulb in the closet. When she saw a white man huddled in the corner, she recoiled, reflexively putting her hands up to shield her face. Her first instinct was to run, but when the man looked more frightened than she felt, she stood her ground.

The man didn't respond. He stood up slowly, and signaled with his hands for her to stay calm.

She confronted him, "What are you doing here?"

She waited for him to speak, her alarm rising by the moment. "Say something."

The man looked straight at her but remained silent. Suddenly, she recognized him. He was the disheveled stranger she'd seen sleeping on the church steps weeks ago.

He kept his eyes downcast. No words came.

She recognized Mo's shirt, the one with a faint grape-jelly stain that never came out, no matter how hard she tried. It might as well have been monogrammed with Mo's initials.

"How did you get that shirt?" She waited for an explanation, but he stood there, mute and frozen. She now understood why Mo had taken food across the street on several occasions. Her uncle with the bleeding heart.

"You can't be skulking around here."

Rosie's thoughts were incoherent. Why was she confronting this lunatic who could hurt her? She fled down the stairs and out of the church, trying to remember when she'd first seen the strange man. Was it the beginning of the school year? Had he been hiding in the church for nearly three months? She felt gullible and angry. She didn't care if Mo was asleep. She marched upstairs and banged on his door.

She had an edge of hysteria in her voice as she shouted through the closed door. "That man! I found that man you've been hiding. The homeless one. He scared the hell out of me."

Mo opened the door in his flannel pajamas. His left cheek showed the creases from a pillow. "Excuse me?"

"What the hell were you thinking? The guy's creepy. He doesn't talk. How could you harbor a nutcase in First Baptist? I can't believe he's been here all this time..."

"Calm down. He's harmless. He's been helping with chores and stayin' out of the way."

Rosie cut him off. "I'm calling Pastor Johnson. We're going to handle this right now."

CHAPTER 16

The next morning, Rosie waited with Mo in Pastor Johnson's vestibule. The radiator had not yet kicked in, and the church was chilly. Jacob, obeying Mo's request to appear, stood in the corner, gazing out the window at the steel-gray sky and the wind whipping through the trees.

Rosie fidgeted, preparing her argument against the stranger. Pastor Johnson hurried into the office carrying a box of doughnuts. "Got here as quick as I could." He looked at Jacob. "Is he the problem?"

He motioned for Rosie and Mo to follow him into the office. He put the doughnuts down, took off his coat, and closed the door, leaving Jacob in the hallway awaiting judgment.

Rosie turned to Mo. "Are you going to tell him or should I?"

"I'm a grown man. I can take care of my own business." He addressed the pastor. "I've let a homeless man stay in the caretaker's room, and he's earning his keep."

Rosie immediately argued. "He spies on the choir from the closet upstairs. There's something wrong with him. He's probably a drunk."

Mo jumped to his defense. "Never seen him drink. He's a lost soul who needs a helping hand."

"But you admitted you don't know anything about him." Rosie's voice racheted up. "What if he's a criminal on the run?

What if he's a pedophile? You want him around Langston?" Rosie had no intention of letting the stranger stay.

"Now hold on." Pastor Johnson spoke slowly. "Let's get the facts straight. Mo, you want to tell me what's going on here?"

Mo recounted seeing the distressed man on the steps of First Baptist, trying to get him to leave, and offering him the caretaker's room for temporary shelter.

Mo made a final point. "He seems like a decent fellow, not a troublemaker. He's lost. You ask me? Something happened to him."

"Why don't we ask him?" Pastor Johnson said. "He's standing outside listening to every word we're saying." He opened the door to Jacob. "Is there anything we should know about you, young man?" he asked.

Jacob remained silent.

Rosie was emphatic. "See? He's off. He doesn't talk. We need to call the police."

Mo disputed her judgment. "I don't see why we have to run him out of town for bein' quiet."

Pastor Johnson held up his hands to calm the argument. "If Mo set him up in the caretaker's room, he's not trespassing. Has he broken any laws?"

Mo shook his head. "No. Matter of fact, he's been helping me around here. Been doin' a good job, too. Did you see the basement? Not a speck of dust."

Rosie's voice dripped with sarcasm. "Hallelujah. The man can use a broom." She looked at Pastor Johnson. "The church cannot be responsible for an obviously unstable man."

"Rosie may have a point here," Pastor Johnson replied. "We don't know anything about him. Maybe the best way to help him is to call the authorities."

Mo again jumped to Jacob's defense. "So they can lock him up? He ain't sick in the head. Sick in the heart, maybe. He's no criminal, and he ain't gonna hurt nobody."

"So now you're an expert on mental illness?" Rosie asked.

Mo knew how to get to Rosie. He stated matter-of-factly, "No sound should be heard in the church but the healing voice of Christian charity."

Rosie heard Pastor Johnson's stomach rumble, and she could see he wanted to put an end to this session. He took a deep breath and announced his verdict: "I'm going to trust my gut here and go with Mo—for now." He held Rosie's gaze. "He's not asking for much. Let him stay for the time being."

Rosie had lost the argument, but at least she would get in the last word. As she gathered her purse and coat, she looked at Mo. "Keep a close eye on him. I don't want to say 'I told you so.'"

Rosie ignored Jacob as she rushed through the vestibule. He was busy looking down at his dirty trousers.

<hr />

That Saturday, Langston happily crossed the street for the Youth Ministry sleepover. Rosie had asked Mo to make sure "Sam" stayed in his basement room during the activities. Rosie got ready for her date with Edmond. Anticipation infused her preparations. She put great care into her hair, makeup, and wardrobe. She was actually looking forward to the evening.

Rosie feared a mildly boring excursion comprising meaningless chitchat and a social pas de deux to determine whether or not she and Edmond had chemistry. But she wasn't bored at all. He'd chosen a charming restaurant in Tuscaloosa with crisp tablecloths and ambient lighting. He ordered a good bottle of wine. While classical music played in the background, he kept the conversation moving. He was pleasant and had a solid sense of humor. He was current in politics and world events. They were mutually entertaining each other when a momentary lull descended on the conversation. She couldn't think of a thing to say and apparently neither could he. Rosie fidgeted with her silverware as if it needed immediate rearranging. She was busy noticing that a tine on her fork was slightly askew when Edmond reached across the table and put his hand over hers. His touch caught her off guard, and when she looked up, his comfortable grin was waiting.

"Tell me something interesting about your students," he said, deftly putting the wheel back on the wagon.

Rosie was relieved to stop talking about herself. She brought up Hansom and the fight in the hallway, and the flow of conversation resumed.

When Edmond offered to walk her to the front door, Rosie felt like she had to take control of the moment. She wasn't ready for a goodnight kiss. She leaned over and pecked his cheek politely. "Thank you for dinner."

She could see that Edmond was disappointed at how cool she'd become. She wanted to explain that her reticence wasn't his fault. Even though the paperwork said that she and Robert were divorced, she hadn't kissed a man since her marriage ended. She was interested in Edmond, but thoughts of Robert had ruined the moment.

Rosie remembered seeing Robert for the first time. She'd gone to the step competition, an annual campus tradition at which fraternities performed step-dance routines. Robert's fraternity performed bare-chested in fatigues and boots to a raucously cheering crowd. Robert was in the middle of the line, calling out the choreography steps for the other dancers. Rosie couldn't keep her eyes off him. He was all raw masculinity, intensity, and charisma. At the post-performance fraternity party, they chatted and danced together, and for once, Rosie didn't feel out of place.

Truth be told, she'd always felt awkward. She'd grown to her full height—five feet, ten inches—over a single summer when she turned thirteen. Although others complimented her willowy build, she felt clumsy and self-conscious. She slumped her shoulders so she wouldn't stand out. In high school, she preferred novels and her mother's quick wit to socializing with peers. Robert was her first real boyfriend, and she gave herself to him completely. She could still conjure the tender desire of those first months of their relationship, when she lived for moments alone with him. Would she ever feel that for Edmond or anyone else?

As she slipped her key into the lock, Mo opened the door. "Seems like a real nice fellow."

She felt like she was back in high school, worried about other people's expectations. "Edmond *is* nice. But nice can be boring."

On paper, Edmond was the perfect match: a teacher, never married, decent looks, a good Christian, and a family man. Rosie wanted time to sort out her feelings.

"Don't be too picky, young lady."

She responded thoughtfully, "I can't afford another mistake. I wasted ten years on one man. Put him through school. Tried to straighten him out. And what do I have to show for it?"

"A wonderful son..."

"Please, Mo. I don't need you or anyone else to tell me that my son is a blessing. If I want to be picky with the men in my life, then too damn bad."

As she walked upstairs, she heard the sarcastic tone of her voice lingering in the living room.

CHAPTER 17

Mo grabbed a quick peek at Sam as they bumped along the road to Walmart. The man was hanging onto his door handle like he was riding a bull in a rodeo.

Mo surrendered to speaking his thoughts. "Damn rains—each year they leave holes the size of soup pots scattered on the asphalt. Makes drivin' unpredictable. You're either swerving at the last minute, or your guts are bangin' up against your lungs. Never mind the fact that the truck needs new shocks somethin' bad."

That Sam was a strange one. Mo could tell that he was smart, and he was good looking too. He had a strong jaw and perfect teeth, but he hardly smiled. The only time Mo saw those teeth was when he was chewing. Mo thought he should get Sam's mind off the road, take his nerves down a notch. The truck's radio hadn't worked in years, so Mo was going to have to hold down both sides of the talking.

"The way I see it, either we get you a jacket and some warm clothes or we're gonna be accused of freezin' you to death. I once knew a man who fell asleep at the bus stop and lost seven of his toes to frostbite." Mo thought that would get a response, but Sam said nothing.

"Well I didn't know him really. I read about him in *Reader's Digest*." Mo stole a quick glance at Sam. "What's with you? Ain't nobody don't pick up the bait of *Readers Digest*. One mention of the *Digest* and somebody usually brings up one of the hero stories, or the one about those folks that ate each other when their plane crashed, or how much they learned from stories like 'I am Joe's Eyeball.' " Mo was so busy filling the air with his one-sided conversation that he took his eyes off the road.

When the truck hit the pothole, he had to use all his strength to avoid losing control of the wheel. The steady flap of the tire turned his chatty demeanor to annoyance as he pulled to the side of the road.

"You hear that? We got a goddamn flat."

Mo got out of the truck, walked around to the front passenger side, and kneeled down to survey the damage. The tire was blown out. He could see clear through to the rim. He stood up and rapped on the hood with his knuckles.

"Okay, gonna put you to work. I need the jack and the spare."

Jacob stepped down from the truck. He looked like a turtle in protective mode. His head was retracted into his sweatshirt and his expression was vacant. Mo motioned with his head toward the back of the truck. Mechanically, Jacob searched the truck bed and bent to look underneath, but when he stood up, Mo could see he was no closer to a solution.

"You never changed a tire?" Mo didn't wait for the response. "Okay, listen up—a man needs to know this kind of thing."

Forty minutes later, the newly shod truck pulled into the Walmart parking lot. Both men had a hint of grease on their hands. As they entered the store, Mo pronounced their destination to the greeter. He could have asked a question, but Mo made a statement of fact. "Winter coats—men."

The old man pointed over his shoulder with his thumb. "Back right corner."

They wended their way through the store, big women's clothing, groceries, sheets and towels, pet supplies, lawn mowers, televisions. Mo continued to fill the air between them.

"This store got everything a body could want...and if it don't, the rest is at Sears. Those two stores and you're set for life." Without warning Mo stopped short at a circular display rack. Jacob almost walked right into him as Mo started rummaging through the jackets. He pointed Jacob to a second rounder with coats.

"You look over there," Mo said. "You're tall enough for a large, even if you are on the skinny side."

Jacob examined each coat. He fingered the material—some were flannel and warm to the touch, some, cool and puffy. When he came to the sole wool coat in the rack, he stopped. It reminded him of his overcoat back in Brooklyn. He pulled the double-breasted pea coat and showed it to Mo.

Mo shook his head vigorously. "That wool don't move," he said as he held up a bright red ski jacket under Jacob's neck. There was a brief moment of assessment and then swift judgment as Mo sucked a tooth. "Don't like this either. You don't look like somebody who'd be hittin' the slopes."

Mo returned the jacket to the rack, picked out a navy parka, and shoved it at him. "Try this one. Won't show dirt."

Jacob unzipped the jacket, put it on, and waited for the sound of Mo's tooth-sucking verdict. "Not bad." Next, Mo handed him a maroon hat and glove combo from a nearby display.

"Take this. You lose ninety percent of your body heat through your head. I read that in *Reader's Digest* too." Jacob turned over the price tag on the jacket: $49.95. How was he supposed to pay for this?

Mo answered the unspoken question. "I'll lay out for you. You can work it off."

Jacob's "thank you" came out without any thought. It was more of a croak than a voice. He hadn't used his voice in the longest time. For so long his responses had been locked inside, and now, without warning, the words slipped out. He wasn't sure if he felt betrayed or relieved by the subconscious mutiny of his vocal cords. He wasn't even sure if he had said anything at all.

Mo's lifted eyebrows told him otherwise. He couldn't hide the shock. His face danced into a smile. "Well how do you like that? He speaks!"

On the way home, Jacob, like a toddler learning how to walk, made forays into speaking. Mo would offer him a conversation starter, a finger held out to balance the lurching child until he was secure enough to venture on his own. Mo found that Jacob was most successful making small talk. In-depth questions about his past prompted a series of shrugs and silences.

Mo pulled up in front of First Baptist. He and Jacob sat in the truck and watched Langston playing basketball by himself in the parking lot. The boy was awkward, downright uncoordinated.

"Glad the boy is smart," Mo chuckled. "'Cause the NBA won't be callin'. "

Mo tapped the horn to get Langston's attention, and Jacob got out of the car in his new winter coat and hat.

Langston dribbled past him and made an unsuccessful attempt at a free throw. Jacob stopped to watch. The boy didn't even hit the backboard.

Jacob remembered Yossi's first attempts at basketball, also clumsy. His son always had his nose in a book, and Julia feared that he'd become a loner. She suggested that Jacob teach him some basketball skills so he could play with the other boys at recess and after school. Yossi's dexterity was limited, but he studied everything about the sport, spouting statistics for players, percentages, and trades like an ESPN analyst.

"Shoot again," Jacob offered as he walked past the boy.

Langston had gotten used to the silence of this strange man, so when he spoke, Langston stopped in his tracks and stared.

"Try again," Jacob said.

"Hey, you can talk?"

Jacob nodded. "Bend your knees."

Langston bent his legs and aimed. The ball arced, hit the rim, slowly circled, and then popped out.

"It almost worked!"

Mo honked his horn again, and Langston put the ball under his arm and headed home.

———✦———

Jacob concentrated on each step as he walked to his basement room. There was something comforting about this space—its sparseness and simplicity. With his brand-new parka still on, he stood in front of the small mirror over the sink and examined his image. He stepped back and angled his body, trying to see as much of himself as possible. He was taken aback by his own re-flection—he looked like a model in a department store advertise-ment. He looked so all-American. He could disappear into this stranger forever.

Jacob stepped toward the mirror, swiping the new wool beanie from his head. His hair was a clump of curls, overgrown and wild. He fixated on his own eyes, searching for a person he knew once existed. The face that looked back was bewildered.

Still in his jacket, Jacob lowered his body to the cot. Within moments, he was asleep.

———✦———

Langston pushed the broccoli around his plate. Mo's plate had nothing but gravy.

"Any more pork chops?" Mo asked.

Rosie got up to clear the table. "You've had enough. Last one is for Langston's lunch tomorrow. Besides, the doctor said only five ounces of meat. Portion control, remember?"

Mo murmured under his breath. "Forgot I was livin' with the food police."

"Did you hear, Ma?" Langston asked. "Sam talked today!"

Rosie looked to Mo for explanation. "I managed to coax a few sentences out of him," Mo admitted.

"What did he say?" Rosie asked.

"He said that the hot water don't work outta the basement spigot."

"I told you, the whole not-talking-thing was an act," Rosie scolded.

"It's not that simple." He took a slice of bread and wiped up the gravy.

"Did he tell you who he is, where he's from?"

Mo shook his head. He got up, stretched his back, and groaned. "Just because a man don't spill his life story don't mean he's tryin' to put one over on you. I'll tell you this much—he's a city boy. Even with all his handiness, he didn't know how to change a flat tire."

"I don't trust him," Rosie said.

"Be that as it may, don't you go pesterin' him with a whole bunch of your questions. Nosy Rosie has no place here."

"I am not being Nosy Rosie," she said defensively. "I have a right to know who's living across the street."

"You don't know what he's been through. Sometimes people are like broken saltines—cracked in pieces. You handle 'em too rough and you get nothin' but dust."

Langston interrupted. "Is there any dessert?"

Mo was happy to change the subject. "Now, *that's* a good question."

Later that evening, Langston was on Rosie's computer downstairs in the kitchen, playing a game that reinforced multiplication tables. He was animated, talking back to the screen, "Nine times nine is..."

Mo wandered into the kitchen. "Eighty-one."

"You sure?"

"Yup. There's a trick to the nine tables. The right answer

always adds up to nine. Nine times nine is eighty-one. Eight plus one is..."

"Nine!" Langston typed in the answer, and the computer rewarded him with a series of blips and bleeps.

Mo pulled the milk out of the refrigerator. "Good. Now I want you to look up something on the computer for me. Look up 'memory loss' on that Google thing of yours."

"There—" Langston pointed to the screen. He started reading the webpage, but Mo pushed him out of the way.

"Go get ready for bed," Mo grumbled as he focused on the screen. "Let me read that."

CHAPTER 18

In the days after the Walmart trip, Jacob spoke more, although he did not initiate conversations or go beyond basic civilities. When Mo asked again about his past, he offered a feeble "I don't remember." He did remember, but he feared that if he spoke, the truth of his past would paralyze him.

With the return of his voice, Jacob thought to contact his mother. But every time he stepped into the pastor's office to place the call, he stopped himself. His mother would never understand how he was living—shaved face, eating *tref*, ignoring all the laws. His mother accepted whatever the rabbi said, that the destruction of his family was part of God's plan. Jacob couldn't accept that way of thinking. He never picked up the phone.

———◆———

Hava hated the thought of returning to the police station, but it was necessary. Each week she checked in diligently with the detective, David Rosenberg, who was in charge of Jacob's case. Hava assumed they'd assigned a Jew because of the circumstances, but this Jew knew nothing about Hava and how she lived. The first time she sat across from him to answer a litany of nonsensical questions, he was eating a ham sandwich, wiping his mouth and smoothing his mustache between bites.

Detective Rosenberg was doing paperwork at his desk. He

raised his eyes to the horizon automatically as he took a bite of his sandwich. He always marveled at the primitive reaction of looking up when eating. The police psychologist had told him that it was a remnant of man's prehistoric self, because that's exactly the moment when self-absorption renders the victim vulnerable to becoming a predator's blue plate special. Even when he was totally conscious of the process, even when he was reading, his gaze automatically swept an imaginary horizon. Instinct was a powerful force.

This time when his eyes lifted, they discovered Hava Fisher staring at him. Hava was one of the many family members who'd lost someone in the bus bombing a few months back. Her son had watched his whole family die. Now he was missing. He walked out and never came back. Rosenberg couldn't blame him, and he couldn't hold extended eye contact with Mrs. Fisher. Even for a seasoned New York detective who'd seen everything, the Fisher tragedy overwhelmed him.

Hava put a Ziploc bag of homemade cookies on his desk. "For you..." There was a momentary silence. "Any word?" She anxiously tucked her hair into her scarf.

Rosenberg admired her tenacity. Every week like clockwork, the same routine. He shook his head and muttered, "Thank you for the cookies," followed by the hope-dashing, "nothing's changed."

He asked the standard queries for a missing person, the same ones he always asked: "Did Jacob have any outstanding debts or legal problems? Was it possible that he was involved with another woman? Was there an insurance policy on Julia and the children?"

She answered all of his questions politely, but she wanted to smash his face with the old manual pencil sharpener he repeatedly used.

"NO," she yelled inside her head. "Jacob was none of these things, you fool! He was a man who loved his wife and children, and they are dead now. He went mad when he watched them disappear. Find him before it's too late...find him." But Hava didn't say any of that aloud.

Each time she visited, she sat with her hands folded on her lap and answered the questions politely. Each time Hava struggled not to weep when she told Detective Rosenberg how much she missed her son. Each time he assured her that they were doing everything possible, but a missing adult who left of his own free will, no matter the circumstances, was not a high priority.

Finally, she asked Detective Rosenberg questions of her own. The desire to know battled against the futility of asking. "Is there any new information about who did this?"

The detective tried to be patient. "We believe this is a political issue. The FBI is in charge. We'll let you know when we have any fresh information."

As she left his office, Hava reached for her cellphone. She called Barbara's home, but Steve picked up. "No news," she told him.

She reported the useless details of her visit with Rosenberg. Since Hava had admitted the truth of Jacob's disappearance, she could talk to Julia's parents with greater ease. Steve was annoyed with the police who offered no clues and was deeply depressed and lonely for Julia and his grandchildren, but he was no longer angry with Jacob for surviving. They were all trying to survive.

——◦•◦——

Jacob sat in a storefront diner. The place was dilapidated, but the food was good and cheap. Since Pastor Johnson had given him a small stipend as compensation for his work, he'd been coming here once or twice a week to eat a meal. He made no attempt to cover his solitary status with a newspaper or a novel. He sat quietly and concentrated on his plate, nodding for coffee refills.

A television was suspended over the high counter that divided the grill from the dining area. One of the waitresses turned up the volume, and instantly the diner came alive. The Atlanta Braves were playing the New York Mets. A few patrons huddled close to watch, commenting on the tight score, and Atlanta's chances in the playoffs. Although the Mets had never been Jacob's team, seeing their uniforms was like a kick in the stomach. He was immediately back in Brooklyn on an oppressive summer day.

New York in August was brutal. It was ninety-five degrees at five p.m., the sidewalks steaming from an afternoon downpour that brought no relief. He couldn't wait to get home, shower, and watch the Yankee playoffs. But when he walked in the door to his Brooklyn row house, the noise assaulted him. The television was blaring a cartoon, Yossi and Miriam were bickering with their cousins, toys were scattered everywhere, and his sister Naomi, pregnant with her third child, was yakking on the phone like chaos was the norm.

"Mommy went to the market," Sarah informed him when he bent down to kiss her head. She was riveted by the exaggerated animal characters on the screen.

Naomi covered the receiver for a moment and patted her swollen belly. "My AC went out. Julia said we could spend the night." Jacob nodded, and she returned to her phone conversation.

After a quick shower, Jacob made his way to the living room and, without a word of warning, changed the channel to the Yankee game. The children—all five of them—objected loudly.

"Daddy! You can't do that," Yossi whined. "We were watching something."

"Go out and play," Jacob said.

Miriam stood up glaring, hands on her hips. "It's too hot. And we were in the middle of the episode."

"The Yankees are playing," Jacob said firmly. His children knew better than to argue with that tone. He scooted the children off the couch and sat down.

His sister's three-year-old began to cry.

"Go to Mommy," Jacob said. He could hear the crankiness in his own voice.

Naomi hung up the phone. "What's going on here?"

Jacob pretended not to hear. He was already listening to the play-by-play. Naomi, balancing the insulted toddler on her hip, her belly popping under her maternity blouse, stood in front of the screen. "Really, Jacob, you could let the kids finish..."

"Bottom of the seventh. No way."

"What do you want them to do?" Naomi asked, clearly annoyed by her brother's intransigence.

"Shhh...the game."

The girls stomped out of the room. Yossi sat on the floor at Jacob's feet, ready to join the secret boys' club.

Now he wondered why he'd been so gruff with them. He wanted a do-over. He'd sit with Sarah on his lap while she named the characters in her silly cartoon.

Why did he care so much about sports? On the day he walked Julia and the children to the bus, he'd been rushing home to watch the Knicks play. His wife didn't know that he was marking his tenth year of sobriety. She didn't understand the importance of sports to him—both watching and playing had been a crucial part of his recovery. In all that time, he had never told his wife about his years of drug abuse and rehabilitation. Those experiences remained a secret, a period of his life that he would never discuss.

Jacob was so lost in his punishing reverie that he didn't notice the waitress standing in front of him, pad and pencil in hand. She'd grown accustomed to seeing this quiet man point to another diner's meal or to a random item on the menu. She was shocked when he ordered in a clear voice, "I'll have the fried chicken, please."

The waitress couldn't see the battle that was taking place in Jacob's mind. With the return of his voice came a growing urgency to assert who he was: Jacob Fisher, son, brother, husband,

and father. An Orthodox Jew from Brooklyn who had witnessed unspeakable pain and loss. A Jew who wasn't sure he believed in anything anymore. Here he was—in the farthest place from Brooklyn that he could imagine—and *no one knew*. He could claim his identity if he wanted, or he could continue the pretense. The aching in his gut told him to ignore the pain, to remain a drifter from nowhere. Being Sam was easier.

He devoured the fried chicken.

⟪⟫

Jacob knocked on Pastor Johnson's half-opened door. The pastor sat at his desk, talking on the telephone. He acknowledged Jacob's presence with a nod. He grunted, sighed, and added an occasional "I understand" into the receiver. Without moving the phone from his ear, the pastor searched the pile of papers on his desk until he found the list of repairs he'd been accumulating. He handed over the list.

As Jacob scanned the paper, he thought of the many times his mother had requested that he use his natural mechanical inclination to fix some noncompliant pipe or wire. Each chore was a mystery to be solved. Where was the wire frayed? Why was the pipe leaking?

When he came back from rehab with new skills, he often recruited his mother as his journeyman. He'd be on a ladder, and she'd be below, handing him tools and giving instructions as if she knew what was going on. The handyman sessions always ended in a running joke. Jacob would recommend that if she knew a better way to fix the problem, perhaps she should be the one on the ladder.

He pointed to the last item on the pastor's list. "Which bathroom?"

Pastor Johnson held his hand over the receiver and whispered, "social hall."

By the time it registered with the pastor that he had spoken, Jacob was already down the hall, gathering Mo's old toolbox, ready to work.

⟶•⟵

Jacob assessed the garden of First Baptist. Mo had gone to Walmart for some mulch. Jacob was weeding the flowerbed to prepare the soil for some hardy winter bulbs. He found satisfaction in pulling the weeds from their roots in the moist, cool soil. He remembered last fall, when he and Miriam had planted tulips against the hedge in the front yard. Miriam was his middle child, and Julia had been insisting that he pay more attention to her. She was the child who shared his love of gardening. Pink tulips were her favorite. She remembered where each bulb was planted and waited impatiently for the green shoots on the first days of spring.

The sound of plastic dragging across cement brought him to the present. He looked toward the noise and saw Rosie struggling to maneuver an overloaded trashcan to the curb. One of the can's wheels was stuck in a crack in the pavement. Frustrated, she tried to dislodge it by kicking the wheel, but the can fell over, spilling its messy contents onto the street.

"Goddammit," she blurted out.

Jacob turned toward her.

"Pretend you didn't hear that," she said. He watched her bend down to deal with the mess of putting the smelly bags back into the can.

She looked up. "You're going to stand there and watch?"

Jacob crossed the street. He bent down and helped her scoop the garbage back into the can. He picked up an empty Cheerios box. "I like Cheerios too," he offered.

Rosie looked at him for a moment.

"They lower your cholesterol," he added politely, pointing to the claim on the box.

"Do cholesterol problems run in your family?" Rosie asked, attempting to draw him into conversation.

Jacob shrugged. Better not to think about where he came from. Yes, Jacob had returned to the world of the speaking, but he did not *want* to talk. Better to say little, to keep his thoughts to himself. He righted the trashcan and put it next to the others on the curb, wiped his hands on his workpants, and crossed back to the church.

Rosie was encouraged by his awkward attempt at conversation. So there *was* awareness behind that blank surface. He had a life somewhere, where he ate Cheerios and people talked about cholesterol. Rosie couldn't figure this guy out. One minute, he was helpful, the next, rude. One minute making small talk, the next, incapable of basic courtesy.

Over the years, she'd had many secretive students in her class, and she'd learned to be patient, to provide the student space until he was ready to talk. It was a slow process, but it satisfied both her curiosity and her need to help. She would apply the same technique to Sam.

CHAPTER 19

The fall semester had flown by. Rosie had adapted to the new curriculum and the school culture, but she was worn out, more than ready for the Christmas break. The students were in the gym for a holiday assembly; she was using the time to grade final exams.

Rosie didn't know what made her walk to the end of the hallway. The janitor's room was open, but that wasn't unusual. Maybe he was getting supplies for a repair or cleaning job around the school. What was unusual was that the door was open only slightly, and the light was off. The janitor was careful to keep the closet locked—it held too many supplies and tools that tempted adolescent mischief. As she approached, she heard strangled breathing from inside the closet.

Her thoughts raced. *Oh Lord, I've heard about kids having sex on school grounds. What the hell do I do now—fling the door open and embarrass all of us?*

Another thought tumbled on top of that. *What if it's not two students, but a student and a teacher? Wasn't that kind of sickness all over the internet?* That's all she needed. Her first year at the school and now she's a witness in some underage sex scandal. Wait—maybe it was the janitor. What if he'd had a heart attack and she was hearing his last gasping breaths? The thoughts pricked her as she walked toward the closet.

She stood outside the barely open door to make sure she was hearing correctly. There it was again—someone was in the closet. She knocked gently. The noise stopped.

"I am opening the door now," she said as a statement of fact. Then she gently swung it open. The light from the hallway spilled in, illuminating a paint-stained sink and shelves of cleaning solutions. Against the walls were two ladders, mops, an industrial vacuum, and a floor-polishing machine. Right in between the vacuum and the polishing machine stood a young man with his back to the door. He stood perfectly still, as if he were pretending to be one of the appliances.

"Are you all right?" Rosie asked softly. The boy said nothing, slowly shaking his head no.

"Why don't you come out here and we can talk?"

He stayed, facing the wall.

"You know it's against the rules for you to be in the janitor's closet."

He kept his back to her. "I needed bleach."

Rosie waited. He turned around. It was Hansom.

"Janine told me that if you put bleach on a cloth and rubbed it on your face, it will clear you up."

"And did you do that?"

"Yes, ma'am."

Rosie flipped on the light and hurried to him. She pulled him to the sink and turned on the faucet. "Wash it off! Wash it off now!"

She helped him flood his face with water. His skin looked raw and painful. She was angry with him for being so gullible, but this was not the place for a lecture. She'd have to report the incident.

Dammit, she thought. *Sex in the closet would have been easier to deal with.*

———◦•◦———

Rosie was at her wit's end. The Hansom incident was upsetting. After school, she'd gone to speak to Kala, but she'd already left for the day. On Rosie's way home she drove past Edmond's house. Good manners dictated that she call first, but her own anxiety necessitated feedback from someone who was familiar with the situation. Rosie had briefly been to his house once before to drop off choir material when he couldn't make a rehearsal. He lived in a white clapboard bungalow with a well-kept yard. She noticed his car in the driveway. She'd use him as a sounding board.

A tiny, well-dressed woman in her sixties answered the door. Maybe she had the wrong house. "Excuse me, is Edmond Scott here?"

"Yes, let me get him. He's unloading groceries."

Rosie extended her hand. "I'm Rosie Yarber. Edmond and I know each other from work."

The woman smiled broadly and held out her hand. "I'm Martha Scott. Edmond and I know each other from childbirth."

The two women laughed politely as they shook hands, and then Edmond's mother folded her arms over her stomach, took a step back, and looked Rosie up and down. "Are you the one from church?"

Rosie was caught off guard. Had Edmond told his mother about her, or was there someone else from church that he was interested in? The thought was disconcerting. Rosie stumbled over her response. "Well...there are a lot of women at church...I'm sure he talks about many people."

"Not unless there are a slew of women named Rosie."

Rosie felt like her arms and hands were flapping about. She was flustered by the woman's frankness and, more than that, unnerved knowing that Edmond had talked about her to his mother. Best to change the subject. "How long are you visiting, Mrs. Scott?"

"Till the end of the year, through the holidays. Why don't

you have a seat? He'll be here in a minute."

She waited for Rosie to sit down on the couch and then sat down next to her. "Can I tell you something you'll need to know?" she said leaning in familiarly.

She didn't wait for an answer. "He likes his food hot, steaming hot."

Rosie wasn't sure what she was supposed to do with that knowledge. "Okay, I'll make note of that." Why had she answered that way? Now it sounded like she and Edmond were involved with one another.

"And he needs a clean towel every day. It makes for a lot of laundry, but that's the way he is. He won't share a towel. He's a clean man."

Rosie didn't know how to react to this piece of intimate information. She'd gone on one date with Edmond, and it had nothing to do with towels.

Rosie was relieved when Edmond came up behind his mother. "I thought that was your voice. Let me introduce the two of you."

Martha lifted up her hand to stop him from speaking. "No need. We already know each other." She winked at Rosie but spoke to Edmond. "Offer your guest something to drink. You were raised better than that."

She whispered to Rosie. "I was just making some hot chocolate...*hot* chocolate," she repeated pointedly. "You'll join us."

Rosie silently berated herself for not calling in advance. She did not want to sit down with Edmond's mother over anything, hot or cold, and she definitely did not want to learn any more secondhand information about his grooming habits.

"Thank you for the invitation, but I have to get home to my son."

Edmond sensed that Rosie was uncomfortable. "We'll do this another time, Mom."

Rosie had one foot out the door. "I wanted to talk to you

about something that happened at school, but it can wait till tomorrow." She waved a quick goodbye and headed for her car before Edmond's mother could object.

CHAPTER 20

Hava entered Detective Rosenberg's office and placed a Ziploc bag on his desk.

"To tell you the truth, I'm tired of baking these cookies for you. You take them every week—and eat them—but you don't give me any information in return. I thought they'd help you remember me and find my son, but you're just a *haser*."

She tossed the Yiddish word for pig at him again for emphasis. "*Haser*!"

Detective Rosenberg smoothed his tie. "Nice to see you too, Mrs. Fisher." Next he smoothed his mustache. "This week I actually do have some information."

Hava wasn't sure she had heard him correctly. "What do you mean?"

Rosenberg looked at her—no expression. She sat down uninvited.

"Is it about Jacob?"

"No."

She let her breath out.

"But we may be closing in on the bomber's identity."

Hava was confused. Had a group claimed responsibility? They'd been waiting for months for some radical group to step forward.

Rosenberg cleared his throat, but there was nothing stuck in it. "The video from the candy store near the bus stop..."

"But you've had that forever. What could be new?"

"We're putting the pieces together. It takes time. We have ten different location videos that we're asking relatives of all the victims to view." Detective Rosenberg spoke softly. "Mrs. Fisher, do you think you could watch this tape and tell me if you recognize someone? I know it's a long shot, but maybe you'll spot someone who knew Jacob and his family."

She sat frozen for several long seconds. She wanted to run away, pretend that he hadn't suggested she view the nightmare. She licked lips that had gone dry and croaked out a question infused with dread, "What will I see?"

"You'll see Julia and the kids." Pain darted across her face. "We need to know if you can identify any of the other passengers."

Hava looked away.

Rosenberg waited for her to look back. "It's all we've got."

Against all logic, she acquiesced.

"We'll do it in the captain's office. I'll be with you the whole time."

Hava adjusted her eyes to the darkened room and squinted at the laptop screen.

A city bus was parked with the passenger door open. Several elderly people hefted themselves onto the bus, one with a cane, then a young woman with a messenger bag boarded.

"Is that who did it...is it in her bag?"

"I don't think so. Keep watching."

Then she saw a young, good-looking African American man in a plaid shirt. But before he could get on the bus, Yossi and Miriam careened into him, knocking a paper bag from his hand. Hava had no breath in her body...none at all. She couldn't hear what they were saying, but she felt their laughter, their banter, their very life. The man politely stepped back as Yossi and Miriam bounded on board. Then Julia, Jacob, and Sarah crowded the frame.

Jacob bent down to hear something Sarah was saying, and then he raised his hand as if taking an oath. Sarah and Julia clambered up the steps. The man with the plaid shirt was the last to board. His child's Batman backpack seemed incongruous. The door shut. The bus pulled away as Jacob stood waving. People walked around him, yet he continued to wave. Then, like in an action film, everyone was blown backward, and the camera swung wildly.

Rosenberg put his hand on Hava's shoulder to offer some small gesture of comfort. It was inappropriate, but she didn't pull away.

"Do you recognize anybody who got on the bus with them... anybody?"

Hava shook her head no.

"We believe he was acting completely on his own."

"Why would he do such a thing?"

Rosenberg shook his head and shrugged. "He may have been a religious fanatic. More likely mentally ill. Paranoid schizophrenic."

She looked at him incredulously. What did it matter? They were all dead, and now her son was probably dead, too. How could he live after witnessing that? The look on Rosenberg's face told her that he understood her fears.

"You have a difficult job, Detective," Hava said.

"Yes, Mrs. Fisher, but yours is harder."

⎯⎯◆⎯⎯

Hava's favorite part of Sabbath dinner at her daughter's house was singing the blessing at the end of the meal. Even as a girl there had always been sheer joy as the gathering erupted in exuberant, table-banging songs to celebrate the day of rest. She was sixty-three years old, and these moments still lifted her spirits. Perhaps the singing felt rebellious, or liberating, or childlike. Whatever the reason, when her family began to sing, she willingly joined in. As her rhythmic pounding on the dinner table escalated, her grand-children grinned at her with the enthusiasm of co-conspirators. She was part grandmother, part pied piper. All of them contrib-uted to the cacophony of human sound and rattling dishes. They sang a joyous Sabbath song, banging the rhythm on the table.

When the song ended, everyone stopped—except for Hava. She wasn't sure how long she had been hammering the table with-out cover of song. She only knew that five frightened faces were staring at her. She summoned super-human strength to control herself and fled the table with a feeble, "Excuse me."

"What's wrong with Grandma?" she heard the oldest grand-child whisper.

"Nothing," her daughter said evenly. "She's got a headache from all the noise."

Hava lowered her body on the twin bed in the small room where she stayed when she came to her daughter's for the Sabbath. Space was a luxury in Brooklyn. Naomi's house was cramped and littered with the detritus of small children: a shoebox of crayon pieces, matchbox cars, a doll with wildly tangled hair and half-but-toned clothes. The children left souvenirs of their existence ev-erywhere. Like Hansel and Gretel, they sprinkled crumbs to find their way back home.

Jacob's children would never come home. She felt the famil-iar tightening in her chest. She tried to put the thought out of her mind, but it was impossible not to replay the sound of Jacob's voice on the afternoon of the explosion. "They're gone, they're gone." He repeated the phrase over and over, and then he didn't speak again.

When Julia and the children died, Jacob was in such pain, in-credible pain, like being burned alive. And Hava couldn't do any-thing to help him. If she was struggling, how was Jacob coping?

She couldn't stop thinking about that program on the An-imal Channel she had seen while trying to distract herself one night. The show had been about animal and insect myths. A viewer thought that if a scorpion was surrounded by a ring of fire and given no way out, it would instinctively sting itself to death before allowing the fire to consume it. The scientists presented the truth: the scorpion was so distraught that it flailed its body around violently, appearing to commit suicide as the fire closed in. Were humans no different than insects? Was Jacob flailing somewhere, waiting for death?

What about all those people who jumped from the World Trade Center on 9/11? Body after body plummeted to earth, determined to control their own destiny rather than endure unbearable pain.

Her daughter Naomi quietly entered the room and sat on the bed. She gently touched her mother's arm. Hava looked directly at her and asked the forbidden question that had been sitting in her mouth for months. "Do you think your brother is alive?"

"Mommy—don't."

She couldn't swallow her thoughts anymore. In a barely audible whisper she confessed, "If that happened to me, I'm not sure I would want to be." Hava saw fear in her daughter's face. Instantly, she regretted her honesty. She'd never intended to frighten Naomi. She simply needed to express her dread out loud.

"It is forbidden," Naomi stated emphatically. "God determines who will live and who will die. We cannot do God's job." Naomi found solace in the black-and-white laws of Orthodoxy, laws that governed her every move.

Hava stayed silent, but she wanted to snap at her daughter. Naomi's religious justifications were nonsense. Hava had questions. She'd always had questions. But pressure from her husband and community—and all the rules and traditions—had squelched her curiosity. For years she'd been a passive wife, maintaining house and home according to religious dictate. The enormity of loss had made her question God's existence, damaging the order of her life.

"Suicide is a sin," Naomi added. "Jacob knows that."

The sound of a baby's hungry complaint filtered in from the other room.

"Go—your son needs you," Hava said, eager to pretend that life could get back to normal.

Naomi leaned in and kissed her on the forehead as if Hava were a feverish child. "Get some rest. I love you, Mommy," Naomi said as she left the room.

Hava's response to the word "mommy" was immediate and visceral. Her chest hurt, as if she'd pulled a muscle deep inside. Instantly, she was catapulted back to the days when she'd ferociously loved her small children: the way they smelled after a bath, her daughter's melodic laugh, Jacob's mischievous grin.

She watched the crack of light under the closed door. When she was sure that Naomi had moved away, she put the pillow over her face and wept. Through the pillow came the heart-rending sound of abandoned hope.

CHAPTER 21

Jacob was painting the door moldings around the church entryway. Lost in the meticulousness of the moment, he dipped and stroked the thick semi-gloss.

Mo stood in the doorway observing him before he spoke. He surprised himself when he commanded, "Put that brush down."

Jacob suspended the brush mid-stroke. He looked up, curious about the order.

"You got that pasty look, what happens to white folks when they stay inside too much," Mo said. "I say we hunt us some rabbit to eat. It's the season."

Jacob's eyes widened in apprehension. Mo's invitation made him uneasy. Orthodox Jews from Brooklyn weren't hunters. And rabbit? According to the laws of keeping kosher, rabbit was forbidden, as it neither had spilt hooves nor chewed its cud. Cows, sheep, goats, and deer were kosher, while pigs, rabbits, and squirrels were not. Although he no longer cared about food prohibitions, explaining why rabbit was abhorrent would bring him too close to the past. Too many words. He went back to painting.

"What, you don't like rabbit?" Mo asked.

"Not my taste," Jacob offered, hoping that would end the discussion, but Mo only became more enthusiastic.

"You probably never had it cooked right. Rabbit can get stringy." Mo smacked his lips and winked, like this was some big secret between them. "I know how to do it tender with tomato sauce and potatoes. Fill you right up! Put that brush down and come with me." Mo took the brush out of Jacob's hand, swished it through the paint thinner bucket, and cleaned the bristles.

Jacob did not resist as Mo led him down to the basement.

"You familiar with a gun?" Mo asked as he reached to the top shelf of the closet in the caretaker's room and pulled down an old hunting rifle that was hidden behind a cardboard box.

Jacob shook his head. "Never used one."

———◦———

Mo and Jacob stood in an old field halfway between town and the woods. It was cold enough to see their breath in the air. Mo lined up a few empty soda cans on a log for target practice like he would with a child, like he'd already done with Langston a few months ago. Jacob looked awkward and clumsy with the rifle in his hands—as if he expected it to pull its own trigger. Mo walked him through the process.

"Now what I want you to do is line up the can in your sights—like we practiced—then breathe out slow. And while you're doin' that, squeeze the trigger."

Jacob followed the directions. The sound was deafening, and it felt like someone had jammed a two by four into his shoulder. The rifle tip jumped skyward, and the kick pushed his body back. He stumbled as he fought to keep his balance. The can was untouched.

Jacob didn't make eye contact with Mo but offered a statement of fact. "Missed it."

Mo sucked on his thinkin' tooth and agreed with a barely audible, "Uh-huh." Then he took the rifle from Jacob and reloaded.

"You know, I never do get when people call huntin' a sport. More like a necessity. I was never interested in a pair of antlers on the wall, and I don't care much for venison—too chewy and a hell of a lot of work to gut the damn thing. But rabbit or squirrel? Well, you're only doin' that to fill your belly. No different from fishin'."

He handed the rifle back to Jacob and corrected his hold on the gun.

"My daddy gave me a twenty-two when I was younger than Langston. Never understood how the rest of the world looked at guns till I joined the Marines."

Mo fine-tuned Jacob's grip. "All right—line 'er up. You want your target right over the sight. Now breathe out and give a gentle, steady pull on that trigger."

Jacob followed his instructions. He shot again. The can's upright posture mocked him.

"Give me that." Mo took the gun from Jacob to reload. Jacob's right ear was ringing and his shoulder ached.

"I guess it's safe to assume that you were never in the military. Combat changes you. You learn to think weapon, not firearm," he mumbled. "Never pull a gun on a man unless you're prepared to use it."

Jacob stood frozen. Nothing about this lesson felt comfortable.

Mo handed the rifle back to Jacob. "You're not much for talkin' today, are you?"

"Not much to talk about," Jacob said as he lifted the rifle into position.

Mo sucked his tooth again. "You got memories and stories. They're in there...just gotta shake 'em out." He tapped the rifle. "Line it up. Breathe out. Squeeze the trigger."

Jacob followed the directions, but he flinched in anticipation, closing his eyes. Click. Nothing happened. He looked at Mo, who was grinning—holding the bullet that he'd pretended to load between his finger and thumb—like a magic trick revealed.

"You're waitin' for the noise and the kick. You're expectin' it, so you get all knotted up. Let go of the expectation."

Mo took the rifle, deliberately loaded it, and handed it back.

Jacob lined up the can in the crosshairs, breathed out slowly, and squeezed the trigger. He hit the can straight through, and it ricocheted off a nearby tree. The sound of the shot crackled through the late afternoon chill.

"I did it," Jacob said with obvious satisfaction.

"Okay. You're ready. Now's the fun part," Mo said.

Jacob rubbed his sweaty palms together.

Jacob and Mo crouched quietly in a thicket, watching a wild rabbit make its way out of the underbrush. Mo tapped Jacob's shoulder and indicated the rabbit with his head. He put his finger to his lips and pointed at Jacob's rifle. Jacob shook his head. He could not pull the trigger.

Slowly and silently, Mo lifted his own gun to the ready position. He lined up the rabbit and clicked off the safety. The metallic sound caused the rabbit to turn toward them, perk up his ears, and freeze. The rabbit's eyes were wide and innocent. Mo pulled the trigger, and the rabbit's head exploded.

A flash of memory physically stunned Jacob. *Sarah looking at him from the back of the bus. The sound of an explosion. The smell of singed hair and blood.* The immediacy of violent death—then and now—merged in Jacob's consciousness. He wanted to cover his head and scream.

Mo's voice pulled him back to the present. Mo slapped Jacob on the back nearly knocking him to the ground. "Right between the eyes...a perfect kill."

Jacob forced a smile. He knew Mo wanted him to be pleased, but all he felt was queasy.

On their way back to town, Mo filled the silence in the car with harmless chatter, no mention of the hunt or the dead rabbit lying in a plastic bag in the back. Even so, Jacob didn't say one word.

Later, in the backyard, Langston watched Mo skin the rabbit.

Mo whistled an aimless tune, his hands bloody and busy at the same time. Jacob stood off to the side. Mo stopped his random tune and attempted conversation.

"It takes a long, slow simmer to make rabbit tender. You've got to spice it up, so it don't get gamey. But if you do it right, mmmmmm...nothin' better."

Jacob, overcome by the sight of blood and the stench of gutted rabbit, began to retch. Mo nodded at Langston, indicating that the boy should offer Jacob some help. Langston cautiously approached Jacob. "You all right?"

"I'll be fine. It was the smell."

"You don't have to tell *me*. Every time he guts a critter I have to breathe through my mouth." Langston held his nose and breathed through his mouth in short shallow breaths. Still nasal, he continued, "Dat way I dond get de daste on my dongue."

Jacob should have laughed, but instead he vomited. Langston pinched his nose tightly and took small sips of air.

Jacob rinsed his mouth with the garden hose, washing away the taste of death.

CHAPTER 22

Jacob carried a timeworn rocking chair from the basement of First Baptist to the parking lot. He set up a work area for himself: tools, sandpaper, cans of paint and wood stain on a small bench. It was a fine December day, unseasonably warm. He rolled up his shirtsleeves and sanded the old chair.

Langston was shooting hoops at the other end of the empty parking lot. He bounced and shot, ducking and weaving, imagining a defender who blocked his moves. Jacob stopped working and watched. The boy dribbled around the basket, faking his imaginary opponent, shooting, and missing.

Jacob closed his eyes. He could see Yossi in dark pants and a white shirt dribbling a basketball down a busy street. He tried to hang on to the picture, but the sound of a ball on asphalt beckoned.

He put the sandpaper down and approached Langston. He held his hands open in front of him, silently asking to join in.

Langston hesitated. "My mom said I should stay away from you."

Jacob said nothing, but he clapped his hands in the universal "gimme-the-ball" signal. Langston gave him an easy pass.

When Jacob felt the dimpled ball hit his hands, he was in familiar territory. He dribbled to the basket and nailed a layup.

Langston was astonished. "Where'd you learn to do that?"

Jacob shrugged. "When I was a kid."

"Were you good?"

"Not in the beginning."

"Who says you're good now?"

Jacob stopped bouncing the ball and laughed.

Out of the corner of his eye, Jacob saw Rosie watching them from her front porch. He dribbled with his right hand, and then shifted to his left. "You've got to dribble on both sides. If you only use your right hand, then you can only go right. The other guy will figure that out pretty quick."

Jacob passed the ball to Langston. The boy awkwardly dribbled with his left hand. "I suck at this."

"So practice until you don't. Otherwise this will happen." Jacob deftly stole the ball and dribbled with his right hand. "Try to steal."

Langston tried to get the ball, but Jacob changed to his left hand. When Langston went in for the steal, Jacob quickly switched back. "Don't watch me. Watch the ball."

They repeated the process, with Jacob dribbling right, then left. This time Langston anticipated the move and managed to steal the ball.

"You do it," Jacob instructed. Langston clumsily attempted the maneuver.

"You need to practice. Dribble with your left hand for one week. Move around while you're doing it. One week. Then we'll work on crossover."

As Langston, awkwardly using his left hand, dribbled toward home, Jacob waved to Rosie, still on the porch. She waved back.

Teaching Langston was the most Jacob had spoken in months. The effort was exhausting. How could he take pleasure in a trivial game? He returned to the monotony of sanding the chair's spindly back.

—◆—

Mo sat in the cab of his truck in the school parking lot, waiting for Rosie to get off work. Brent High School was originally a one-story brick structure built in the 1930s. It had been remodeled and expanded in recent years, with a graceful new entry, larger windows, and a second-story addition to accommodate new classrooms. Mo watched the students leave the high school in groups of twos and threes. These kids knew the latest fashions: the boys sagged their pants and wore jerseys of their favorite NBA players. The girls wore short skirts or skin-tight jeans and skimpy tops, like pop stars in music videos. The boys looked like their clothes were one size too big, and the girls looked like their clothes were one size too small. To Mo, they all looked like they could be on the streets of Hollywood, not from a small town in Alabama.

When he'd been in school, he wore pressed trousers and a button-down shirt in the warmer months; in the winter, the same pressed trousers with a V-neck sweater. Hair was kept clipped, close to the scalp. Girls wore skirts and blouses. Most of them spent Saturday afternoon straightening their hair for the week ahead. By the time Mo left for Vietnam, school dress had changed completely. The kids grew out Afros. The girls wore bell-bottom jeans that showed off their developing curves. He smiled at the memory.

Mo felt his stomach rumble, and his thoughts turned to tonight's dinner. He had left some steaks marinating in the refrigerator. The potatoes were peeled and ready to be boiled and mashed. Mo's thoughts then moved to Christmas, only days away. He mentally reviewed his menu for the big dinner—always good to stick with tradition. Even when Rosie was living in Birmingham, she'd come home for Christmas. They'd developed a nice routine for the day—he made the ham and the sides, and she'd set the table and make dessert. That girl could sure make a mean pie. Mo was so lost in his daydream of Christmas dinner that he didn't see Edmond come out of the building. Edmond rapped on the roof, startling Mo into the present.

"Hey, Mo. What are you doing here?" He reached through the open window and shook Mo's hand.

"Came to get Rosie. Her car's in the shop."

"I could have given her a ride."

Mo changed the subject. "You doin' anything special for the vacation?"

"Spending Christmas with my mother. What about y'all?"

"Church. Cookin'. Eatin'."

Edmond was surprised. "You cook?"

"Damn right. And I'm good at it too. But I leave the pies to Rosie." An awkward moment passed until Mo added, "So it's only you and your mother on Christmas?"

Edmond nodded.

"The two of you want to come for dinner?"

When Rosie left school she saw Edmond standing by Mo's truck. He saw her too and lifted his arm in a wave. She acknowledged him with a quick nod of her head. Before she got to the truck, Edmond ran around to the passenger side and opened the door. "My mom keeps asking if you're going to stop by again. She's driving me crazy." He imitated his mother. "That girl looks like a good catch."

Rosie pulled herself into the truck. "Yes, I'll bet she has a checklist for all the women who stop by."

"There's not as many as you might think," Edmond said, amusing himself. "Thanks again for the Christmas invite, Mo. I'll ask my mother to make her scalloped potatoes."

Rosie gave a quick sharp look at Mo and smiled at Edmond as he closed the truck door. When they pulled away, Rosie turned to Mo. "Really? You invite people to our holiday dinner without asking me first?"

Mo pretended not to hear her.

Rosie's laptop sat open on the table with her Christmas playlist filling the kitchen. Mo dotted his sweet potato casserole with brown sugar and butter. Rosie opened the oven and took out the fragrant ham, so that Mo could slip the sweet potatoes in to caramelize. The counters were filled with side dishes: green beans, coleslaw, and collard greens. The small kitchen could barely accommodate the two of them, and the sink was filled with dishes, pots, and pans. Mo looked longingly at Rosie's pecan, apple, and pumpkin pies, happy that there'd be leftovers for the next week.

"So tell me again," Mo asked. "What's wrong with having Sam?"

"You already invited Edmond and his mother."

"Then one more person at the table won't make a difference."

"I don't want that man at my holiday table. He's your charity case, not mine." Rosie dragged a stool to the far cabinet and reached for her mother's good silver that was kept in a wooden box. "All those long silences. He makes me nervous."

Mo was emphatic. "Man shouldn't be by himself on Christmas Eve." And then the final touch, the comment he knew would convince her, "Not very Christian of you."

Rosie remembered Mo using those very words about Robert the first Christmas after their divorce. Including Robert in the family Christmas seemed like a good idea—Robert shouldn't be alone for the holiday, and Langston would enjoy having his parents together. On Christmas afternoon, after Robert returned to Birmingham, Langston had a full-blown temper tantrum. He misinterpreted his parents' kindness to each other as proof that they were getting back together. That Christmas was a disaster.

Rosie sighed as she opened the box. The silver was tarnished. She'd have to polish everything before she could put it on the table. More work. Mo's recrimination echoed in her head. The image of Jacob patiently teaching basketball skills to Langston intruded.

"All right, Mo. You win. Invite him. And can you go pick up a pint of heavy whipping cream before the stores close?"

"I don't mind. Could use some air," Mo said as he reached for his jacket.

Although they weren't often physically affectionate, Mo kissed Rosie on the cheek as he left the kitchen. Christmas made Mo more sentimental than usual. From the kitchen window, she watched him get into his truck. He'd always been so youthful, his movement like a man half his age. Although his folksiness sometimes grated on her, she loved him dearly because he was her Uncle Mo—and because he was the last of her parents' generation. Feeling emotional, she turned up the volume and sang along with the holiday songs.

Sitting down to polish the silver brought back memories of Christmas with her parents. Her mother would be a nervous wreck as the dinner approached. She never was much of a cook, and there were some disastrous experiments over the years. Her father always invited enough guests to fill the small dining room, and he was too busy writing his Christmas sermon to offer any help. Mama insisted on pulling out her best china and silver year after year. Rosie was so proud when her mother let her carry the dishes into the dining room.

Langston interrupted Rosie's thoughts. He came in with a half-built Lego rocket ship. "Look, Ma."

Rosie pulled off the polishing mitt and wiped her hands on a dishcloth. "That's really something," she said sincerely.

"Come see the launch pad. I finished it already."

Although the guests would be arriving soon and the table was not perfectly set, she allowed herself this moment with her son. She followed him into the living room. The tree twinkled in one corner, and Langston's Legos took up most of the floor space. She resisted the urge to straighten up and sat down on the floor to admire his creation.

———◆———

Jacob was replacing a bulb in the twinkly Christmas lights around the church sign when Mo pulled up in his truck. "Doin' a last-minute run to the market. C'mon. You can pick up some supplies for the weekend."

Jacob climbed into the cab. Mo chattered all the way to the market—about the weather, Rosie's pies, Christmas spirit. Jacob offered an occasional listening noise, a barely audible "uh-huh" that filled the conversation spaces and bridged Mo's rambling monologue.

Jacob followed Mo into the Winn Dixie supermarket. The place was filled with people and holiday excitement.

Mo grabbed a shopping cart outside the door. "Damn carts. I always get the one that only goes left. Maybe I'm meant to buy stuff that lives on one side of the store."

The tinny sound of an ancient recording of "It's a Holly Jolly Christmas" played over the store's sound system. All of the personnel and some of the patrons wore Santa hats. The store manager casually placed one on Jacob's head accompanied by a hearty "Merry Christmas."

Jacob had never worn a Santa hat, never mind been encouraged to enjoy a Christian holiday. His first instinct was to take off the hat, but he thought it might insult Mo. He was relieved when Mo leaned in and quietly told him to remove the hat because he looked like a fool. He scooped it off his head in one swift motion, reminding him of the way he'd remove his *kipah* before he got into bed each night.

That one thought catapulted him back to his bed in Brooklyn. He remembered the way Julia asked him to rub her lower back for a minute before she fell asleep. She never actually used words, merely turned her back to him and pressed her body close. Recalling that unspoken ritual made his throat tight.

Mo continued his steady stream of chatter as they moved along the dairy aisle in search of whipping cream.

"You know, Rosie and me were talkin'. Sure would be nice if you'd join us for Christmas dinner." Mo waited to see if Jacob would respond. He gave it a second and added, "Langston asked too."

For a brief moment Jacob considered the offer. But then he thought there might be rituals or references to Jesus, and he wouldn't know what to do. He had no gifts to give, nothing to contribute to the holiday meal. He didn't want to expose himself to some embarrassing, awkward situation.

"You tell them that I appreciate the thought, but no thank you."

Mo picked up a lonely Christmas decoration that languished on a nearby display shelf, kitschy electric candlesticks with "Jesus Loves You" in red glitter. He looked at the price. Then by way of explanation, he told anyone in earshot, "If you wait till the last minute, the price comes way down." Mo placed the decoration in his cart.

He and Jacob were immediately distracted by the voice of a young mother shrieking at her toddler. The runaway child careened through the store, his tantrum gaining momentum as he pinballed off carts and displays. The customers froze and watched the boy's growing hysteria.

The boy slammed headfirst into Jacob's legs, grabbed onto his thigh, and looked up. The toddler wailed, his face contorted with fear at the sight of a stranger. Jacob reached down and pried the boy's hands loose. He handed the tearful child to his fast-approaching mother. The child buried his head in his mother's neck.

The embarrassed mother offered a hurried "thank you" to

Jacob. Then she admonished her child, "Jacob Tuttle, behave your-self or Santa Claus is gonna skip our house this year." The boy's muffled cry of objection faded as the mother-son duo walked to-ward the exit.

Mo shook his head. "Nobody keeps kids on a short rope any-more." When he looked to Jacob for confirmation of his opinion, he saw a look of anguish on Jacob's face. "You all right, Sam?"

All Jacob could hear was the sound of his own pulsing blood inside his head. He needed to hear his name aloud. He didn't want to pretend any longer. He tightened his mouth and rubbed his forehead as if he could wipe the thought away.

Mo was stunned by the words he heard next.

"Not Sam...my name is Jacob."

CHAPTER 23

After Mo dropped him off at the church, Jacob immediately went to his basement room and sat on the narrow cot, staring at nothing in particular, trying to make sense of his own behavior. He hadn't planned to tell Mo his real name. It slipped out. So he was no longer Sam the drifter, but Jacob the stranger. Mo had tried to extract more information out of him on the way home, but Jacob stated repeatedly that he didn't remember. He decided to conceal everything beyond his first name—he wasn't ready to be Jacob Fisher again. He might never be ready.

In the dark silence of the caretaker's room, his identity didn't seem to matter much. Without removing his puffy down coat, he lay down on the bed.

There was a soft knock, not so much a knock as a light kick with the tip of a shoe. Jacob stood and opened the door. In one hand, Langston tried to balance the full plate of food that his mother had prepared. In the other were the electric candlesticks that Mo had purchased at the last minute from the grocery store.

"I have food for you," Langston said as he handed Jacob the plate, "from my mom."

Langston looked around, noticing that the room was dark. "Were you sleeping?"

"No. I was thinking."

"I don't know why you won't come over for dinner. You're all by yourself on Christmas."

"I don't mind, really."

"Well at least you should have a present."

Langston placed the plastic decoration on the small bedside table and plugged it in. "Ta-da," he sang with a flourish of his hand.

The words *Jesus Loves You* flashed on and off, filling the darkened room with alternating red and white light, first the red *Jesus* then the white *Loves You*, then both together. Langston and Jacob stared at the lights, momentarily transfixed. Langston broke the silence.

"Uncle Mo told me your name. Can I call you Jacob now?"

"Sure."

"The lights on this thing are cool."

"They are. Thanks. And thank your mom for the food. You better get back so you're not late for dinner."

Langston replied, "See you later...Jacob."

Jacob closed the door behind him and sat with the plate of food, the blinking decoration illuminating his solitude. As he stared at the colored lights, a powerful image surfaced. Jacob willed the memory to come to life. The red lights became red flowers on a table, the white lights morphed into candles, and there stood Julia, eyes closed, hands circling the flame of the Sabbath candles. Jacob felt whole. He wasn't alone anymore.

Jacob longed for these sweet scraps of recollection. He remembered Friday afternoons in Brooklyn, when he'd come home early from teaching. The house would smell of roasting chicken and yeasty challah bread. He'd enlist the kids to straighten and organize their small home. Toys were put in boxes, books returned to shelves. Yossi took out the trash while Miriam set the table. Sarah would wait for him by the piano.

Jacob would stay in this dream if he could, but the reverie only lasted seconds. He took a deep breath, sipped some water, and switched off the electric candlesticks. He could not possibly be farther from home, from who he was. After so many months, he needed to hear the voice of someone who knew him, someone he loved.

In the darkness, Jacob made his way to the pastor's office. He opened the door and picked up the telephone. He was ready to hear his mother's voice. He dialed and let the phone ring, imagining his mother on the other end. He could see her sitting on the couch in her apartment, surrounded by books, photos of grandchildren, and the knickknacks she had accumulated in a lifetime. Hava answered quickly.

"Hello?"

He was tongue-tied. He longed to be with family—the people who knew him in his "real" life, before his world disintegrated.

"Hello?" Hava demanded.

Jacob couldn't bring himself to speak. What could he possibly say? *I'm alive...don't worry.* Perhaps she was better off thinking he was gone forever. His old world meant suffocating pain. Breathing came easier here. He gently placed the receiver back in the cradle.

Jacob returned to his small room and paced. He needed some distraction from these thoughts or he truly would lose his mind. He took his plate and climbed up the steps from the basement. Standing in the dark on the front steps of the church, he could see directly into Rosie's house. Framed through the window was a bountiful holiday table with people sitting down for dinner. His fear of feeling uncomfortable weighed less than his fear of being alone. He crossed the street.

———※———

Hava shook the can of Pledge and sprayed the piano in Jacob's living room. She worked the cloth across the surface and took in her distorted reflection. She'd hoped that polishing his furniture would be distracting. Instead, she found herself repeating the *Sh'ma* over and over again. *Sh'ma Yisrael, Adonai Eloheinu,*

Adonai Echad. "Hear, O Israel: the LORD our God, the LORD is one." It was the first prayer a Jewish child would learn—and repeat every night at bedtime. When Hava babysat the children, she'd listen to them say it before her final goodnight kiss. The prayer was a requirement, but it was never intended to run continually and obsessively in a woman's head—of that she was certain.

The *Sh'ma* states that Judaism, above all, requires a monotheistic belief—one God. But Hava was at her wit's end. One God? What God? She kept repeating the prayer because she hoped it would bring her back to believing in something. She might as well have been reciting "Hickory dickory dock, the mouse ran up the clock" for all the comfort her monotonous prayer provided.

These past few months, she'd sought solace in the counsel of the rabbi, but too often she found herself watching his mouth, nodding as if she were registering his words. Her thoughts were jumbled and incoherent, wandering in ten different directions and nowhere at once.

Since she'd seen the tape in Detective Rosenberg's office, she relentlessly played the event moment by moment on her mind's screen. She saw the explosion again and again, as if mentally viewing the tragedy would somehow change the results. *Sh'ma Yisrael, Adonai Eloheinu, Adonai Echad.*

⸺◆⸺

Edmond and his mother brought their half-filled wine glasses from the living room into the dining room, and they all took their places at the table. Mrs. Scott was wearing the most dreadful Christmas sweater Rosie had ever seen: Santa and the reindeer flying over a house, each reindeer with a bell sewn on his neck, so she jingled when she walked. While Rosie appreciated a man who was close to his mother, all that information about his eating and grooming habits had ruined any possibility of a "sweep-me-off-my-feet" romance.

Rosie sat down and looked at the table, ready to enjoy herself. Mama would have been proud. She had pulled it off—a perfectly set table, fresh flowers, glowing candles. After the obligatory compliments from Edmond and his mother, Mo signaled for the group to join hands in prayer.

Mo looked at Langston. "You want to start?"

Langston knew what was expected and began sincerely. "Dear Jesus, this is Langston Yarber, and I want to say thank you for my family, and for the food, and for the super-builder Lego set that I think I'm gonna get."

Rosie looked at Langston with an indulgent smile. Tonight she would not correct his grammar. The other guests responded warmly with "Amen."

Mo looked across the table to Edmond. "Anything you'd like to share?"

Edmond winked at Langston, "Thank you, Jesus, for the striped silk tie that I think I'm going to get." Then he looked at Rosie. "And thank you to Rosie and her wonderful family, who have welcomed the Scotts to their holiday table."

Rosie knew they were all waiting for her response to Edmond's compliment.

Mrs. Scott piped up. "Heavenly Father, thank you for the gift of my son, Edmond, and for his new job here in Brent. It feels so right to be part of this family at holiday time."

Rosie felt the burn of that last hint. She liked Edmond well enough, but he wasn't pursuing her with any urgency. Hearing his mother's blatant suggestions felt like courtship by proxy.

Mo's benediction was straightforward, impersonal, and yet deeply felt. "Lord, thank you for the blessings of Christmas and for the bounty of food we are about to eat." He stood to slice the ham. "Now, who wants the end piece?"

Before anyone could answer, there was a knock. Langston jumped to open the door. There stood Jacob, holding the full plate that Langston had brought to his room. He was still in his work clothes, but he had combed his shaggy hair.

Langston, genuinely happy to see Jacob, pulled him into the dining room. "You changed your mind." He looked at his mother. "Hey Mom! Jacob is here."

Jacob looked at the startled faces gathered around the table. Mo stood carving the meat, while the other guests passed steaming side dishes. The air was filled with the aromas of food, fragrant candles, and pine from the Christmas tree.

Rosie looked accusingly at Mo. She couldn't believe that Sam—or Jacob, or whoever he was—had shown up after refusing her earlier invitation. Her table was perfectly arranged, the meal was proceeding smoothly, and now he walked in? Did the man have no manners? While she got up to get a place setting from the sideboard and Mo pulled an extra chair to the table, Edmond introduced himself and his mother.

Mo patted the added seat neat to him, and Jacob put his plate down. Mo nudged Rosie under the table.

"I'm glad you decided to join us. You came in time to eat," she said with forced politeness.

Langston piped up. "Wait! We can't eat until Jacob offers his thanks."

Rosie tempered her son's enthusiasm. "Be still, Langston. We don't want to put him on the spot."

Mo jumped to Langston's defense with a conspiratorial wink. "Sure we do." He turned to Jacob. "It's our Christmas custom to go around the table and give thanks. You don't wanna break tradition."

Jacob looked at the candles glowing on the table and the expectant faces of his hosts. Rosie was apprehensive. Was he going to say something embarrassing? Was he going to say anything at all?

Jacob spoke, "Blessed are you, oh God, who has kept us alive and allowed us to enjoy this season...this shining moment in time."

The beauty of his words touched her. This "shining moment in time" was a simple truth for all of them. She studied his face, trying to understand what might be going on behind his clear blue eyes. The stranger suddenly seemed different to her, no longer vacant or passive. She had no way of knowing that Jacob had offered the English version of a Hebrew prayer of gratitude spoken on holidays and special occasions.

The smell of biscuits burning in the oven brought her back to reality. "Damn!" She jumped up and grabbed the pan.

"She always burns the biscuits," Langston whispered to Jacob. "You have to cut off the bottoms." Langston returned to his sweet potatoes.

Rosie noticed that Jacob ate everything on his plate.

After dinner, the guests carried the dishes to the kitchen. Mo rolled up his shirtsleeves and shooed them all away. "I've got a system," he announced, "and it includes y'all gettin' out of the kitchen."

Langston led Jacob into the living room and showed him his Lego spaceship. Jacob sat on the floor and let the boy ramble on about his creation. While keeping up the small talk with Edmond and his mother, Rosie watched Jacob and her son playing on the floor.

CHAPTER 24

The rain had been relentless all afternoon and showed no signs of easing. The rising puddles were ankle deep. Rosie stood in the doorway of the main building of Brent High, eyeing the distance to her car in the faculty lot. She'd forgotten her umbrella, and, to make matters worse, she had a stack of essays and no room in her book bag. She tucked the essays inside her coat, took a deep breath, and sprinted for the car.

The rain pelted her car on the way home. At one point, she had to pull over because the windshield wipers didn't work fast enough, and she couldn't see. She hoped that Mo had the good sense to drive over to pick up Langston.

A few blocks from home, she spotted Jacob walking toward First Baptist. He carried a plastic supermarket bag in each hand, and he was soaked to the skin. She remembered his face at the Christmas table. Rosie pulled over and opened the passenger window.

"Hop in. You look like you could use a ride."

Jacob looked down at the water streaming from his clothes and hair. "Are you sure?"

"Don't worry about it." She leaned over and opened the door. There was a long, awkward moment of silence as Jacob settled into his seat and pushed his matted hair from his face. Rosie quickly filled the air with small talk. "If I didn't have a leak in my roof,

I'd love the rain. It makes me want to go home and curl up in bed
with a good book."

"Do you read a lot?" Jacob asked.

Rosie was interested. "Well, you're making progress. That's
the first time you've asked me a question." She smiled at him.
"When I was little, my mother took me to the library every two
weeks, and I'd check out a stack of books. I'd usually finish them
all before the two weeks were up."

Rosie stopped at a red light. The rain fell stubbornly, the wipers beating in a steady rhythm. She stole a side glance at Jacob.
"Do you have a favorite book?" It was a question she often used
with a troubled student. A discussion of favorite books or movies
could lead to a more open conversation.

Jacob smiled. "I like biographies and memoirs."

"Anyone in particular?"

Jacob nodded. "Teddy Roosevelt, Churchill, Miles Davis,
that kind of thing."

His face fell, as if he'd admitted some terrible secret. Rosie
watched him, not sure how to move the conversation forward. He
turned away and looked intently at the road.

In the silence, the rain pounded the roof. This guy was definitely off-kilter. Those long silences and blank stares indicated a
troubled mind. Even a homeless wanderer should have the good
sense to find a better place to land than Brent.

Rosie noticed the water dripping off Jacob's nose and ears.
Self-consciously, he used the back of his hand to wipe off the
moisture. A horn beeped impatiently from behind. The light had
changed to green. She signaled her apology to the driver with a
wave of her hand.

"I'm sorry. I'm ruining the seat," Jacob said.

"It's only water," Rosie responded without the usual critical
edge to her voice.

She pulled over in front of First Baptist. As Jacob opened the door, Rosie added, "I have lots of books you can borrow. I might even have some biographies."

Their eyes locked.

"Thanks for the lift," he offered as he escaped her scrutiny.

Rosie opened the front door to the sound of a video game filtering in from the living room. She filed away her thoughts about Jacob and turned her attention to home: Langston, dinner, and the damn leak in the roof. She set up a new bucket under the maddening drip and warmed up some stew for dinner.

Later that night, after Langston was asleep, a new cold front pushed through the already sodden town, bringing heavy winds and another drenching rain. She could hear the steady plinking sound of drops falling in the plastic bucket. She sat at the kitchen table with a cup of green tea and opened her laptop to check Facebook before settling into her tenth graders' essays on Robert Frost.

She looked at the recent posts from her friends in Birmingham. Most of them were uninteresting—pictures of meals, homemade cakes, and babies with sunglasses. As she scrolled mindlessly, a message came through from Edmond. Rosie hesitated. She didn't want to accept his friend request. She wasn't ready for him to see all those pictures of Langston and his father. She signed off quickly, hoping he'd think she didn't see his request.

Rosie meant to correct the essays, but her mind drifted—to Jacob, alone in the church basement as the storm passed. She felt sorry for him. It must be lonely to be down there by himself, hour after hour, with nothing but an old transistor radio to pass the time. Even during daylight hours when he was busy, he was alone. She wondered what it would be like to be the only white face in a tight-knit African American community. She took out a legal pad and wrote down some notes: *Jacob (Something), Educated, Good with children, Hard-working.* Then she added some questions to the list: *City? Carpenter? Handyman?*

Rosie turned back to the essays, forcing herself to finish. She glanced at the list and added a final question: *man vs. self?* Although she still didn't know the cause, Jacob's battle seemed to be internal. His mystery fascinated her. She was Nosy Rosie, after all.

Before she went to bed, she emptied the bucket in the living room.

CHAPTER 25

After nearly a week of rain and gloom, Rosie awoke on Saturday morning to bright sunlight streaming through the blinds. She took in the sounds and smells of home—cartoons in the living room, pancakes on the griddle, coffee in the pot. She dozed for a few more moments, luxuriating in not having to rush through the morning. A loud banging startled her into consciousness.

She stood at the top of the stairs and shouted down to Mo. "What the hell is that?"

Mo looked up from the griddle and pointed to the ceiling. "Jacob. He's fixing the roof."

"Did you ask him to do that?"

"No. He showed up this morning. Maybe he's psychic."

Rosie dressed quickly and went outside. The roof was drying in the morning sun. She watched Jacob pull the worn shingles off and inspect the flashing around the chimney. He was sure-footed, easily keeping his balance as he worked. He had stripped down to an undershirt, which showed his well-formed muscles and athletic physique. For the first time, Rosie noticed that Jacob had a body. Flushed with embarrassment, she felt like she'd walked in on him while he was in the shower.

He seemed completely absorbed in the repair—competent and confident twenty feet above the earth. She watched him for a few moments before shouting up to him, "You be careful up there." He acknowledged her with a nod and returned to his work.

———◆———

Although he'd been at First Baptist for many months, Jacob still preferred to stay in the shadows as much as possible. He did not seek contact with others, finding he had little to say. A few congregants raised their eyebrows when they saw him, wondering how the church had enough money to pay a second handyman. When the pastor explained that Jacob was working for room and board, they backed off.

Each week, the sound of the music pulled him to Tuesday choir practice and the Sunday-morning service. The simple harmonies, the passionate voices, and the infectious rhythms resonated in his gut. The music was familiar, even if the lyrics were foreign.

The melodies brought him back to a simpler time—sitting with Lenny on his hand-me-down couch, the ancient turntable spinning, listening to the history of jazz. He remembered Lenny's face, eyes closed, head nodding, clutching his prized recording of "Black, Brown, and Beige" by Mahalia Jackson and Duke Ellington. That was Jacob's introduction to gospel, but it was only a recording. What he heard at First Baptist was the real thing.

Jacob pictured the record collection that Lenny had willed him lining the shelves of his boyhood bedroom. He'd kept the records in the same chronological order that Lenny had—from the early days of ragtime and blues, to Dixieland and swing, to the great vocalists, and on to the more improvisational jazz of Miles Davis, John Coltrane, and Herbie Hancock. The records were vinyl, in their original jackets, worn with use.

He remembered how his parents had fought about his "inappropriate" taste in music. His mother had been his champion, arguing with his hardheaded father that listening to Lenny's records was a temporary phase to be tolerated. He could see his mother standing by the door of his bedroom in her pastel housecoat, exhausted, waiting for him to turn off the music and go to sleep.

His mother. He had not allowed himself to think of her since the day he'd tried to call. She would have had her sixty-fourth birthday since he left. He pictured her at the kitchen sink at his own home, bathing one of his babies—was it Sarah who was kicking and splashing and making his mother laugh? He smiled at the memory. He missed his mother's all-encompassing love, but he did not miss her stifling anxiety.

His mother. Trench had called her in desperation from the emergency room. He'd waited for her to arrive and then he disappeared. When Jacob finally gained consciousness, there she stood, her scarf half off her head, asking the doctor to repeat over and over exactly why her son was in the hospital.

"This is a mistake," Hava told the doctor. "My son doesn't do drugs. He doesn't even smoke cigarettes."

Jacob recalled the hysteria in her voice. The doctor offered to show her the chart, but Hava swatted it away. "He comes from a good home. Two parents who love him. A fine education."

The young doctor assured her she was not alone, that many children from good families get in trouble with heroin. He explained the treatment and offered some hope. When Hava finally accepted the doctor's assessment, she blamed Trench for Jacob's downfall, demanding that he be arrested. Even when the doctor explained that Trench had saved her son, Hava wouldn't apologize for her anger.

Jacob's father never came to the hospital. After a confidential conference with the rabbi, Aaron learned that Jacob wasn't the first observant boy to fall prey to addiction. In fact, the problem was so pervasive that a reputable rehab program had been established in Israel. Nonetheless, the family had to conceal Jacob's transgressions from the community. He was weak, and this character flaw would make him unmarriageable. Aaron made plans to ship his son off for a year, away from the bad influences.

Jacob realized he was more like his father than he thought—Aaron had wanted to avoid gossip about his son's addiction, while Jacob wanted to avoid the look of pity on peoples' faces. In Brooklyn, the laws of his religion would tell him how to eat, pray, and grieve—all within the tight framework of his insular community. In Brent, Jacob was free for the first time in his life. His anonymity gave him freedom—freedom from religious obedience, from public opinion, and from any obligation to the concept of God.

Jacob pushed all thoughts of home away and concentrated on the music.

Each week Mr. Day, the choir director, introduced different selections. The congregants listened to the choir with their whole beings, clapping in rhythm, raising arms in praise, and shouting responses. When Rosie came forward for her solo, her voice was clear and authentic. The service could not be more different from his Orthodox synagogue in Brooklyn. In Jewish worship, the individual moved through the scripted, unchanged prayers at his own pace, and the cantor would occasionally bring the congregation together with ancient liturgy or responsive song. There was little visible emotion. The Sunday-morning service at First Baptist, by contrast, was a communal sharing of both pain and joy.

Jacob looked forward to the Sunday service. He'd settle into his secret perch in the alcove above the chapel before the congregants began filing in. The men wore suits and ties. The women looked like a flock of brightly colored birds as they greeted one another, bobbing their heads to kiss cheeks and admire children. They wore an array of gemstone-colored suits and dresses, surpassed only by flamboyant hats perched atop well-coiffed hair. It appeared that some of the women even wore their hats over wigs. His mind leapfrogged to his wife.

Julia's greatest bone of contention with Orthodoxy was the

sheitel—the wig. It was required that an observant married woman cover her hair to indicate modesty. As the Muslim woman dons the *hijab* when she leaves her home, so does the religious Jewish wife tuck her hair away. For everyday errands in the outside world, a fashionable cloche or colorful scarf would do, but for Julia to look presentable in any public social situation she had to wear a *sheitel*. Her natural hair had always been unmanageable—everything from corkscrew curls to loose ringlets. Any moisture in the air, and the strands on her head would coil.

She complained that the *sheitel* was hot and itchy. No wonder the older women all cut their own hair so short. She wore her wig only for synagogue or dressy occasions. She couldn't wait to get home and free the *sheitel* to roost on its wig stand in her closet. Her wild curls and a scarf were good enough for her immediate family. Jacob would have loved her if she didn't have a hair on her head.

To distract himself from the memory of Julia, Jacob focused on the arriving parishioners who filled the chapel with energy. The little girls twirled in party dresses with flouncy skirts, while the young boys tugged at ties and fidgeted in their polished oxfords. Even the adolescent boys, who usually wore baggy jeans and T-shirts, dressed up on Sunday.

This Sunday he watched the Christian ceremony of baptism. A young couple cradling a new baby stood beaming in front of the congregation. The mother was dressed in a bright blue dress, barely squeezed into its slim cut. Jacob could see that she'd recently been pregnant—her belly hadn't yet returned to its natural shape, her hips strained at the fabric, and her breasts were milk-filled and waiting. The father stood proud in his brown suit, new shirt and tie, and shined shoes. His face was a beacon of light as he tentatively took the tiny infant from his mother's arms and handed him to the pastor for the blessing.

"Please note that young Tolliver, like his parents, has dressed for the occasion," Pastor Johnson said as he lifted the baby so all could see his tiny tuxedo T-shirt. The congregation cooed, and the baby wailed.

The pastor turned to the parents. "Your presence today indicates your dedication to raising this child in the ways of the Lord."

The crying infant. The milky mother. The nervous father. He recognized the primal, instinctive sensation of pride and paternity. He had cradled Yossi, his firstborn, at his bris, the ritual circumcision performed eight days after the birth of every Jewish male. Julia cried throughout the ceremony, fearing the pain to her newborn son. But after she nursed him, she could see that he hadn't suffered.

As the congregation filed out, Mo leaned into him. "They're servin' good food in the social hall after this is over."

Jacob turned to Mo, his voice trembling. "I am a father."

"What are you talkin' about?"

Jacob responded, "I know that feeling." He gestured toward the father holding the infant. "I've done that."

The unplanned confession scared Jacob. Why was he telling Mo what he wanted to hide? He bolted for the exit, needing fresh air. Mo followed.

Jacob felt wild and frightened. This man was being kind and compassionate and all Jacob wanted to do was run. If he told Mo about his family, he'd have to tell him everything. No more hiding, no more pretending. Mo placed a hand on Jacob's shoulder to steady him, but Jacob cut him off.

"Let me be."

Mo, surprised at Jacob's intensity, raised his hands in surrender. "Take your time."

Jacob muttered quick thanks and left.

⟫⋅⟪

Rosie was putting away dishes when Mo came into the kitchen

carrying some loose dirty clothes. He approached the washing machine and began fiddling with the dials.

"I'm gonna throw Jacob's dirty clothes in the wash. Man's only got three shirts, and two of them used to belong to me. He's been rinsin' them out in the basement sink. And they ain't gettin' clean."

Rosie got up. "Let me do that. Last time you did the laundry, everything turned pink."

"I didn't think one red sock could do that much damage," Mo said, grinning.

Rosie took the clothes from Mo. "Does he talk to you?"

"This morning at the baptism—clear as day—he said he was a father," Mo said.

"Just like that?"

"The service musta jogged his memory."

"That's all he said? No details?"

"If I push him, he shuts down. He opens the door a crack, but he don't invite anybody in for coffee and cake."

"He's a strange one. I can't figure him out," Rosie said as she stuffed the clothes into the washing machine, but Mo was already halfway up the stairs and out of earshot.

Maybe Jacob wasn't at all what she thought. She looked at the label of the shirt he'd been wearing when he arrived: *Meyer Brothers, New York.*

Later that night, Rosie sat at the table, sipping tea and reviewing her lessons. She couldn't keep her mind on school. The legal pad with the list of Jacob's characteristics rested next to her. She added *father* and *New York* to the list.

———⊰•⊱———

Jacob stood in the doorway to the empty sanctuary. The room smelled of wood and people, leftover hints of Lemon Pledge mingled with perfume and aftershave from the congregants at the last worship. The smells had become familiar, yet he was far from content. In the last few days Julia and the children had taken up residence in his thoughts. The memories were clouding his eyes like swarming gnats. He filled his waking hours with manual labor so his exhausted body could fall asleep at night.

He crossed the sanctuary and sat at the piano. His hands caressed the shape of the casement. There was nothing fancy about this old upright: It had dings, scratches, and fingerprints all over the wood. Although he'd dusted it many times in the past months, he'd never tried the keyboard.

Jacob leafed through the sheaf of music that sat on top. He studied each piece for a few moments. Then without conscious effort, he read the music, humming each melody, until he found the bluesy hymn that had been replaying in his head.

In his world, the world he had come from, the world he now purposefully ignored, liturgical music was unchanged. Chants and melodies had been handed down for thousands of years. Little innovative music was written for worship. Both prayers of lament and those of celebration were instantly recognized by Jews the world over. Here, in this new world, worship and creativity were intrinsically linked.

Jacob set out the music for the song that had intrigued him, sat down at the piano, lifted the keyboard cover, and played. He played the melody line with his right hand. After a few moments, his left hand added the chords. The action was natural and unforced.

He didn't realize that Rosie was standing in the sanctuary doorway as he played. He began to sing the lyrics in a pure and full-voiced tenor. Rosie moved toward the piano.

Jacob stopped abruptly when he became aware of her presence.

"Don't stop."

"I had the song stuck in my head."

He lightly played a line from the hymn. The notes hung in the air.

"Such a beautiful melody," Rosie offered as she moved closer.

Jacob stood up awkwardly. Rosie showed him the neatly folded laundry. "I brought you clean shirts."

She couldn't resist asking, "How long did you study piano?"

Jacob gently closed the keyboard cover and looked directly at Rosie. He knew she meant well with her concern, but he couldn't engage. One question would lead to another, and he would have to claim his history. He chose to continue his deception. "I can't remember."

He could tell she didn't trust him. He wanted to placate her. "I studied music my whole life, mostly classical." He launched into "Clair de Lune" by Debussy. "But then I learned about jazz." He segued into 'Take the 'A' Train" by Duke Ellington. "And that turned me from someone who studied music into a musician." He finished the segment.

There was a long moment as the final chord hung in the air.

"You should play the piano more often," Rosie said. She placed the laundered shirts on the nearest pew and left.

Jacob did not move to claim his shirts until he heard the front door of the church close behind her.

CHAPTER 26

Rosie had been waiting all day to talk to Kala. She intercepted her in the teachers' lounge and requested a confidential meeting. Kala's office was the repository for all things behavioral at the school; every sort of problem was handled behind her doors, from learning and psychological issues to suspected abuse in a student's home. As a school guidance counselor, Kala had heard it all. Her insight—and pragmatic advice—was invaluable.

Rosie took a moment to gather her thoughts. She wasn't sure if she was stepping on uneven ground with her concern for Hansom. There was a fine line between helping and butting in.

"Listen, Kala, I have an issue with one of my students, and I'm not sure about the best way to handle it."

Kala put her pen down and waited for her to continue.

"Hansom Willis...he's getting the emotional shit kicked out of him. I notice that during passing periods, he sticks close to the lockers so he won't have to bump into anyone. They make fun of everything about him—his skin, his name, his effeminate behavior. The other day I found him in the janitor's supply room putting bleach on his face to clear up the acne."

"Bleach," Kala said with no inflection, the one word a statement of fact.

Rosie nodded, "He's floundering and needs help. I don't know where to get it. His grandmother has zero resources."

Kala typed notes from the conversation into her computer. "Is he ostracized by other students?"

"He's got one friend, another oddball who jousts with the pack. Janine Marshall. The heavyset girl who always wears black. She was the one who suggested bleach. No ulterior motive. She meant well."

"Why don't you call his grandmother?" Kala suggested. "Maybe there's something going on at home?" Kala jotted down the phone number on a Post-it and handed it to Rosie.

Rosie opened Kala's office door and hesitated. "Can I ask you something else—not school related?"

"Ask away," Kala responded patiently. She knew that a "door handle" question was often more pressing than the educational matter, especially if it was about a teacher's personal life.

"Remember I told you there was this mysterious guy working at my church?"

Kala nodded.

"Well, I've got red flags waving all over the place."

Kala pressed her fingers together in a peaked triangle, leaned forward, and listened. Rosie pulled out her notes. She told her everything she had gathered about Jacob. "I can't figure this guy out. He doesn't talk for weeks, then he tells us his first name but nothing else. Makes out like he doesn't remember his past. But then it turns out he can fix anything, teach basketball, *and* he plays the piano. Is he bullshitting us?"

Kala took a deep breath and then answered in her gentle Mumbai accent. "Sometimes a person can remember how to perform skills, like playing piano or shooting baskets, and not remember specifics about his past. Rare, but it does happen. Usually this behavior is caused by physical or emotional trauma. It's like the hippocampus is stuttering. The hippocampus is the sorting center for memory."

Rosie absorbed the information. She'd expected Kala to tell

her that she was gullible, but instead she was saying that Jacob might be genuine.

"How long will this stuttering business last?"

"Depends on what triggered him. He might never remember or he could suddenly recall everything. Or...maybe he knows who he is, but he's choosing not to tell you." She paused for effect. "Or he could be bullshitting you completely."

"What if he's on the run, or a con man, or an addict?"

Kala took her glasses off, cleaned them, and put them back on. "Yes...and maybe he's drifting because something happened. Sometimes people are so desperate, so hopeless, that they go 'down river.' They get on a raft and let the current take them wherever it goes."

"Is that from Hindu philosophy?" Rosie asked.

"No. From life." Kala smiled.

The image of Jacob floating down a river felt right. Rosie wanted to find out what had pushed him into the current.

———◆———

She thought about what Kala had told her about Hansom for days, and then she decided to take action. She had to do something to help him, and getting him medical care to clear up his skin would be a good first step. She took out Kala's note and called Hansom's grandmother. The recording on the other end informed her the number was no longer in service.

Rosie took the address from the school's file and drove to his grandmother's house. She had known, by the address, that Hansom had little money, but she was alarmed at how far below the poverty line he lived. His grandmother's home was little more than a shanty. The roofline was crooked, the exterior hadn't been painted in a generation, and old bed sheets covered the windows. There was no hint of lawn or garden, just lumpy spots of dirt and wayward patches of gone-to-seed grass. She sat in her car for the longest time. Going uninvited to a student's house verged on crossing the line.

As she approached the front door, she stepped carefully on the termite-ridden front porch. Rosie knocked on the door. It rattled in the loosened framework.

The frailty of the door reminded her of the children's story of the three little pigs. *I will huff and I will puff and I will blow your house down.* Good Lord, was she the big bad wolf? Rosie knocked again, this time more loudly.

"Use your damn key," she heard an old woman say from within.

"It's not Hansom, Mrs. Fredericks. I'm Mrs. Yarber, Hansom's English teacher. I want to talk to you for a few minutes."

"Hold your horses. I'm moving slow today."

Rosie waited for what seemed forever until the door unlocked and gradually swung open. Hansom's grandmother sat in an old wheelchair. A worn bathrobe with faded daisies barely covered her obese body. Her white hair was thin, revealing patches of shiny scalp. Her feet had been squeezed into slippers below her swollen legs.

"Well, what did you want to talk about? Is he failing? The boy's dumber than wood. My daughter was on drugs when she was pregnant. I think it fried his brains," the woman said as she rolled herself backward into the room.

"No, ma'am. Hansom is doing fine in school. He's a bright boy."

The grandmother snorted.

"Then why are you here?" she asked, her heavily lidded eyes narrowing in suspicion. "Did he do something wrong?"

"No, ma'am. He's well behaved. I want to talk to you about..." Rosie stood in the doorway. "Can I come in? This is personal and we should talk about it privately."

The grandmother rolled herself closer to the door to block

the entry. Still, Rosie saw plenty from the doorstep: a tattered corduroy couch dominated the living space, with a rickety card table and four folding chairs. The table was piled high with old magazines and newspapers. The beige carpet was ancient, buckled and stained with the grime of wheelchair tracks.

She looked Rosie up and down. "We're private enough right here."

Rosie began, "His acne needs to be treated. I would like to take him to a doctor, and I need your permission."

The grandmother took in a deep breath through her mouth and exhaled through her nose. Her entire demeanor went steel cold. "My family don't need charity."

Rosie continued, "I'm concerned that Hansom is being bullied at school."

"That boy knows how to take care of himself. And if Hansom needs a doctor, he gets one. Who the hell are you to tell me that I'm not taking proper care of that child? Next thing you're gonna have the county take him away because the boy has pimples? That's my grandchild!"

"That's not what I said, Mrs. Fredericks. I want to help him."

"Well, we don't need your help. Me and Hansom do fine on our own. Now you get your scrawny behind out of here and don't you come back." She swung her huge leg at the door, slamming it in Rosie's face.

Rosie didn't know whether to hang her head in defeat or bang on the door and threaten. She turned to go and realized that Hansom was standing a few yards in back of her, his arms filled with groceries. His face was a confusion of fear and embarrassment. He had heard the encounter.

"I just wanted her permission to take you to a doctor for your skin," she explained.

"Yeah. Well, you pissed Grandma off," he muttered as he walked past her into the house.

Rosie noticed the contents of the grocery bags: bread, milk, eggs, and adult diapers. Grandma didn't take care of Hansom. He took care of her.

CHAPTER 27

Rosie was so preoccupied with her frustration about Hansom that driving home was automatic. She didn't notice Robert's parked car and was caught off guard by seeing him sitting on the front steps of her house. His presence startled her, and the way her heart jumped in her chest was unsettling. Damn if she didn't still find him attractive. She dredged up old memories of his deception and bad husbanding. Once she rallied the familiar animosity, she stepped from the car.

"And what brings you here unannounced?" she asked as she walked by him and put her key in the door. "Langston's not around today. He went to a friend's house...and I'm not changing his plans to accommodate your whim."

"I didn't come to see Langston. I came to see you."

Rosie stood on the steps and gave him a good long look. "You need money." She waited for the predictable excuse and request.

Robert half grinned, "No, I don't need money."

"Are you in some kind of trouble?"

"Not a bit. I came to see you specifically. May I come in?"

Rosie pushed open the front door and Robert followed her inside. She made a weak attempt at courtesy. She offered food and a cold drink. Robert declined and waited for her attention.

Feeling awkward, Rosie put her hands on her hips and pressed her point. "So why did you drive all the way here?"

"I've been trying to work through some of my problems, and I think I figured it out."

Rosie's arms moved to cross defensively over her chest. Robert took a deep breath. "I want us to try again. We had a good thing, baby, and I want to see if we can make it work."

Rosie was stunned. His suggestion was the furthest thought from her mind. Before she could respond, Robert put his arms around her.

"I have missed you more than you know," he whispered in her ear. His hands moved down her back and rested on her waist.

Rosie's feelings were a conflicted jumble. How dare he be so familiar with her body, and yet how comforting the familiarity felt. She missed loving him and having a complete home, and yet she was satisfied being her own person and no longer a victim. She pushed him away and stepped back.

"You're not good for me," she said quietly.

"I *wasn't* good for you, but I'm sober now."

"It's so much more than that."

His eyes narrowed. "Okay then," he said. "You can't say I didn't try." And with that he walked out.

Robert intentionally left the front door open, and Rosie knew why. He wanted her to run after him, to beg him to return like she had so many times before. But she didn't move. She stood absolutely still, listening to him walk to his car, waiting for the sound of the motor turning over, and anticipating the grind of tires on asphalt.

When she was certain that he'd left, she closed the front door and locked it. The click of the deadbolt acted as emotional punctuation.

———◆———

That night, Rosie cooked spaghetti with meatballs, Langston's favorite. She welcomed the distraction of chopping and preparing.

Langston wolfed down his dinner without a compliment and escaped from the dinner table to practice basketball in the last moments of daylight.

After dinner, Rosie crossed the street for choir practice. In the dusk, she noticed Langston shooting baskets with Jacob. A moment of wistfulness settled on her shoulders like a lightweight scarf, familiar but unnecessary. When Rosie was a child she had a tendency to embellish. Uncle Mo would always pose the question, "Is that a real story or a 'wannabe'?" which was his way of asking, "Are we dealing with truth or fantasy?" When Rosie saw how much Langston enjoyed playing with Jacob, she experienced a clear moment of "wannabe." She wished someone like Jacob was his father.

Edmond pretended not to be waiting for her at the church entrance. She could tell it was a charade because she saw him look at her, then look away, then look back again with exaggerated welcome. Was he interested or not? More importantly, was she interested in him?

"Are you free on Saturday?" he asked. "I've got tickets for the symphony, an all-Mozart program."

Without looking at him, she responded, "All the way in Birmingham?"

Rosie heard the edge in her own voice.

"It's only fifty miles."

Langston made a basket, and Jacob high-fived him. Once again, Rosie observed the easy connection between her son and Jacob.

Edmond followed her gaze.

"Okay, then...you think about it. We need to get in for rehearsal." Edmond held the door open for her, and Rosie forced a smile.

Before she entered the church, she cupped her hands around her mouth and hollered instructions toward the basketball hoop:

"Langston! Enough! It's a school night."

—◦—

Jacob observed the rehearsal from the last row of the sanctuary. It had taken him weeks to feel comfortable listening to the choir from the back row instead of the loft. The choir members were connected to their music, and his presence was that of interloper. In the past month, Jacob had begun to feel more familiar to himself. He attributed that sense of ease to his growing relationship with Langston. The boy made him laugh, and his willingness to be coached gave Jacob an hour to look forward to each day.

Mr. Day kept running the sopranos through their part, but when the choir combined, the sound was off. The sections didn't balance. Attempting to ascertain the problem, Mr. Day asked that only the tenors sing.

From the back of the room came Jacob's voice, escaping his throat before he realized he was singing. So pure was his sound, so plaintive and powerful, that everyone else stopped singing. Jacob trailed off when he realized no one else was participating.

Mr. Day suggested, "Well, you can't sit all the way back there—it throws the rest of us off. Move up."

As Jacob walked to the choir he thought of a long-ago childhood toy, Wooly Willy, a cartoon face with iron shavings that were pulled into position by a magnetized stylus. He felt like those magnetic scraps, being dragged by some unseen hand to the front of the church. He sat with the other tenors.

Jacob hardly noticed that two hours passed. Mr. Day called the practice to a close. Wordlessly, the choir members came together, joined hands, and swayed. Ill at ease and unsure of what was expected of him, Jacob got up to leave.

Rosie waved him into the prayer circle next to her. As she took his hand she leaned in. "You are exactly what this choir needs."

CHAPTER 28

Hava sighed deeply as she arrived at Jacob's row house. She was surprised how much she missed her daughter-in-law. She'd been suspicious of Julia in the beginning. Jacob brought her to the house not long after they met. Hava could see that they'd fallen in love. Julia had been a kitchen Jew, assimilated and non-observant, identifying her religious connection with chicken soup and bagels and lox. Her parents had brought her up to believe that religion was narrow-minded and superstitious. Like many others of her generation, she had sought spiritual understanding in yoga classes, self-help books, and late-night philosophical discussions. Hava worried that Julia wasn't good enough for her son, that she would never fit into their world.

Julia was not the type to accept doctrine blindly. Hava listened to her objections and assured her that observant Jews knew what was going on in the outside world but chose not to live in it. Instead, they preferred a life of gratitude and consideration for the needs of others. In time, Julia couldn't deny the appeal.

Jacob was a kind and patient teacher. He was strict in his own observance of the laws and expected Julia to be the same. Under his tutelage and with his mother's help, Julia came to understand the Orthodox way of life. At Jacob's urging, she began keeping the Sabbath and holidays required by the Jewish calendar. Over several months, Hava taught her to incorporate the many blessings for daily life and to keep a kosher home. A wedding date was set.

———◦◦◦———

Hava took the mail from the box and unlocked the front door. She added the envelopes to the considerable pile on the entry table and looked around the house—untouched since the explosion. Sara's dollhouse made her short of breath and dizzy.

She forced herself to finish the chores. She ran a dust rag over the furniture and went to the backyard. She swept the fallen leaves and pushed them into a garbage bag. She unrolled a garden hose hidden in a pot. The shrubs would die if they didn't get watered twice a week. As she turned on the hose, Jacob's neighbor, Frank DeFazio, stepped out of his house.

"Hello, Mrs. Fisher," he said tentatively.

"Frank."

She acknowledged him but didn't want a real conversation. Perhaps saying his name out loud would be enough, and he would go about his business. No such luck.

"You know there were some detectives here the other day asking questions about Julia and the kids. They asked about Jacob, but I didn't know what to tell them," Frank said. "I hope that's okay."

"They're very thorough." She was still hoping Frank would go away.

"Have they found anything?" he asked. He stood there as if he was thinking about every word, his right hand jiggling change in his pocket. Hava couldn't bear the tension, nor did she want to talk about Detective Rosenberg's latest investigations. She shook her head.

Hava uncoiled the hose and turned on the water.

Frank cleared his throat. "Those hoses are a pain in the neck."

"I should let his garden die?" she said, her voice filled with irony and sadness.

"No, not at all. You know, Mrs. Fisher, there really is no need for you to come over here all the time...I can do that for you."

"It gives me something to do while we wait."

"I understand," he said as he walked away. He turned back again. Hava thought to herself, *now what?*

"Me and Donna light a candle for them every Sunday at Mass." He jiggled his pocket change again. "Is that okay, you being Jewish and all?"

Hava wanted to hug him for his bumbling generosity, but all she did was offer a perfunctory, "Thank you."

———◆———

Back in her own kitchen, Hava dusted the countertop with flour and pushed her hands into the pile of wheat, sugar, and eggs. She kneaded the newly risen dough into a malleable lump, rolled out three long tubes, and braided them together in a loaf. Most Shabbats, Hava bought her challah from the bakery. Every once in a while she made her own. Lately, the never-ending occupation with housework had led to a feeling of emptiness and insignificance. What personal or spiritual growth was there in washing dishes, cleaning the floor, or the labor-intensive process of making bread? Yet, as she anchored each section of dough to the other, she recited the required blessings and a sense of calm settled on her.

As Hava wove the dough together, she was reminded of the meaning behind each section of the braided challah. Truth, peace, and justice were carefully intertwined. Each needed the other to function. Her daughter-in-law, Julia, had once learned to make challah at her side. Hava now imagined that she was teaching her granddaughters, Miriam and Sarah, the same way she had taught their mother. She told them of each braid's purpose. She explained aloud to the girls that the woman of the house was referred to as the *akeret habayit,* the foundation of the home. Her granddaughters were so real to her that she became distraught when she noticed that she was alone in the kitchen.

Hava awoke from that night's sleep having dreamt that she had gone to the *mikvah*, the ritual bath of purification that all married women who menstruate were required to observe. She was sixty-four, and her body no longer linked her to a monthly cycle—it hadn't for twelve years—but the dream had been so vivid that she lifted the crook of her elbow to her nose to see if there was any lingering hint of the rosewater moisturizer that the *mikvah* provided. Clearly, the dream had been her subconscious desire that time be rolled back—her husband asleep beside her, the children protected and safe. What could she do today to keep from feeling sorry for herself? What mundane distraction would keep her from believing that Jacob's way of dealing with his loss had been to take his own life?

When her own husband died, she thought the sadness would kill her. She was afraid to be alone in their bedroom because she might inhale some lingering remnant of his physical being. Grief became familiar, the only place she felt comfortable and loyal to her husband's memory. She would scrape the wound over and over again to make sure it stayed fresh. Slowly, in the tiniest of increments, she let an emotional scab form. Even so, she would start each day crushed by the reality that, against her will, she continued to breathe.

In time, her pain eased and she admitted—guiltily—that she enjoyed her freedom. Although she had run their household without complaint, Aaron had been a demanding husband. She was always concerned with his needs, his schedule. Now she liked sleeping in, having scrambled eggs for dinner, and watching television programs that he would have labeled immodest. Yes, he had been funny and loving, but he was often opinionated and temperamental, too. Now she was her own boss.

Loss was a complicated tangle of emotions.

If Hava were honest, she would admit that she had emotionally separated from her husband long before he died. Jacob was the reason for that. For the longest time she suspected there was something wrong with her son, an illness or hidden genetic malfunction or, God forbid, a mental instability. He was bright, and yet he couldn't study. He was personable and yet constantly argumentative. At first she attributed those qualities to adolescence, but puberty came and went and the qualities lingered, taking root, changing her child, and frightening her. When she attempted to involve her husband, he dismissed her concerns, declaring Jacob immature. Hava became hyper-vigilant and perpetually anxious.

Aaron had no patience for rule breaking or experimentation. He blamed everybody else for Jacob's flagrant truancy and abrogation of Orthodox dictates. It was her fault, his friend's fault, but most of all, it was Jacob's fault. Her husband ranted and bellowed, screaming at Jacob that he was flawed.

Jacob's response was to prove him right. He had lived away from them for a year when Hava got the phone call that altered her life. Some man named Trench called to tell them that Jacob was in the hospital. She was beside herself with frenzied disbelief. Although visibly upset, her husband refused to get out of his chair and talk on the phone. When he forbade her to go to Jacob, it took her less than thirty seconds to make up her mind. She covered her head with a scarf, put reading glasses in her purse, and headed for the hospital.

Finding your child in a hospital bed was one thing, but discovering that he was a junkie who tempted death repeatedly was nearly incomprehensible. Very little of that night was ordered in her head. It was a random jumble of doctors and social services.

She did remember the young social worker who sat with her in the hallway. She kept saying that alcohol and drug abuse was a disease, a fatal illness. She said that it was important for Hava to understand that chronic heroin addiction ended in one of three ways: prison, madness, or death.

Hava sat by Jacob's bed throughout the night, praying that none of those alternatives would claim her only son. In the morning, when she was sure he would live, she called her husband and told him that if he did not arrange for the best possible rehab for Jacob, she would no longer be his wife.

CHAPTER 29

Jacob wasn't sure why he woke from sleep. Not the usual reasons. No voice had been calling him from his subconscious. No vague memory of smell and touch prodded him awake. He was fully alert and didn't know why. He closed his eyes and concentrated on a rasp of whispered voices in the dead of night—conspiratorial and unfamiliar. The sound of breaking glass came from inside the chapel.

Jacob slipped from the safety of his woolen cocoon. The night air wicked away any remnant of comfort. He fumbled into pants, a flannel shirt, and shoes. He reached for the hunting rifle on the closet's top shelf. He stood perfectly still, head cocked to the side.

Soundlessly, Jacob moved toward the voices. He stopped outside the sanctuary to take in the sounds: loud thuds, breaking glass, and drunken laughter. He cautiously moved up the stairs, the weight of the rifle heavy in his hands. In the chapel, the moonlight illuminated the broken pews, a shattered stained-glass window, a spray-painted devil's pentagram over the mural of Jesus, and two men, one covered in tattoos, the other clearly a tweaker, a meth addict, with rotting teeth, and open sores on his face and arms.

Jacob stood unseen in the shadows.

The tatted guy was the leader. He was thick limbed with a shaved head and a bull neck; his arms and chest said he lifted weights daily. He read dangerous. Every inch of visible skin, from wrist to jawline, was covered in ink. Even from a distance Jacob could make out a fanged rattlesnake in strike mode. The snake wound its way up his arm and to the back of his shaved head, where it spit out a black swastika, like some giant poisonous spider ready to sting. He wielded a baseball bat. The broken glass and pews were his doing.

Tweaker was pissing on the steps to the pulpit. His urine smelled foul, like something had crawled inside him and died. The air smelled bitter, like chemicals.

Jacob was hyper-aware of his own body. He could hear his legs brush against each other as he moved forward. He could taste his own fear as he shifted the rifle into ready position and slipped off the safety. Mo's words echoed in his head: "Never pull a gun unless you are prepared to use it."

His hands shook, and his heart pounded. If he pointed his weapon, the incident could easily escalate. He decided to back out slowly and call the police. That was when Tweaker reached for a rusty metal container. As he splashed the contents on the wooden pews and lectern, Jacob recognized the distinct smell of kerosene. If he didn't stop them, the church would go up in flames.

Jacob placed the rifle out of sight, leaning it against the last row of pews, and stepped out of the shadows. "You need to leave."

The vandals stopped mid-action.

Swastika spoke. "Who the fuck are you?" The man moved toward him.

Jacob's body tensed for physical confrontation. He maintained eye contact with Swastika, but he could see Tweaker puff up his chest and close in.

A sane man would have run for help. Jacob didn't. In that instant he was sure he would die. That was what he wanted. He had known for months there was nothing to live for. He would let someone else do the job for him—his version of suicide by cop.

Jacob planted his feet. "This is a house of God. Get out."

Swastika flashed a mock smile and touched his chest in sarcastic apology. "If we knew it was a white church, we woulda minded our manners."

"You're an asshole," Jacob growled. "Get the fuck out."

Swastika's grip tightened around the bat. "This prick doesn't know how to show respect. Come on, nigger lover. Let's play."

He swung the bat at Jacob. He should have stood there and welcomed the blow, but his arms instinctively moved to protect his head. Swastika checked his swing when Jacob cowered, then changed position and violently shoved the end of the bat into Jacob's gut. As he doubled over, Swastika smashed the bat into his face. Jacob gushed blood from his nose. He stumbled, reeling backward from the force of the impact. He tried to stop himself, but the momentum took him down. Stunned, he watched his blood drip on the floor.

Jacob heard the sound of Tweaker's kick before he felt it. The steel-tipped work boot landed in his ribs. Excruciating pain. He started to lose consciousness. Through the haze of battered submission, and against his will, the instinct to survive took over. *Live, goddamn it. Live.* Jacob saw the rifle he'd placed against the back of the pew. He'd have only one chance to use it.

Tweaker stood over him. "Get up and talk to me with respect." They were intent on shaming him until the end.

Jacob pulled himself up, using the pew as leverage. As his hand cleared the back of the pew, he grabbed the rifle and spun toward his attackers, pointing the barrel at Swastika's chest.

The room erupted. Tweaker lunged for his legs and Swastika closed in. Jacob lurched to the left, and his rifle discharged. The sound of the shot shocked all of them, giving Jacob a nanosecond to steady the weapon on Swastika's heart.

The man held his hands up in a take-it-easy stance. "You don't look too familiar with that rifle, buddy."

Jacob stood his ground.

When Tweaker took a step closer, Jacob switched his aim. In that instant of hesitation, Swastika charged. Jacob flipped the rifle from Tweaker back to Swastika and pulled the trigger. Swastika shrieked in pain. He fell to the floor holding his shattered leg.

Jacob pointed the gun at Tweaker. "Don't move."

———◆———

Mo awoke for the second time that night to use the bathroom. Damn prostate. As he returned to the warmth of his bed, he heard a gunshot. His body tensed. There was no mistaking that sound, and it came from across the street. He looked out his window and saw a light on in the chapel and a beat-up truck near the entrance. He heard a second gunshot. He unlocked the aluminum box underneath his bed, took out his shotgun, and ran across the street as quickly as his seventy-year-old body could take him.

Mo swung open the chapel doors to a sight he could never have imagined: Jacob was pointing the old hunting rifle at two skinheads. One of the men clutched his leg, trying to stop the flow of blood. The church was in shambles—pews destroyed, stained glass in shards, murals defaced. The distinct smell of kerosene mixed with urine, blood, and gunpowder hung in the air.

Mo immediately took charge. "What the hell is going on here?"

He took the rifle from Jacob's trembling hands, all the while keeping his own shotgun pointed at the intruders.

Mo ordered Jacob, "Go over to Pastor Johnson's office and call the police."

Jacob tried to move, but his legs wouldn't obey. As adrenaline ebbed, his body registered the blows of bat, the impact of boot.

Mo brought his shotgun closer to Tweaker's chest. "You boys should know that I was a US Marine, and I ain't afraid to pull a trigger."

When Rosie heard the gunshots and saw the light in the

chapel, she called the police. Within minutes, she heard sirens. Throwing on clothes, she ran outside. A patrol car arrived at the same time as the paramedics. She waited with them, shivering in the cool night air, until one of the officers gave an all clear.

When Rosie entered the church, she was relieved to see Mo standing calmly to the side. Jacob was soaked in sweat, and the blood from his nose was smeared on his shirt. The police had cuffed the intruders, and one of the paramedics had tended to the wounded vandal. The other medic was examining Jacob while a police officer peppered him with questions.

Although the medic declared him unharmed, Jacob couldn't narrate the chain of events, as if his sequencing switch was turned off.

Mo intervened. "Why don't you officers come back tomorrow? Jacob will be happy to answer your questions when he's feelin' better."

Mo surveyed the damage. "We can put this place back together. Nothin' so bad we can't clean it or fix it."

Jacob walked mechanically toward the basement stairs.

"You sure you're okay?" Mo asked. He continued even though Jacob didn't respond. "Go back to bed. That's what I'm gonna do."

CHAPTER 30

With only the light of the moon coming through the tiny window in the caretaker's room, Jacob stood at the sink and washed his battered face. He heard a soft knock. He opened the door to Rosie, her face full of concern. He moved away from the door, giving her room to enter.

"You all right?"

The words hung in the air. Jacob stood stone-still, head down, shoulders slumped. "I shot a man."

"Why are you ashamed?" Rosie asked. "I'm grateful for what you did."

Jacob blinked rapidly. "I had every intention of killing that man...at the last second, I changed my mind."

Rosie responded matter of factly, "Then you didn't have every intention."

His thoughts twisted and swirled. Was he coward or hero?

The assault on Jacob's nose sent a small dribble of blood slowly down his mouth. He held a washcloth in his hand, so disconnected that he didn't clean his face.

"The medic said he'll be fine...unfortunately," she continued. She pointed to his face. "That looks like it hurts." Jacob shrugged.

"Sit down," she ordered. He sat like an obedient child. Rosie took the washcloth from his hand and rinsed it in the sink. She gently wiped the blood from his face. He winced but allowed her to touch him.

A tremor went through his body. "It was the *sound* of the rifle." He said the word "sound" with loathing. "The *sound*...made me think of my life before." It was as close to the truth as he could venture.

Rosie sat down next to him on the narrow cot, their legs touching. He longed to tell her that it wasn't the rifle he was hearing. He wanted to explain. He wanted the words to come out of his mouth in a verbal purge of personal horror: *my family—my whole family—was killed in front of me. My wife and children died, and I couldn't stop it.* But his mouth didn't form the words. The thoughts filled every cell of his body, but the words stayed trapped in his chest.

He closed his eyes to dodge Rosie's judgment. She touched his shoulder in compassion.

Eyes still closed, Jacob visited the fantasy of rescuing his family. Moments before the explosion he raced onto the bus and demanded that they leave. He picked up Sarah and forced Miriam, Yossi, and Julia to get off the bus.

In his fantasy, the bus still exploded, but his family was safe.

In his fantasy, he comforted them and they clung to one another.

In his fantasy, they lived.

He opened his eyes and looked at Rosie. "When I was real... before I came here...what if..." he mumbled, the pain obstructing his words.

Rosie acknowledged his urgent desperation. She spoke to him soothingly. "You're real now. You protected us. You're a good person."

"I don't know what kind of person I am," he erupted. "I'm made up. No beginning, no end."

As quickly as the anger appeared, it was replaced by sorrow. Vulnerable, childlike, Jacob sat on the cot with his hands open in front of him, imploring. His long-buried despair surfaced. He cried—desolate, inconsolable. Rosie held him, quieting and comforting him as she would a tearful child.

Rosie kissed his damp cheeks, his forehead. "Shhh, it'll be okay. You'll figure it out. You're a good man. A good man."

Rosie held Jacob as tears flooded his face. She again kissed his forehead, his cheeks, repeating over and over, "You're a good man."

Jacob turned his head as she kissed his cheek. Her lips landed on the corner of his mouth. He should not have kissed her back full on the mouth, but he did. Rosie pulled away, and he could tell she was embarrassed. But when she looked up, he held her gaze. Gently, his hand held the back of her head. He drew her face to his. He kissed her again. Her body welcomed him. Rosie would have no idea that while making love to her, Jacob had summoned the essence of Julia.

———◦◦◦———

When they finally separated on the tiny cot, Rosie rested her head on Jacob's chest. He mindlessly traced the curve of her back. She savored the moment—she didn't realize how much she'd missed this feeling of being held and cherished. Jacob's face was swollen and red where he had taken punches, but within moments, he was asleep.

Rosie woke up when first daylight filtered through the small basement window. Her thoughts were muddled. She looked at Jacob, his face in sleep so different than it was last night. Yes, the connection had felt right—good, in fact—but she questioned her judgment. Her loneliness had caused her to act on impulse. In the intensity of the moment, she'd lost her self-awareness, switching off her analytical voice to become a physical being, a body with needs. In the light of day, her recklessness was replaced by shame. If she left now, no one would ever know she'd been there. She could forget that physical desire ever happened. She pulled her tangled clothes from the floor and dressed in silence.

———————

Mo had finally given up on sleep—too much commotion. He showered and dressed. The reflection in the mirror over his dresser pleased him. He was damn proud of himself for the way he handled the situation last night. Not bad for an old man. He was about to put on some coffee when he heard the front door open and footsteps quietly climb the staircase. He heard Rosie's gentle step in the hallway and the bedroom door shutting behind her. Clearly, she'd been out all night.

Rosie came downstairs a little later than usual. Mo and Langston were already deep into their cereal bowls.

"Hey, Mom," Langston said, "Uncle Mo told me what happened last night."

"Yep, there was quite a bit of excitement."

"If I'd have been there, I would have karate chopped them," he said, shoveling a last spoonful of cereal into his mouth.

"That woulda finished 'em off," Mo agreed.

Rosie looked out the kitchen window toward the church. Mo waited till Langston finished his breakfast and went upstairs to retrieve his backpack.

As he rinsed the cereal bowls, Mo began his interrogation: "What are you doin' with Jacob?"

"We've been talking."

"Nothin' more?"

Rosie's hackles went up. "What does that mean?"

"I thought you didn't like him."

"Then why is it your job to say I do?"

Mo tried another tactic. "Look, he's a fine person. I like him, I do. But you know how it is in this town. People will start flappin' their lips about you."

Rosie's voice trailed off as she walked up the stairs. "Judge not, lest you be judged. Condemn not, lest you be condemned."

Mo called after her, "You don't have to go all biblical on me. I'm tryin' to help you here."

CHAPTER 31

Rosie welcomed the distraction of Brent High School after the violence at First Baptist. The incident had not yet been reported on local television, so she was able to block out her confusion over the night with Jacob and concentrate on school. She found a note in her teacher's box on folded paper:

> *Dear Mrs. Yarber,*
> *I don't care what my grandmother says.*
> *I need your help.*
> *Hansom*

This presented a problem: the guardian said no, but the student said yes.

The registrar's desk was at the back of the school's main office. Rosie approached the prehistoric woman who safeguarded all school records. She was eating some kind of Tupperware lunch that reeked of broccoli. Rosie's stomach turned.

"Lydia, could you tell me when Hansom Willis turns eighteen?"

Rosie waited patiently as the woman wiped her mouth and punched the request into her computer.

"Three weeks from today," she said with half hiccup, half burp.

Hansom would technically be an adult in three weeks, so as

of then it wouldn't matter what his grandmother wanted.

Rosie spoke as she walked into Kala's office: "Tell me I'm interfering and I should mind my own damn business."

Kala looked over the top of her glasses. "Does your scathing self-assessment have anything to do with me?"

Rosie bulldozed to her point. "If a kid lets me know that he wants my help for an elective medical treatment, but the guardian says no, and I find out that the kid turns eighteen in three weeks—what do you suggest I do?"

"Who is it?"

"The Willis kid. I contacted his grandmother about getting him some help for his skin. She turned me down—rather rudely, I might add. He left me this note today."

Rosie handed Kala the note. She read it quickly and gave it back. "Wait until the day after he turns eighteen and offer help again."

Kala returned to her work.

"That's what I thought. But I need to get him to a doctor who will treat him pro bono. The kid has no money."

"So this *is* about me?" Kala teased.

"It's more about your husband."

Kala smiled. "Okay, you're right. You're an interfering biddy and you should mind your own business." Kala's Bombay accent made the whole exchange comical, but Rosie knew she'd get what she wanted. Kala would persuade her husband to treat Hansom without charge.

—————

Mo and Jacob were cleaning the church. They swept up the broken stained glass and covered them with sheets of plywood. They worked silently, each engrossed in his thoughts. A chaotic battle raged in Jacob—guilt for betraying Julia, affection for Rosie, and disgust with his carnal needs.

Mo rambled on. "You know, sometimes if you make things look right on the outside, people get to believin' that things are gonna be right on the inside. I read that some big professor at one of those fancy schools did an experiment that proved it. He had a bunch of folks hold a pencil in their teeth when they watched a cartoon. Like this," he said, biting down on a ruler from the toolbox. He gripped the ruler lengthwise between his teeth, forcing his face into a jack o' lantern grin.

He quickly removed the ruler and continued talking. "And another bunch watched the *same* cartoon regular, no pencil. Damn if the people holdin' the pencil in their teeth didn't think the cartoon was funnier that the do-nothin' group. Why do you think that was?" Jacob waited for Mo's conclusion. The old man was a breathing archive of *Reader's Digest* articles.

Mo paused dramatically, and then drove his point home. "Because the group holdin' the pencil already had their mouths in a smile. See, sometimes things work from the outside in."

Jacob nodded in agreement but didn't offer a comment. Instead, he moved to the pews to examine the splintered wood that had absorbed the gunshot.

"You and Rosie seem to be getting along." Mo tried to take any edge off his voice, like this was simply another topic of conversation. Jacob said nothing.

"She's been through a lot. Deadbeat husband and all."

Jacob pretended not to hear Mo's prattle and addressed the work at hand. "These pews need a few pieces of mahogany and a good sander."

Mo looked straight at him and sucked his tooth.

CHAPTER 32

Rosie parked her car in the spot reserved for visitors in the Brent Police Station parking lot. Sergeant Michaelson, the officer who had handled the break-in, sat behind his desk. In front of him were two computer screens: one showed current police activity; the other was for Michaelson's own research. When Rosie walked in, he stood up and shook her hand.

"Sorry for the mess," he offered, clearing a few files from a chair so Rosie could sit.

Michaelson reviewed his notes: the break-in, the destruction, the shooting. Jacob's version of the events made sense, but Michaelson was concerned that Jacob couldn't verify his own identity. He had no driver's license, no credit cards, and no passport, and he was unable or unwilling to supply a last name. Fortunately, Mo had spoken highly of Jacob's character.

"The case is pretty cut and dried. Those two have extensive records, and we have plenty of evidence against them," the sergeant added.

Rosie wanted to use Michaelson as her confessor. She wanted to hang her head and admit that she'd slept with a man whose full name she did not know. Rosie, who wasn't a risk taker, had allowed her neediness to override her reason. But she didn't say anything revealing. Instead, she asked, "How do I find out who Jacob is? He says he can't remember how he got here. Or why."

Michaelson sighed. "Do you know how many people go missing each year? Tens of thousands. Some are foul play, but most are folks who got sick of their lives and walked out. Maybe he doesn't want to get found."

"Someone must be looking for him. Isn't there a list of some kind?"

"Mrs. Yarber, I wish I could help you. This is a huge country, and we're a small-town police force. You're better off checking with the FBI. They keep a database." He jotted down a website address on a Post-it and handed it to her. "Public information. Look for yourself."

As she got in her car, she again considered the possibility that Jacob had run away from something. Kala said he could be bull-shitting, but he didn't seem like a fugitive. He was helpful and brave, risking his neck to stop the skinheads. Clearly his problems were beyond her ability to comprehend. She should stop rummaging in Jacob's mess of a life and try to move forward with her own. He had to leave. She needed to patch him up and help him find his way home. It would be best for everyone.

Later that night, after the dinner dishes were put away and the lesson plans reviewed, Rosie opened her laptop. She tried the FBI website that Sergeant Michaelson had suggested and began to scroll through the thousands of faces—every age and every race—that made up the database. Even after she narrowed her search to white males between thirty and forty, there were still thousands of faces. At first, she read the short blurb on each missing person; then, growing weary, she scrolled through the pictures. The sheer volume of people frustrated her.

Langston came in the kitchen and opened the refrigerator.

"What are you looking for?" Rosie asked.

"I don't know. Somethin' good." Langston flopped in a chair. "I'm bored."

Here she was occupied with all these missing sons and

daughters while her own son was right there under her roof, asking for company. She was always so busy—with lessons and essays, cooking and cleaning. Not tonight.

"Me too," Rosie agreed. She shut down the computer. "How about a game of Crazy Eights?"

Langston's face lit up. He loved games of all kinds, but cards were a favorite,

Rosie hugged her son and rocked him side to side, "Have I told you that you are one terrific kid?"

Langston groaned. "You tell me every day."

"Close your eyes." He complied. Rosie kissed his lids. "Do you know what that means?"

Langston shook his head, wiping the kiss away.

"It means that I love you. Only people who love you will kiss you on the eyes." She released him and grabbed the playing cards from the kitchen junk drawer. "But that doesn't mean I'll let you win."

⸺•⸺

As the rain fell steadily outside, Jacob worked to erase any traces of the damage at First Baptist. He fixated on the immediate gratification of smoothing the grain and restoring the woodwork. He was pleased that the new pews looked nearly identical to the old ones.

He reconstructed the other night in his head as he meticulously fitted pieces of mahogany onto the beat-up pews. He remembered the noise in the church as the vandals broke the windows. He saw their angry, drunken expressions and felt their blows to his head and stomach. He saw himself pointing the gun at the tatted intruder.

His thoughts turned to Rosie—the taste of her mouth, her raw energy and need—and his own fierce passion. That had been real, so real that he couldn't stop thinking about it. His thoughts—of the vandals, of his own desire for death, of his need for human contact—tumbled over one another, vying for dominance.

Jacob was startled from his reverie when Mo came in. "I hope this'll be my last trip for supplies," Mo said as he shook the rain from his hair and clothes. He inspected Jacob's completed work. "Nice job."

Rosie came in right behind Mo.

"Hey Rosie," Mo said.

Jacob's greeting was awkward. "Hello."

Rosie kept an upbeat tone. "How's it goin'?"

"Should have most of this place back in order by Sunday," Mo said proudly.

An uncomfortable silence followed. Rosie studied her feet while Jacob ran his hands over a rough patch of wood.

Mo made a self-conscious excuse. "Well, I gotta check on... something."

He hastily left the chapel. Rosie moved closer to Jacob and admired his work. "You can't tell the difference."

"Can you hand me that *schlissel*?" he asked.

"The what?"

"I meant the wrench." Jacob looked down at the pew, busying his hands while his mind raced. He'd slipped and used a Yiddish word.

"Why did you call it a *schlissel*?" Rosie tried to make her mouth say the strange-sounding word.

He deflected the question, "That's the first thing that popped into my head."

She rummaged around the toolbox and took a deep breath. The words came haltingly. "I need to talk to you about the other night."

Jacob looked at her. He remembered the hollows in her neck that he had kissed, the nutty smell of her sweat.

Rosie filled the silence. "I don't know what got into me. That was crazy. I don't do things like that. You don't know anything about me. And I don't know anything about you."

Jacob nodded in agreement. They had no business being together.

As she handed him the wrench, their hands touched.

Her body language was rigid and unyielding. "I made a mistake. That...can't happen again."

Jacob nodded.

Rosie turned away. "I have to go."

As he watched her cross the street, he felt an aching in his chest. He desired Rosie, but he longed for Julia. Thinking about his beautiful young wife threw him into a cauldron of self-loathing. He'd been intimate with another woman. He felt the powerful weight of guilt and the regret that his life could go on when his family was gone.

⁕

The house was quiet. Langston was in his room doing homework. Mo was watching football in his bedroom. Rosie poured herself a glass of chardonay from a bottle that she kept in the back of the refrigerator. After so many months of keeping her emotions in check, she wasn't ready for this tempest. She waited for the warmth that usually came after a few sips of wine.

Rosie had always liked puzzles. She was good at them. The prepackaged jigsaws with pictures of the Grand Canyon challenged her. Making sense out of a mess of random pieces could keep her occupied for hours. The more she learned about Jacob, the more he reminded her of one of those jigsaws. She could see there was a whole human being in front of her, but she didn't know how to put him together.

She took out her legal pad with the notes about Jacob. She added "*carpenter*" and "*German? Amish?*" to the list of his attributes.

CHAPTER 33

Hava hoped that a trip to the supermarket would take her mind off what Detective Rosenberg had told her. He'd called to tell her that DNA evidence from the bomber in the bus explosion had identified a recently released prison inmate, with a history of mental illness. No political organization had claimed him, nor had he left any letter or recording to further a cause. He'd missed the last meeting with his parole officer and hadn't filled his medication prescription in months. Detective Rosenberg had been right all along—the bomber was a deranged rogue. At least there was an explanation, even if it was insanity.

Naomi's new baby had forced Hava back into the world. The colicky infant distracted her with his round-the-clock needs. She still had a knack for calming a baby. She swaddled, sang, patted, and paced so he could relax into sleep. Naomi was grateful for a few hours of peace, and Hava could divert herself from unhealthy thoughts. Her grandchildren were refuge, but thoughts of her own son always intruded. She missed him desperately.

She had decided to stop looking for answers. She'd gone to see the rabbi for counseling, and he spouted the same platitudes that he said at every funeral or *shiva*. She argued with him—she couldn't accept that God had a plan that involved so much loss and suffering. But she also couldn't face a world without God. For all of her sixty-four years, she'd found comfort in the rituals and restrictions of religious life and joy in belonging to a community. So she decided to stop searching for a benevolent God—the one she believed in before the tragedy—and get on with living. When issues of faith entered her head, she pushed them away and focused on minutiae.

Hava had always enjoyed shopping for food. She'd walk up and down the aisles hoping to be inspired. Sometimes she'd bring home an interesting piece of produce to try in a new recipe on her grandchildren. Last week she made spaghetti squash with tomato sauce. Only the toddler really thought it was spaghetti. The other children knew they were being duped.

Hava caught a glimpse of herself in the refrigerator case when she rounded the frozen food section. She almost didn't recognize the reflection, and the response to her own image unsettled her. Once, years ago, she and her husband had celebrated an anniversary at a fancy kosher restaurant on the Upper West Side. The back wall of the dining room was mirrored, and as they entered Hava saw her own reflection. For one split second it didn't register that she was looking at herself, and she remembered thinking that the "other" woman was beautiful. Now she noted that the other woman was nice-looking—but no longer beautiful. She fixed her headscarf and straightened her blouse as she appraised herself.

A voice with a heavy Yiddish accent startled her. "Are you practicing for the fashion parade?"

Hava immediately recognized eighty-year-old Rivka Edelman and laughed off the old woman's comment. She gave her a quick hug. "How are you, Rivka?"

"How should I be when I have to schlep around by myself getting food for the week?" Rivka waved her arthritic right hand over her shopping cart. In the cart sat one loaf of bread, one quart of milk, instant coffee, two cans of tuna, three bananas, a dozen eggs, and toilet paper.

"Where's your daughter?" Hava asked.

"Her youngest boy has a kidney stone, and she's over him like an eagle. How could a twenty-year-old get a stone?"

Hava fell into Rivka's rhythm. "I don't think kidney stones ask about someone's age before they visit."

"Nothing asks for permission before it visits. Look at my hand." Rivka held up her left hand, which had a large bruise covering the back. "I woke up three days ago and I got this thing on me. I asked the doctor what it was. Maybe I bumped myself in the night? I move all over like a jumping bean. Maybe I banged it on the nightstand? You know what he said?"

Rivka didn't wait for an answer. "He said that it comes from old age and that he hopes *he* lives long enough to get one."

Hava couldn't get a word in. The old woman kept yammering as if she hadn't talked in months.

Rivka held up two fingers. "Do you know what this represents?"

Hava shrugged. Why bother trying to respond?

"It's the number of husbands I've had. Izzy died, and two years later I married Abe—a good man—one bad hip but otherwise perfect. It was a shock when his heart gave out. He was only eighty-four. I would look around for another one, but I don't want to wash someone else's socks again." She took a breath and continued her monologue. "You're younger than me. You shouldn't be alone. Have you talked to the rabbi? He knows people."

It took Hava a moment before she realized that Rivka was suggesting that she ask the rabbi to set her up in a marriage.

"Rivka, I'm nowhere near ready to meet someone. It's less than a year since Julia and the children—"

Rivka cut her off, "Nobody's saying you shouldn't wait out the year—but then what? It's your responsibility to be a good Jew, and you know what good Jews do? They choose life."

"Yes, you're right," Hava said. She was willing to acquiesce to any nonsense to get rid of this busybody and go on with her day. Rivka squeezed Hava's arm hard enough to leave fingerprints and shuffled her cart down the aisle.

What an insensitive and ridiculous person, thought Hava as she rubbed her arm. *Who would the rabbi suggest I marry anyway?*

"Nonsense!" she said out loud as she smoothed her skirt.

As Hava unpacked her groceries, she found herself thinking about Rivka Edelman's suggestion. The idea left her cold. She thought of the few divorced men and widowers she knew in the community—the ones who were appropriate for her age were either repulsive or ancient. Her husband had been an attractive man and a good provider. Only as a father did he fall short.

Hava never felt that her husband was to blame for his poor parenting. Aaron was the only son of Holocaust survivors who damaged him with repeated stories of suffering and loss. Even after decades in the United States, his parents kept to themselves. They lived in constant fear of persecution and passed that anxiety on to their child. Aaron's own fears turned inward to depression and outward to anger. Jacob had been his primary target.

Jacob's paternal grandparents died before he was born, but his father relayed their stories, passing survivors' guilt and dread to a third generation. Naomi was an easy child, compliant and passive, but Jacob tested the limits. Aaron kept his son in line through harsh criticism and constant punishment. But Jacob's natural ebullience and curiosity could not be contained. As soon as he was old enough to walk home by himself, he started exploring. In retrospect, it was only natural that Jacob would rebel completely.

By sixteen, Jacob's interest in music propelled him away from Torah study and family. Aaron was adamant that Jacob was on the wrong path. Jacob argued with his father, point for point, validating his choices with facts and the corroborating opinions of others. Although Jacob was not a weak person, the daily barrage of attacks eroded his sense of self. To survive, he left home. Hava pretended to give him free reign by looking the other way and secretly providing him with money.

Jacob descended into random couch surfing and substance abuse. Hava believed that his involvement with drugs came from disappointment. And she, his mother, had disappointed him more than anyone else. He must have known deep down that she thought his music was frivolous. She had often told him, "You love music, but you're not a musician." How could she know what he was, what he could achieve? Her inability to believe in her son seeped into his life and poisoned his soul. Drugs dulled his disillusion.

Eventually, Aaron found out that Hava was giving Jacob money and banned him from the house. When he overdosed, Aaron begrudgingly found a rehab program in Israel. As soon as he finished detoxing, Hava packed his bag, picked him up from the hospital, and put him on a plane to Tel Aviv. His father never even said goodbye.

The program was called Yitziah, or the Way Forward. A well-respected American rabbi, himself a former addict, ran Yitziah like a kibbutz, with all members handling the chores and upkeep, food and laundry. Other than prayer services and daily Torah study, the program followed the outlines of secular twelve-step programs, with lots of group sessions and individual counseling. A full year was mandatory, necessary to facilitate real behavioral change. Jacob could call home only once a month. If his father answered, he'd immediately pass the phone to Hava.

Jacob was miserable. The drugs were out of his body, and he resented the program's regimented routine. He didn't understand why he had to be stuck in a rehab facility so far from home. That first phone call, he begged Hava to let him return to Brooklyn. She hung up before his tears destroyed her resolve. The second month, he told her how much he hated the endless and repeated confessions of drug use and debauchery. He wasn't like the other people. The third call hinted at transformation. He'd found a therapist who understood him and an elective, woodworking, which he truly enjoyed.

Over time, he led prayers and read Torah for the group. The rabbi singled him out for the beauty of his voice and encouraged him to act as the rehab community's cantor. Jacob slowly rediscovered his connection to tradition and ritual, becoming fully observant. Hava secretly worried that it was one addiction replacing the other.

———————

In his sixth month of rehab, Jacob was summoned to the office. As he walked into the rabbi's private sanctum, he knew there was trouble. The rabbi motioned for him to sit.

"There is no easy way to tell you this," the rabbi stated. "Your father died today on his way to work. Massive heart attack."

Jacob's mouth felt scorched, and he slumped into the chair. His father was gone. He remembered his father beaming at him when he cogently analyzed a Talmudic text. He also recalled his father's face shouting at him, followed by door slamming, shoves, slaps, and ultimately, humiliation. He remembered the day when his father's face registered defeat—he'd tried to break Jacob and failed.

The dry mouth turned into that inexplicably appealing metallic taste he'd have in his mouth after shooting up. When he was high, he forgot how he'd disappointed his parents. Although he'd been clean for more than six months, he craved that feeling of euphoric indifference.

The rabbi could see the confusion in Jacob's face. "We can arrange for you to go home to be with your family."

"I can't go back yet," Jacob said quickly. "I'm not ready. They will have to bury him without me."

CHAPTER 34

Rosie wasn't one to pace. If something bothered her, she bit her cuticles or slid the small cross on her neck back and forth on its chain. Today, however, she was pacing. From inside her kitchen, she could see Jacob setting up a ladder to paint the church. Looking at him made her anxious. She wanted to ask him for a favor.

An idea had been slowly forming. Hansom was good with his hands. He'd whittled the bird she kept on her desk. Jacob was clearly adept with tools and woodwork. If she could convince him to take an interest in Hansom, the boy might pick up some skills and feel valuable. Rosie stopped pacing. She made up her mind to broach the idea, and if Jacob was hurt because of that whole sex thing, then so be it.

—◦•◦—

Out of the corner of his eye, Jacob could see Rosie cross the street and head in his direction. Maybe she'd change course and he could elude her. Nothing had been the same since the night they connected. That word struck Jacob as sterile, but that's what they had done—connected, not only in a completely satisfying physical sense, but also in some perfectly human symbiosis. As Rosie approached, he became overly interested in his paint bucket. He continued painting like a bad actor in some poorly staged play.

"Good morning," Rosie said, straining to sound casual.

"Morning," Jacob responded. An eternity of silent seconds

passed.

"I have a student who could use your help."

Jacob stopped painting and listened.

"There's a kid in my class who has a difficult home life. He's good with his hands...likes woodworking. I was hoping to send him around so you could teach him a few things."

Jacob remembered the gentle face of his counselor in the rehab program in Israel. Unlike the other counselors, Gil was a secular Jew, a successful cabinetmaker and business owner. He, too, had battled heroin. Jacob welcomed the distraction from endless hours of group meetings and therapy. Working with his hands had been an important component of his recovery. Jacob would be happy to share those skills.

"Anytime," he offered.

"Thanks," Rosie said. "I'll let you know when."

She relaxed against the post and instantly pulled away, the entire back of her shirt covered in wet paint. Jacob tried to stifle his guffaw. The laugh escaped through his nose, shooting a small bubble of snot all the way onto the front of Rosie's shirt. He was embarrassed, but she was horrified, not knowing what to clean first—the back or the front. She flapped her hands in disgust and hopped about like a frantic bird. Jacob yielded to full-out laughter, and then Rosie laughed harder. Eventually the two were bent over, gasping for air.

———

Word of the skinhead incident quickly spread through Brent. In a small town where not much happened, a racially motivated attack was big news. The local paper reported that the men had come all the way from Mississippi. They had vandalized another church, held up a liquor store, and stolen the beat-up truck.

Most Sundays, First Baptist was full. Today, it was overflowing. Other than the plywood sheets that covered the window openings once filled with stained glass, everything had been repaired.

Jacob took his place in the tenor section of the choir. After the shooting, he'd thrown himself into work. He looked at Rosie sitting with the other sopranos, her attention fully given to prayer and song. Her short natural hair accentuated her perfectly symmetrical features and high cheekbones. Jacob had a powerful desire to touch her, to feel her warm body and gentle breath, but she'd been clear that that would never happen again.

After the introductory hymn, Pastor Johnson stepped to the podium. Once the congregation stopped buzzing, he began. "Having others to share our burdens is the unspoken gift of belonging to a congregation. Last Thursday night, every one of us shared the burden of hate, when vandals defiled property and threatened our house of worship."

He paused for dramatic effect. "But look around—you will see little out of place. That is because we have a hero among us. That hero is our friend Jacob, who put his fear aside and acted for the good of this community." He gestured toward Jacob. "On behalf of the entire congregation, I offer you thanks and benediction."

The congregation applauded. Jacob looked down at his lap, overwhelmed by the pastor's erroneous adulation. He had wanted to die, not be a hero.

Pastor Johnson nodded to the choir director. Mr. Day signaled for the choir to stand. Their voices blended in joyful celebration.

※

Rosie kept her body facing forward. She willed herself to keep her mind on the music. The task was impossible. She recalled the way Jacob's hands, roughened by manual labor, had felt on her body. They had pleased each other without words or instructions, a natural coming together of two souls. Robert had always been so critical of her lovemaking. Jacob made her feel sensual and desired.

Perhaps the mystery surrounding Jacob created some of the attraction. But whatever the source of his allure, Rosie had allowed Jacob to chip away at her hard-won wall of defense.

After the fiasco of his last visit, Robert had been contrite. He stayed in touch via phone but knew better than to ask for a visit with Langston until Rosie cooled off. He apologized repeatedly for his irresponsible behavior. He'd gotten a new job and was trying to turn his life around, even sending delinquent child support payments. When Robert finally asked for an overnight with his son, Rosie could not object. Langston adored his father.

This time, when Rosie and Langston crossed the street after the Sunday service, Robert was waiting for them. He got out of the car to give Langston a big hug. He wore crisp jeans, a pastel button-down, and new Nikes. He looked like the old Robert, polished and smooth. Rosie waited with him on the sidewalk while Langston went to retrieve his overnight bag. Then she noticed a pretty woman—flat-ironed hair, big sunglasses—sitting in the passenger seat of Robert's car.

"And who is that?" she asked. She couldn't mask the hostility in her voice.

"Denise, my new girlfriend." Robert signaled for the woman to get out of the car. "We met at AA. She's been dying to meet Langston."

Denise got out of the car, giving a tiny wave to acknowledge Rosie as Langston came barreling out of the house.

"Langston, this is my friend Denise," Robert said. He turned to Rosie. "I'll bring him back on time, I promise. Are you okay with Denise?"

"Absolutely not—but what can I do about it?"

Langston jumped in the backseat, and Rosie leaned in to buckle his seatbelt. Denise got back in the passenger seat and turned to talk to the boy.

Rosie smiled and waved feebly as the car pulled away.

Inside she was fuming. How dare Robert bring a new woman into Langston's life? The boy needed to spend time with his father, and this Denise would only get in the way. His "new friend" had fallen for Robert's bullshit, just as she had. The man knew how to put on a show, and Langston was an effective prop. Damn Robert. She wanted to pull back the curtain and reveal him for the fraud he was, but she refused to inflict more pain on her son. Her job was to protect Langston.

⸺◆⸺

After working late at school, Rosie pulled up in front of the house and noticed that the lights were on at the church. Mondays were usually quiet—no choir practice or youth ministry. After the exertion of his Sunday sermon, Pastor Johnson always took Monday off. Muttering to herself about the electric bill, she crossed the street and entered the chapel.

Jacob was seated at the piano, humming, playing, and writing on a piece of paper.

Jacob was so engrossed that when Rosie came in, he didn't notice. He tucked the pencil behind his ear and played with both hands. He stopped and made corrections on the page. When he looked up and saw her, he was embarrassed and abruptly stopped playing.

"I saw the lights on. No one's supposed to be in here right now," Rosie stated.

"Sorry. I had this song in my head and I had to get it down."

Jacob played a few bars, watching her face intently as his hands worked the keys. "It's not quite there yet, but..."

"Turn out the lights when you're done," she said curtly.

Jacob continued to play.

As Rosie opened the door, she stopped and listened. "The melody is beautiful. I'd like to hear it when you're finished."

The chapel door closed behind her. Jacob plunked out a *bum, bum, bum, bum, bum, bum—bum-bum*. The notes rattled his memory. It was the same childish finale that he'd played with his daughter Sarah so many months before.

He sat in silence remembering Sarah—her fidgetiness on the piano bench, her compassion for all living things. He let the memory wash over him. He closed the piano.

Jacob tinkered with the song every night after chores were done and the church was quiet. The act of composing absorbed him. There were so many aspects of creating music that felt natural and familiar: the blues progressions he'd learned from Lenny, his fingers on the keyboard, the transcribing of both clef and treble on the page.

He developed the lyrics carefully, matching the sounds of the words to the melody. The words were based on a meditation, a melody he'd sung with his students back in Brooklyn. How strange that here, in Brent, he could weave together Talmudic teachings, Hebraic melodies, and gospel rhythms.

The following week, Rosie met Jacob before choir practice to listen to the song's progress.

"You know, every year we sing a traditional hymn for Gospel Sunday. It's boring. What if you played your song for the choir?"

Before Jacob could refuse her suggestion, the doors to the chapel opened and the choir members filtered in.

"That's not why I wrote it," he said.

Rosie ignored him and beckoned Mr. Day to the piano. "You should listen to this. It's really good."

CHAPTER 35

Pastor Johnson had finished his last phone call for the day and shut down his computer. As he put on his coat, he made small talk with Rosie, who waited by the buzzing copy machine. She was making copies of Jacob's song for choir practice.

She handed him a set of the sheet music. "Jacob wrote it."

Pastor Johnson looked at the page. "I don't know anything about melody, but these are beautiful lyrics." Then he pointed to some squiggles at the top of the page. "If I'm not mistaken, those are Hebrew letters."

"Really? What does it say?"

"I have no idea."

The choir was waiting for her. She'd look into this Hebrew thing later. She gave the copies to Mr. Day and took her seat with the sopranos.

Choir practice ran smoothly. Jacob looked apprehensive when Mr. Day distributed the sheet music for his song, but his fears dissipated when the choir responded positively.

After prayer circle, Rosie watched Jacob talk to Mr. Day about some changes in the song's arrangement. They were both enthusiastic, gesticulating about the harmonies and the flow of the song. But it wasn't Jacob's physical animation that caught her interest. The vibrancy came from within him. Jacob was alive and engaged, fully in his element.

Edmond watched Rosie watch Jacob. What was that look on her face? Pride? Friendship? Attraction? Her expression made him uncomfortable. Territorially, Edmond touched her arm and redirected her interest to him by asking a mundane question about school. Her answer didn't matter. She was talking to Edmond now. That's what mattered.

Hansom waited for Janine in their usual spot, the far corner of the yard. He scanned the throng of students looking for his friend. Today he'd brought Double Fudge Oreos, a snack she loved. He'd surreptitiously used a portion of his food stamps to buy them and had managed to hide the purchase from his grandmother. Janine always shared her food with him. The cookies were deserved payback. His arm shot up to wave her over when he spotted her. Janine saw him. Their eyes connected, and he waved again.

He expected her lopsided smile and a nod of acknowledgment as she made her way over, but instead she turned her head away and back to the boys surrounding her. The sound of derisive laughter rose from the group. He told himself their joke wasn't about him. When the group looked in his direction, and another chorus of insulting laughter catapulted toward him, he felt the ache of rejection. Hansom sat alone, his hand covering the cellophane-wrapped Oreos. Without deliberation, he threw them in the trash.

After lunch, Rosie waited for Hansom to pass by so she could catch his eye. She crooked her finger and indicated that she wanted to talk to him.

"Hey Mrs. Yarber."

"Hey Hansom." Rosie hated the way the whole country now used "hey" as a greeting, but she wanted him to feel comfortable, not corrected.

"You know, I can't stop admiring that bird you whittled for me."

Hansom shifted his body uncomfortably. "Thank you. It wasn't even that good. I can do better."

"I was thinking. You have a natural gift for woodworking, and I know somebody who is skilled in that field. He's looking for an assistant. He would train you at first, so no money while you're learning, but once you have it down, I bet you could pick up some cash."

Hansom fiddled with the straps on his backpack. "Okay, I could do that. I don't work on Thursdays."

"Good. Then this Thursday after school would be perfect. His name is Jacob, and he'll meet you in front of the church at four."

Hansom mumbled his agreement and moved on as the bell rang.

Rosie used her free period at school to do some sleuthing. The mystery of Jacob's identity continued to intrigue her. She had new information. Why were there Hebrew letters on his sheet music, and what did they mean? She found the number for the Birmingham synagogue and made an appointment with the rabbi for the next day.

Rosie had never met a rabbi before. She had known Jews—a few of her teacher colleagues at the high school in Birmingham— but they weren't religious. Once one friend had invited her to a Passover celebration, and she'd been deeply moved by the retelling of the story of the Exodus.

Of course she'd seen Jews in movies and television. She pictured the rabbi as a bearded old man in a dark suit. She was surprised when a sandy-haired man in khakis and a casual dress shirt opened the door of the rabbi's office at Congregation Emanu-El of Birmingham. He introduced himself as Rabbi Klein. At first glance, he looked like he was recently out of college. But when she looked behind his trendy tortoise-shell glasses, she saw that he was probably closer to her age.

Rabbi Klein ushered her into the office, offered a cold drink, and made small talk. When they sat, he quickly got down to business. "So what can I do for you?"

She pulled out Jacob's sheet music from her purse and pointed to the Hebrew letters in the corner. "I want to know what this means."

He quickly answered, "That's the Hebrew abbreviation for *Be'ezrat Hashem*." It literally means 'with the help of God.' It's a sign of faith. Orthodox Jews put it on everything they write." The rabbi examined the lyrics. "Who wrote this?"

"Jacob. He's someone our church took in. Turns out he's a musician."

"You know, the expression 'a narrow bridge' has been around for a long time. This Jacob has done a nice job of interpreting the idea."

Rosie listened intently as the young rabbi explained the origin of the expression. He told her about a famous rabbi from the nineteenth century, Rabbi Nachman of Breslov, in the Ukraine. The phrase "All the world is a narrow bridge, and we should not be afraid" was part of his teachings.

When he handed the music back to Rosie, he asked, "This Jacob...he never mentioned being Jewish?"

"No. Never."

"Interesting. You know, there are groups of Jews all over the world who live according to Rabbi Nachman's teachings," he said. "He believed in the power of music. Joyful celebration connects man to God."

Rosie smiled. "Amen to that."

Rabbi Klein grinned and took a pen from his shirt pocket and a pad of scratch paper from his desk. He wrote three letters in Hebrew and explained, "The Hebrew word for 'faith' is *emunah*.

The root for *emunah* is made of three letters: *aleph - mem - nun.*"

He then wrote the three English equivalents underneath the Hebrew: A - M - N. *"Emunah,"* he repeated. "Amen means faith. Every time we—all religions—say 'amen,' we are simply saying 'faith.' "

Back in her car, Rosie took out the legal pad with the list of Jacob's characteristics and added *Jewish* to the list. As she drove home, she felt energized. Her research into his past was finally paying off. Tomorrow she'd tell him what she had discovered, and maybe that would jog the truth free.

Hansom was eager to get to work at McDonald's. The manager had promised him the drive-through window tonight, and that always made the time go faster. Sometimes he'd pretend he was from another country. As the customer pulled up to the window, he'd read back the order in an accent. He modeled his voice on old TV movies that he watched with his grandmother.

Tonight he was British all the way. *"Thet will beeya two burh-ghars, three lahge freyes, and two koe-lahz."*

As he handed the order through the pass-through, he heard familiar contemptuous laughter.

In the driver's seat was the student who beat him up in the hallway.

"Well, what do we have here? It's Hansom, the faggot with a face like a maggot."

The other guys rolled down the windows and checked him out.

"What was that stupid accent? You trying to pick up some fairy to fuck?"

"I'm working," he responded, trying to sound professional.

"He's working! He's a workin' girl. You mean you're using the McD window to pimp out your gay ass," the driver continued. The backseat was roaring, egging him on for more.

"You're holding up the line," Hansom stated again, trying to keep the hurt out of his voice.

"No I'm not. You were hitting on me. You think I'm a fucking fag."

More laughter from the car.

"There are people behind you," Hansom insisted.

"Tough shit. I'm complaining to the manager that you were using the drive-through to hit on customers. Everyone saw you take out your dick and ask me to suck it. They're gonna fire your ass."

Hansom couldn't stop the tears from coming. "That's a lie and you know it."

There was a flash. One of the guys in the car had taken his picture with a cellphone. Hansom heard their taunts as they pulled out into traffic.

Hansom knew what that picture looked like. Him with his stupid McDonald's uniform and hands on his hips, crying like some indignant girl.

It would be all over Snapchat and Instagram tomorrow. He was a dead man.

———⊰•⊱———

On Thursday afternoon, Jacob scanned the bench he'd arranged in the churchyard. On it were the handyman's essentials harvested from the church's toolbox: various hammers, pliers, and wrenches, a manual wood saw, and an assortment of nails and screws. Jacob wasn't sure how much this kid Hansom knew of the basics, but it couldn't hurt to start from the beginning. He vividly remembered how Gil, his woodworking counselor in rehab, had taught him to tell a Phillips screwdriver from the others.

"It's the *goyisha* one," he said, using the Yiddish for non-Jew. "It has a cross on the head."

He'd avoid that explanation with Hansom.

Jacob was eager to meet the boy. He kept scanning the street and checking his watch. Rosie had confirmed the time with him. The kid was twenty minutes late. That would be the first lesson—respect other people's time. He filled his wait productively, organizing the loose nails that had mysteriously accumulated at the bottom of the toolbox.

Ten minutes later, he put all the carefully displayed hardware away. Jacob was disappointed. Hansom wasn't coming.

CHAPTER 36

After quizzing Langston on his spelling words, Rosie crossed the street for choir practice. She grabbed the legal pad with all her notes about Jacob. She wanted to have a word with him before the others arrived.

When she walked into the chapel, he was seated at the piano. "Listen to this." He played a few notes. "We'll start with the altos"—he played a few more notes—"then add the bass."

She approached the piano as he continued. "Everyone will expect the sopranos to lead, but I'll have them do harmonies." He played with both hands. She heard the beauty in the blending of the notes.

Jacob stopped and smiled. "Thank you for bringing my song to the choir."

"My pleasure," she stuttered, unsure how to bring up the real reason for her early arrival at practice, the knowledge she'd garnered from Rabbi Klein.

Edmond, Mr. Day, and a few of the other choir members entered the chapel, so she took her regular seat in the soprano section. Although she was bursting with new insight into Jacob's past, she was afraid to ruin his newfound joy. She'd show him the notes on her legal pad tomorrow. What did one more day matter?

At practice that evening, Mr. Day announced that they had to make their final decision for Gospel Sunday. Almost immediately, the choir divided into two camps: one to sing Jacob's "Narrow Bridge" and the other "There Is a Balm in Gilead," one of their most popular Sunday worship songs. The dividing lines were fairly predictable, with the exception of Edmond. The younger choir members made their case for new material, while the older ones wanted to stick with tradition.

Mr. Day opined that traditional songs usually placed better in the competition. "A new arrangement, yes, but a new song? Pretty risky."

The hour was growing late, and Mr. Day put the decision to a vote. Even though Jacob abstained, his song was chosen by a slim margin. He felt the heat rising in his face as choir members congratulated him. He quickly slipped out so he wouldn't have to join the prayer circle.

<hr />

The house was quiet when Rosie walked in. As much as she wanted to go straight to bed, she couldn't resist the temptation of Facebook. She was disappointed that there were no comments or messages from her old friends in Birmingham. Moving to Brent had been a good decision, but she missed her friends and the stimulation of a city. Absentmindedly, she clicked over to her emails and then the FBI database.

Rosie scrolled through many pages of faces. She passed the picture of Jacob that she'd seen earlier but hadn't recognized. This time she paused and looked carefully. She read the text and zoomed in on the bearded face. Rosie held her breath. She had found Jacob.

From the FBI picture, she then Googled "Brooklyn bus bombing." With another click, she looked at the headline from *The New York Times* of the previous year: "Thirty-two Perish in Terrorist Attack." She read the text over and over and then found a sidebar with a photo of Jacob's wife and children: "Mother and

Three Children Die on Bus, Leaving Father and Community Bereft."

So his name was Jacob Fisher: an Orthodox Jew from Brooklyn, a teacher and a cantor, a husband and a father—with no living wife or children. She couldn't imagine anything more painful than losing your family. But the newspaper article said he witnessed the explosion. That was beyond comprehension.

Rosie finally understood what he had lost, and how he had become so lost himself. She closed the computer and wept.

She had trouble falling asleep that night. She should have been proud of herself for putting together the clues to Jacob's identity, but instead she felt burdened. She hated being the only one who knew who he was. It was too late to go back now. How could she tell him that she knew what happened? And when could she tell him?

Look what Nosy Rosie had discovered. Again, she questioned her motivation—why had she been so driven to pry? She hated to admit that she had feelings for this man. But she did. He was wounded—certainly not his fault—but wounded all the same. Why was she trying to fix something that could never be repaired?

Some time in the middle of the night, Rosie made a decision. She'd tell Jacob what she knew and accept the fallout. But she'd wait a few more days, until after Gospel Sunday, for selfish reasons. The choir needed him.

CHAPTER 37

Rosie felt she was moving forward with her Hansom project. She'd waited until he turned eighteen, then she called Kala's husband, who'd graciously agreed to treat Hansom for no charge. Now all she had to do was arrange to get him there. His grandmother would blow her top when she discovered the deception, but Rosie could handle her. In their conversations, Hansom had revealed that he did all the shopping and housework. He still held the part-time night job at McDonald's. No wonder the kid fell asleep in class. He was responsible and inappropriately burdened. Bad skin was only a small part of his problem.

She was gratified that she could help the boy with a practical solution. Wouldn't he feel better about himself if he could hold his head up high? Maybe he'd even live up to his name. She was concerned that he hadn't shown up for the meeting with Jacob, and he'd been absent for two days. Rosie decided to go by his house to tell him about the doctor's appointment. She'd pretend that she was dropping off an assignment.

As Rosie turned the corner to approach Hansom's house, she saw the street filled with gawking neighbors, a police car, and a bright red paramedic truck, lights flashing. Her stomach dropped. Here she was bringing the kid good news about something as trivial as his skin, and his grandmother was dying. She got out of the car to see if she could help. He could use a friendly face. As she approached the huddle of neighborhood gossips she caught tidbits of news.

"His grandmother was having trouble breathing."

"She wasn't making sense."

"She was shrieking for help."

Rosie walked through the people toward the house, but her legs refused to move when she heard the next sentences.

"I heard his grandmother found him kicking."

"She couldn't get out of the chair to cut him down."

"Her screams sounded like someone was killing her...an awful sound, just awful. Leon had to break down the door to get to them."

Rosie ran toward the house. A police officer stopped her. "Are you family?"

"I'm his teacher."

The grandmother's wheelchair appeared in the doorway. She was wearing the old ratty daisy robe with a wrap on her head. Rosie heard her panicked wailing as the paramedics wheeled out a gurney.

"I ain't lettin' no one take that boy away from me. No one takes him away from me. You hear? He's my blood. He belongs with me."

Hansom was on the gurney. The paramedics were pumping him with a manual breathing pump.

Rosie could barely process the possibility that he was dead when all attention fixed on her.

The grandmother was pointing and accusing. "It's her. That evil woman killed my boy...she made him unhappy with who he was. It's her fault."

Amid the chaos, Rosie pushed her way to the paramedics who were urgently ministering to the limp teen. The snippets of conversation began to make a picture: Hansom had taken his own life, and now the old woman blamed her. Rosie felt the shock of losing Hansom and the fear of somehow being responsible. If she had minded her own business, Hansom would be alive.

One of the paramedics muttered a steady count as he pumped the breathing device. His partner pushed the gurney forward. Rosie's reasoning returned. Those would be wasted efforts if Hansom was dead. Either he was still alive or they were hoping to bring him back. She scanned his body for cues. Ever so slightly, one of his hands twitched. It was a barely perceptible movement, but she noticed. They wouldn't have to bring him back from the dead. He was still living.

The paramedics loaded the gurney onto the ambulance, and Rosie said a silent prayer of thanks for the neighbor who had broken down the door.

The next day, all of Brent High was buzzing with word of Hansom's attempted suicide. Rather than let the rumors and half-truths explode, Kala and Principal Hayes called for an assembly to explain what had happened. In recent years, the dynamic of public education had changed to accommodate tragedy. Counselors were prepared to handle all forms of trauma. Kala had been suggesting for months that the district initiate a curriculum on bullying. It took this boy's torment to make them take her seriously.

After the assembly, Rosie went to have a word with Kala in her office. Kala had been in touch with the psychiatric hospital in Birmingham, and Hansom was doing as well as could be expected. He was in good hands. Hospital staff had begun the evaluation process.

"Did I meddle too much?" Rosie worried. "His grandmother blamed me."

Kala's unruffled demeanor quieted her self-reproach, "It will take time to sort out what triggered him," she explained calmly. "Certainly, you are not responsible."

Despite Kala's words of comfort, she felt guilty. Paying extra attention to the boy was supposed to help. Her meddling had backfired. Why was she always trying to fix people? Instead of being the hero, she'd been the catalyst for damage.

The bell rang, and Rosie had a class to teach. As she left the office, Edmond entered. He looked tired and preoccupied. He'd been up all night trying to get information about Hansom's condition. After a comforting hug, Rosie and Edmond agreed to meet after school. They both needed to talk.

———◆———

Edmond brought back a doughnut to share along with their coffees. For the first time since she'd seen Hansom on the gurney, she felt hungry.

"I talked to his grandmother," Edmond confided. "They're holding him on a thirty-day psych evaluation but...who knows. He's already eighteen. Most likely they'll let him be in charge of his own life."

"Is that a good thing?"

"I don't know."

"I'm thinking about going to visit on Saturday," Edmond said. "Do you want to come?"

Rosie was afraid to see Hansom, but she couldn't admit it. Despite Kala's reassurance, she needed to shake off the feeling of responsibility.

"Of course I'll go. He needs us."

CHAPTER 38

The following Sunday, the First Baptist community gathered in the church parking lot to get ready for the trip to Birmingham for the Gospel Sunday competition. Although the spring weather in Brent usually fluctuated between blazing hot and freezing cold, the day was mild—scattered clouds in a crystal-blue sky.

Parked in the lot was a large school bus draped with a hand-lettered sign for "GOSPEL SUNDAY." The entire community was there: young and old, choir members, deacons, and clergy. They carried baskets and picnic boxes for the gathering afterward.

Langston and a few of his friends shot hoops at the far end of the parking lot. Although it was confining to play ball in their Sunday best, the kids were clearly having fun. When Langston got the ball, he scored. His basketball skills had greatly improved.

Mr. Day loaded the freshly pressed choir robes into the rear of the bus and then took his place behind the driver. Jacob shepherded the young boys onto the bus. Mo and Rosie, carrying a cooler, boxes, and bags for the picnic, were among the last to board. Jacob helped Rosie secure the cooler on the overhead rack. Rosie had been avoiding him since she found out about his past. The timing had to be right for such a powerful disclosure. She didn't want to cause him further pain.

Rosie looked at him. "Are you ready?"

Jacob responded, "A little nervous."

She sat down next to Langston while Jacob looked for an open seat.

Langston scooted closer to the window, "Come sit with us."

"If it's okay with your mom?"

Rosie moved in and patted the seat. The bus pulled out of the parking lot. Jacob tried to keep his thigh from knocking Rosie's, but the bumpy ride forced them to touch. She pulled her leg away by pretending to straighten her skirt. She moved slowly so the action wouldn't be offensive.

By the time the bus reached the main highway, congregants and choir members joined together in song. Rosie was relieved she didn't have to talk.

On their way to 16th Street Baptist in Birmingham, Rosie told Langston about the church's importance in the history of the South. It had been a meeting point for desegregation and voting-rights activists. In 1963 the Ku Klux Klan had detonated a bomb under the steps of the church, killing four young African American girls who were at Sunday school. The anger that the incident generated galvanized the civil rights movement.

"You should ask Uncle Mo what life used to be like. When he grew up, Brent was still segregated. Our folks couldn't even drink out of the same water fountain as white people. It was against the law."

Jacob listened as attentively as Langston. He knew so little about African American history. Although he'd studied US history in high school, the rabbis glossed over anything controversial or "irrelevant" to the world of Orthodox Judaism.

Jacob expected 16th Street Baptist to be a larger version of First Baptist in Brent, but this was light years away from that simple clapboard church. It was a lushly landscaped, neoclassical brick structure on a broad downtown boulevard. Out front was a sign, "Welcome to Gospel Sunday." Inside was a majestic sanctuary—cavernous ceilings, row upon row of polished wooden pews, a magnificent pipe organ behind the choir loft, and a mezzanine with extra seating.

There was a palpable feeling of expectation in the air. Clusters of people, dressed in their finest, greeted one another in the parking lot jammed with cars and buses. License plates revealed that some church choirs and their supporters had come from hundreds of miles away. Many participants knew each other from previous competitions. They backslapped and hugged in greeting.

Once inside, Jacob saw that the church was filling rapidly. Mo and Langston found seats in the front row of the mezzanine.

Langston could hardly contain his excitement. "I know we're going to win. I can feel it in my bones."

"You're not old enough to feel anything in your bones. There's some pretty stiff competition here."

The various choirs sat in roped-off groups, each distinguished by the color of their robes. First Baptist quickly settled into its assigned pews, the singers fidgeting with the bright yellow overlays on their purple robes. The audience fell silent the moment 16th Street Baptist's pastor stepped up to the podium. Pastor Shields was an imposing figure, barrel-chested and well over six feet tall. His voice rumbled out of his body as he introduced this year's judges. They included a music professor from Spelman College, a congressman, and the longtime host of WPRZ's "Gospel Hour." Each was greeted with a polite smattering of applause. Twelve churches were competing, but everyone knew the trophy would likely go to one of the top three: the Prince of Peace choir, Calvary Baptist, or 16th Street Baptist.

The Prince of Peace choir, some forty singers, sang a traditional Southern gospel song. Its closing chorus, with its strong harmonies, low bass, and bright falsetto, brought the audience to its feet.

Calvary Baptist, last year's winner, was a smaller group, only twenty. Their robes reflected African roots, with bold swaths of primary colors and graphic designs adorning their dashikis and headdresses. Their sound rang with percussion and the jubilant celebration of East Africa.

The youth choir from 16th Street Baptist sang in a contemporary urban gospel style. While the lyrics had a spiritual bent, the song sounded more like the ubiquitous hip-hop on the radio. Mo rolled his eyes at the lengthy rap about faith and Jesus, while Langston drummed on his seat's armrests.

Finally, First Baptist was called to the podium. Mr. Day led the choir in Jacob's song "Narrow Bridge." Each of the choirs was impressive, but emotion set First Baptist's performance apart from the rest. When Rosie sang her solo, the entire church came alive.

"We're gonna win," Langston whispered. "Mom is so good."

The singers returned to their seats while the judges, heads together, conferred. Langston crossed his fingers and offered a silent prayer. The audience grew restless as the judges deliberated. Finally, the radio host handed Pastor Shields a folded sheet of paper. He took the stage to announce the winners.

Mr. Day had warned the choir that an unfamiliar song could take them out of the running, so when First Baptist came in third, he was delighted. He never thought they'd place at all. Langston couldn't understand why third place was considered a success. Hadn't they lost?

Jacob found Mo and Langston as they left the church. Langston couldn't contain his disappointment, and tears dripped down his face. He put his head inside the neck of his shirt to hide his feelings.

Mo said to Jacob, "They should mark up a boy's shirt in sections like they do the cow map in the meat department. The sleeve is for cleanin' your mouth, the cuff is for your nose, and the bottom is for wipin' sweat off your face. But the neck of the shirt, that's for when feelings get the better of you and you have to go all ostrich on the world."

Mo looked at Langston and shook his head. "I may be fuzzy, but I do recall being a boy." He sucked his back tooth hard and walked away.

Jacob crouched down next to Langston. "It stinks, doesn't it?"

Langston nodded, and his head popped out where it belonged. He used his cuff to wipe his nose. "I don't know why God let us lose. I prayed all the way through the song. Well, almost all the way. In the middle I started clapping and forgot I was praying."

"God had nothing to do with it. I think we lost because the judges liked Calvary Baptist's song better. Maybe we weren't as good as we thought."

Langston stared at Jacob. "So God wanted Calvary Baptist to win again?"

"Nope. They won because they did a better job...or someone slipped the judges an extra slice of cake," Jacob said under his breath.

Langston giggled. Jacob always made him feel better.

⊰·◆·⊱

By the time they arrived at the park, the prospect of copious amounts of food and socializing had turned disappointment into celebration. Each church group set up its own buffet tables and emptied vast quantities of homemade dishes out of coolers. The older children played Frisbee, baseball, and jump rope. The toddlers chased each other between the picnic tables and their mothers' skirts, and the seniors congregated on camp chairs in the shade.

As people walked by, they shook Jacob's hand and offered words of congratulations.

An elderly woman with a hat the size of a platter and a walker festooned with purple and yellow ribbons approached Jacob. "The minute they picked your song, I knew we were gonna win somethin'."

Jacob demurred, "It was Mr. Day and the choir."

"Stop being so modest. Who woulda thought a skinny white boy could make such a big sound?"

She beckoned him to move closer and whispered in his ear, "That judge from the Gospel Hour? He was smiling so hard I thought his face would crack." Jacob laughed and kissed her cheek.

Suddenly he was hungry, very hungry. He'd been too anxious to eat earlier. The loaded picnic table beckoned.

Edmond and his mother were circling around the pies, admiring all the choices. When Edmond saw Rosie commandeer a table, he approached.

"Room for two more?" he asked.

She looked up from her plate. "Sure."

Langston could hardly contain himself. He bolted down a few bites of food, stood up, and bounced his basketball impatiently. Jacob worked on his plate, and Edmond seized the opportunity. "Now that we're done with Gospel Sunday, I'm sure you'll be moving on. Where do you plan to go from here?"

His tone was demanding and oppositional. Rosie stopped eating, and Edmond's mother reached over and patted her son's hand, signaling him to be quiet. The table was immediately strained with tension. Edmond conceded to civility. He turned to Langston.

"I had skills back in the day," Edmond said. "Let's shoot around."

Langston shook his head. "Me and my friends are already playing Jacob."

Rosie was annoyed with all the men at the table. Langston was the least complicated target. "Me and my friends?"

Langston immediately corrected himself. "My friends and I."

Revising Langston's grammar sidetracked Rosie from correcting his rudeness to Edmond. She watched Langston dribble the ball as he made his way to the basketball courts. Jacob hastily wiped his mouth and followed.

She offered an apologetic, "Raising a child is like domesticating a wild animal."

"Edmond was never rude as a child," said Mrs. Scott. "He was polite and well spoken." She punctuated her superiority by adjusting the collar on her blouse.

All Rosie wanted to do was watch Jacob play ball with her son, but manners dictated that she turn her attention to Edmond and his mother. She'd never quite grasped the meaning of the word "fussbudget," but after knowing Edmond's mother she understood exactly what it meant. She felt smugly satisfied when she noticed that Mrs. Scott had deposited a visible thumbprint of grease on her blouse.

CHAPTER 39

Mo was putting away the picnic gear in the kitchen. After a near-perfect day, a cold front had moved in, and a light rain was falling. A layer of melancholy descended on him. Now that Gospel Sunday was over, what would he think about?

Rosie carried a sugar-crashed Langston up the stairs and tucked him into bed. She changed into her sweats and came back down.

Mo held up the cooler. "Where the heck does this thing go?"

"Way up on the shelf in the pantry."

She dragged a chair from the table to reach the top shelf of the overstuffed pantry. Mo handed her the cooler. "Crazy to have something that you use once in a while take up so much space."

Rosie was suddenly serious. "Uncle Mo..."

Mo stopped. "Uh-oh. You never call me Uncle Mo unless you mean business. What'd I do wrong?"

"You didn't do anything. I need some ideas...some advice."

As far back as he could remember, she'd never asked anyone for advice—not her mother, not her father, and certainly not him. Mo sat down opposite her. He figured something had happened with that jerk of an ex-husband.

Rosie took some folded papers out of her purse. She handed him the first sheet of the yellow legal paper. It was the list of Jacob's qualities and characteristics. Mo fumbled around for his reading glasses and studied the page. He couldn't make sense out of the random words: *carpenter, father, handyman, musician, teacher, New York, Jewish.*

Mo was puzzled. "What is this exactly?"

"Jacob's characteristics. What I've learned about him."

"I imagine he knows most of this about himself."

"I've been doing some research on the internet, and I'm pretty sure I figured it out. Who he is and what he's running from."

She handed him the printout from the missing-persons database. Mo studied the picture for a minute. "I'm glad he got rid of that beard."

Rosie forced a smile. "That's not all." She handed him the article from *The New York Times.*

Mo scanned the article and exhaled slowly. "He watched his whole family die."

"This is why he's so shut down."

Mo sucked his tooth. "Most likely."

"How do we tell him that we know?"

Mo looked at her.

Her throat was thick with sadness. "You tell him. I can't."

He took another moment to peruse the article. He pointed at the bottom paragraph. "Says here he's got a mother. I'll bet she's the one who reported him missing."

"How do you survive that kind of loss?"

Mo shook his head. There was no answer to the question.

⸻◆⸻

Rosie couldn't sleep. She felt the exhaustion in her limbs and in the small of her back, but she couldn't turn her mind off. Although she'd read the article a dozen times, she'd never thought about his mother. This woman had lost her daughter-in-law and grandchildren, and then her son disappeared. She thought of Langston safely asleep upstairs in his bed. Jacob was someone's son. His mother must be inconsolable.

She would contact Jacob's mother and ask her to come to Brent. The decision brought a moment of relief, quickly followed by doubt. If she asked Jacob for permission to contact his mother, it would be obvious that she knew his identity. He could disappear again.

She tiptoed downstairs at three a.m. and turned her computer back on. It didn't take much effort to find Hava Fisher, Jacob's mother, in Brooklyn. She wrote down the phone number and the address and forced herself back into bed.

The next morning, Rosie reached for her cellphone during her free period. She went as far as punching in the area code before she came to her senses. To Jacob's mother, Rosie was a complete stranger, and the situation was far too complex to explain over the phone. A letter felt formal and disconnected. Rosie couldn't imagine a single day without Langston. She felt obligated to travel to Brooklyn, to find Mrs. Fisher, and to tell her about Jacob face to face.

—◆—

Rosie arrived at JFK on a late spring morning. In Brent, her rose bushes were already in full flower. Here, there were only tiny buds on the trees, and a frigid wind was blowing. She taxied into Manhattan and checked into a midtown chain hotel. She remembered visiting New York with her mother when she was twelve. It was a whirlwind of sightseeing—as many museums and churches and historical sites as her mother could fit into a weekend. She remembered looking through the tour bus window at the hordes of people racing down Fifth Avenue. Where were they all going? Twenty years later, she felt the same way—too many people, not enough trees. No matter how hard she tried, she couldn't hear any birds.

After a quick shower and change of clothes, she headed to the subway. The letters and numbers and directional signs overwhelmed her. She was embarrassed to ask a stranger for help, so she used her phone to figure out the stop closest to Mrs. Fisher. She needed to take only one subway to get to Brooklyn.

The train was overheated and claustrophobic, and her sense of adventure had become deflated by worry. What kind of a stupid scheme had she undertaken? Why hadn't she called Jacob's mother or written her a letter, instead of embarking on this wild goose chase? What if the woman wasn't home? Coming to New York was another meddlesome plan, poorly thought out and poorly executed.

When Rosie emerged into the sunlight of Jacob's neighborhood, she was overwhelmed. The flow of humanity on the sidewalk moved her forward. Brooklyn was a wild mixture of skin color and unusual garb. Latin music blasted from a small grocery store. Indian women in saris pushed strollers. Groups of uniformed children walked to a parochial school. The smell of something deliciously Asian hung in the air, making her stomach growl. All the people walked with purpose—work, shopping, school.

She pushed away any earlier reservations about her mission. She'd carry out her errand, even if it felt foolish. She stopped a young woman for directions. With a heavy Russian accent, the woman pointed the way. The first few blocks were diverse, but then the neighborhood became distinctly traditional, the Orthodox corner of Brooklyn. She saw women in long skirts with scarves on their heads, and a sea of black-suited men with beards and hats. She had no way of knowing that she'd passed Jacob's synagogue, the kosher bakery where he shopped, the corner where he last saw his family. She mentally rehearsed what she would say when Jacob's mother opened the door.

Rosie found the five-story brick apartment building where Mrs. Fisher lived. Deliverymen, struggling with a brand-new refrigerator, had propped open the entrance. She skirted around them, quickly found Mrs. Fisher's apartment, and knocked.

Rosie sensed movement behind the door and spoke tentatively to the peephole. "Mrs. Fisher?"

"Whatever you're selling, I'm not interested."

"I'm not selling anything, Mrs. Fisher. I know your son—Jacob. I need to talk to you." The words tumbled out in a heap, nothing like she had planned.

Hava opened the door slowly, drying her hands on a dishtowel. "You know Jacob?"

Rosie noticed that Mrs. Fisher's hands were trembling as she held the door open.

"Yes."

"Is he alive?"

"Yes, Mrs. Fisher. He is very much alive."

Hava mumbled a blessing and motioned for Rosie to come into the well-ordered apartment. Rosie noticed a wall of books, an upright piano in the corner, an oil painting of a Jerusalem landscape, and a schoolchild's drawing.

"Sit, please," Hava stammered.

Hava adjusted her headscarf and smoothed her skirt. They studied each other. Rosie noticed that Mrs. Fisher's eyes were the same shade of blue as Jacob's.

Rosie told Hava everything—finding Jacob lost and disheveled on the steps of First Baptist, the weeks of silence, living in the church basement, and his work as a handyman. But she did not tell Hava about her personal relationship with Jacob.

Hava interrupted, hurt in her voice, "Why didn't he call me?"

"I don't know."

"So why did he send you?"

"He didn't. I came on my own. Jacob has no idea that I'm here. I found you on the internet after reading an article about your family's tragedy. He's never told me anything about his past."

She took out her cellphone and showed Hava a picture of Jacob with Langston. Hava had never seen Jacob's adult face without a beard, but there was no mistaking the image. Her son was alive. Hava's hand covered her mouth.

"Where are my manners?" Hava asked. "You've been traveling all day. You must be starving."

Within minutes, Rosie was sitting at the kitchen table with a slice of coffee cake and a cup of tea. Hava kept looking at Rosie, waiting for more information.

Rosie repeated everything she knew about Jacob, and then Hava pulled out one of her photo albums. She narrated the story of her son's life: excelling at the yeshiva, leading his basketball team to school championships, his beautiful singing voice, marrying Julia, and the three children. Rosie studied the pictures of Julia. She hadn't expected her to be so beautiful.

Hava stopped turning the pages. "Is he doing drugs?"

"Drugs?"

Hava went deeper, telling Rosie about Jacob's problematic relationship with his father, his disappearance once before, and the overdose. "Thank God, his father shipped him off to a rehab center in Israel before anyone found out. At the time, I thought my husband was heartless, but *Baruch haShem*, Jacob returned a changed man."

Hava took several deep breaths. Rosie could see she was fighting to control her emotions. "When he disappeared, after the...explosion... I was terrified that he couldn't handle his feelings, that he went back to drugs."

Rosie sighed. "These months...not knowing where he was... must have been torture for you."

Hava offered a wry smile. "For me, worry is a permanent state of mind."

Hava returned her attention to the photo album, to the tangible evidence of her son's goodness. She showed her pictures of Julia, the wife who had made a fine home and given him beautiful children. Rosie learned their names: Yossi, Miriam, and Sarah.

The older two looked like their mother. Sarah definitely took after Jacob.

"I made a book for each of my grandchildren, pictures from infancy until a few weeks before their..." Her voice trailed off, and her eyes again filled with tears. She couldn't even say the word "death." Silently, she turned the pages of the photo album on her lap.

Rosie told Hava about the Jacob that she knew. She led her through the clues that had helped her solve the mystery and brought her to Brooklyn. She told her about Jacob's kindness to Langston. Then she told her about Jacob joining their church choir.

Hava was shocked. "I can't believe it. My Jacob sings gospel?"

"Our church placed third in a gospel festival with a song he wrote for us."

"Jacob *writes* gospel?"

"Yes."

Hava twisted her wedding ring. "The song he wrote—did it have Jesus in it?"

"No Jesus."

Hava lowered her voice. "Is he a Christian now?"

"I don't think he's anything."

Hava shook her head. "This whole conversation is beyond my imagination."

Rosie continued. "The song he wrote is about how the world is a narrow bridge."

"Jacob didn't write those words."

"I know. A rabbi told me."

Hava swallowed hard and touched her throat.

"You've been through hell," Rosie reached across the photo album to touch Hava's hand.

"Why did you come all the way here? You could have called," Hava asked.

"I'm a mother, too," Rosie said softly. "Your son needs you, and I was afraid you wouldn't believe me."

Hava registered the truth aloud, "My son needs me."

"Come to Brent with me."

Hava didn't hesitate. "I need to pack."

CHAPTER 40

After Hava put her small travel bag in Langston's bedroom, she was ready to see her son. She wanted to put her arms around him—even if he was a grown man. She remembered Jacob when he was a child. He'd been so in love with life and eager to discover the world.

"Eema, I heard a song in my head, here's how it sounds."

"Eema, how come when we go to the bakery, I get hungry even when I'm not?"

Jacob had always challenged the family's adherence to Orthodoxy—rules for every aspect of daily life, customs that isolated Jews, all that praying. His father told him repeatedly that the Jewish people did not survive persecution only to be wiped out by a lack of discipline. All Hava could do was love her son and give him what he wanted. Later, she learned her permissiveness made her the "enabler," the one who kept making excuses for his behavior and protecting him from his father's wrath.

Jacob stayed in rehab in Israel for a full year. By the end, he sounded strong on the telephone, though Hava still worried. When he returned looking like his old self—full beard, the clothing of Orthodoxy—she offered a prayer of gratitude. She never brought up his willful absence when Aaron died. They talked about Aaron only in vague terms and rose-colored memories.

The fact was that Jacob had chosen to remain in the Orthodox community. He'd trained as both a teacher and a cantor. He'd brought Julia into their way of life, and then the children came, creating so much joy. She was sorry that Aaron hadn't lived to see their son so completely reformed.

From what Hava could gather from Rosie, her son had post-traumatic stress syndrome, like a soldier coming back from war. In those long months in Brent, Jacob had never talked about his losses, moving through time like a sleepwalker. The road back to normalcy would require him to confront those unspeakable moments, to tell the stories of his family and to grieve openly. Hava wished the job of grounding him had fallen to someone else. Forcing him to relive the day his family perished would be like tossing a rock into still water. Not only would the stone descend, but it would also create ever-expanding outward ripples on the water's surface, compounding the effect. Ramifications lay ahead. She was sure of that.

Hava checked her reflection in the mirror. She hoped Jacob could remember her before sorrow etched her face. She forced a smile and armed herself with the photo album from home. Rosie led her across the street and into the chapel.

Jacob was painting the window trim on the western side of the chapel. After the stained glass had been replaced, the molding looked beaten and old. He stood on a ladder and painstakingly attended to the details of repair. He was humming as he patched, sanded, cleaned, and painted—the picture of a contented man at work.

The women stood for a moment, acclimating to the muted light, the silence interrupted only by the faint humming. Hava took in the church: the pews, the stained glass, the mural of Jesus, and the wooden cross over the pulpit.

Rosie gestured. "There...that's Jacob."

Hava watched him. He was dressed in coveralls and sneakers, his head, uncovered, his face, clean-shaven. But the familiar profile gave her resolve.

"I'll get him for you," Rosie offered.

Hava squeezed her hand. "No, this is my job."

"I'm across the street if you need me," Rosie said, closing the chapel door behind her.

Hava walked purposefully down the aisle to the man on the ladder.

Jacob continued to work, humming to himself. She waited, willing Jacob to feel her presence.

"Ya'akov?" Hava said, calling him his Hebrew name, the name they had used at home when he was a boy.

Jacob reflexively turned toward his name. It took a moment for him to place her. He searched and re-searched her face. His mother was in Brent, standing before him. How could this be?

Jacob stepped down off the ladder and stood in front of her.

She tried in vain to stop the tears. "You shaved your beard... you've changed."

"I'm sorry," he murmured, his voice unsteady. "I'm so sorry, Eema."

In his apology, Hava understood that he was not as void of memory as Rosie supposed. His distance had been a choice.

Jacob struggled to find words. Hava put her arms around her son. He let her hold him. "Is there somewhere we can talk?" she asked.

He beckoned her to follow. They walked in silence down the basement stairs to the stark caretaker's room. He pulled a stool out for his mother, motioning for her to sit. He sat on the bed.

"So this is where you've been hiding all these months," Hava said. Although she was pretending to make lighthearted conversation, her voice betrayed her.

Jacob looked down. "At home, everywhere I looked there was Julia...or Yossi...or the girls. I couldn't breathe."

"So you ran away," Hava stated flatly.

Jacob nodded, using his sleeve to wipe the tears from his face.

"You ran away to *goyim*?" Hava asked, using the Yiddish word for non-Jews.

"I didn't know where I was going. I turned off all thoughts of home. I thought if I wasn't there, then they weren't there, and it never happened," he stammered. "I didn't allow myself to think about them."

"Thinking about them will help you get to the other side." Hava tapped the photo album.

She moved next to him on the bed, opening the album.

Jacob turned his face away. "Please don't do this to me."

"You need to remember them when you were happy. It's good to remember."

Reluctantly, Jacob opened the book. Hava watched him absorb the photos of Julia and the children frozen in time: laughing at a birthday party, playing in the snow, hiking in the mountains. Tentatively, he touched the crinkles around Julia's eyes when she laughed, Yossi's oversized ears, Miriam's odd-toothed smile, Sarah's mop of curls. He gasped for air as the enormity of his grief hit him with full force.

"I loved them so much," he whispered, his voice muffled by sorrow.

Hava nodded. "And they loved you."

Jacob's mouth opened in anguish, as if he had suffered an excruciating and incomprehensible injury, but no sound emerged. He rocked back and forth. Then he took a deep breath, covered his face, and keened, an eerie, high-pitched wail, part strangled scream of torment, part futile plea for relief. Hava was frantic to take away her child's pain. She held him tightly. She couldn't protect him, nor could she could make this agony go away. All she could do was rock with him and weep.

Hava had been so keyed up with the anticipation of seeing Jacob, but here he was, altered and confused. The past two days had been draining—traveling to this strange place, to a part of the country she'd never even imagined. She thought she had grieved for her daughter-in-law and grandchildren, but the wound was still gaping. She felt so weary she could hardly hold her head up.

Hava had her son, and for that, she silently thanked God.

———◆———

Hava's sleep was restless and disturbed. When she heard Rosie leave for work, she gave up and went downstairs. When Langston walked in, Hava was sitting at the breakfast table with a cup of coffee. He stopped in the kitchen doorway and backed up, nearly running into Mo.

"There's a white lady sitting in the kitchen!" he whispered to Mo.

"I told you that Jacob's mother was here."

After quick introductions, Mo left to walk Langston to school. As Hava rinsed the breakfast dishes, she saw Jacob sitting on the church steps. She crossed the street.

"Let's walk," she said.

His strides were long, and Hava struggled to keep up. She waited for Jacob to speak, but he was clearly in no mood. The most he offered was to point out some of the landmarks of his life in Brent: the market where he bought his supplies, the café where he ate an occasional meal, Langston's school. After twenty minutes, they circled back, and he told her gruffly that he had work to do.

Hava knew the excuse of work was only that—an excuse. Although she envisioned herself a hero bringing Jacob back to reality, she had, by necessity, inflicted pain. Even so, after months of worrying about him, she found comfort in his presence. She was willing to accept his anger.

———◆———

Jacob had enjoyed Brent, the simplicity of his days cleaning and fixing, playing ball with Langston, being near Rosie. He suspended his grief by becoming a vacant man without family, past, or home. Now he was required to mourn, to feel.

His brain struggled to remember. His body led the way. There were memories that brought him to his knees: the way Julia pursed her lips when she braided Miriam's hair, the way Yossi tried to slap the top of the door jamb every time he walked from one room to another, Sarah's annoying four-year-old way of asking why. The barrage of memories enveloped him, and he needed to sit on the ground. The weight of his body, the recognition of all that was gone, was too heavy a burden.

Jacob could see that his mother was hurt that he had rejected his faith. Returning to Brooklyn and his old way of life would be intolerable.

⟩⟨

Over the next few days, Hava tried to connect with Mo, Rosie, and Langston. The conversation stumbled. Sometimes they'd all talk at once, but more often there would be ragged patches of uncomfortable silence.

Mealtimes were odd to say the least. Hava explained that to keep kosher she could eat only vegetables and fruit, so the table was a strange assortment of baked potatoes, steamed broccoli, carrots, and melon. Hava ate with plastic utensils and paper plates. Jacob no longer cared about keeping kosher, and he ate whatever was offered him. Hava flinched when he reached for the pork at dinner.

After dinner one night, Jacob couldn't wait to get out of Rosie's house. He'd been in a foul mood all day. He was raw, as if someone had sandpapered his very soul. As soon as the meal was over, he hurried across the street to his basement room. Agitated, he yanked off his shirt, wadded it up, and threw it on his bed.

He rubbed his arms and paced. His hands repeatedly went to his head, his chest, his neck, and then back to rubbing his arms again. He felt manipulated, used, and enraged. The cyclical motions lessened his anger.

After Jacob left that night, Rosie worried that she'd overstepped boundaries. Since Hava's arrival, Jacob had been distant. He would have been better off without her snooping around. She should have told him that she'd found out about his past and let him contact his mother when he was ready. Foolishly, she'd brought Mrs. Fisher here, and now Jacob was disintegrating. Rosie had moved to Brent to make her life less complicated, and here she was, entangled in someone else's turmoil.

Impulsively, Rosie left everyone in her house cleaning dishes and followed Jacob back to the church. She could never fully understand the depths of his grief, but she could read the signs of devastating rage, the struggle to accept a reality that could never be acceptable. His anger was also a product of shame. By bringing his mother to Brent, she had humiliated him. Rosie understood humiliation.

During the last gasps of her marriage, right before she kicked Robert out, she had felt blind rage. Robert stayed out late, absented himself on the weekends, and made excuses filled with holes. He picked fights, like a little boy waiting to be caught and punished, so he could justify his outrageous behavior. When Robert finally confessed that he'd fallen in love with someone else, Rosie flashed white-hot. With all her strength, she heaved a wine bottle against the wall, smashing it inches from his head. She watched him cower as the red liquid dripped down the paint and seeped into the carpet, staining it irrevocably like their marriage.

As quickly as she'd become angry, she became pathetic. That was the only word for it. She wailed about being hurt and victimized, begging him to stay. The final humiliation came when she took his hand and placed it between her legs, trying to entice him. It was her fault that he cheated. She wasn't pretty enough, seductive enough. The look of revulsion on his face landed like a sucker punch.

Rosie stood outside the door to Jacob's room. She could hear him pacing back and forth and mumbling. The sounds were guttural and enraged, his voice rising and falling as if he were arguing with someone. She knocked on the door and opened it at the same time.

Jacob couldn't contain his wrath. "Aren't you supposed to wait for someone to acknowledge your presence before you come barging in?"

"Sorry…I—"

"—thought I was a child, so you treated me like one," Jacob said.

He had never snapped at her this way. She stood there trying to gather her thoughts. He grabbed his crumpled shirt off the bed and put it on, not bothering to button it. Rosie didn't know if his action stemmed from a lingering sense of propriety or the need to cover his vulnerability.

"What do you want?" he demanded. There was hardness in his voice she had never heard before.

"Nothing, I was…nothing," Rosie stammered. In truth, she had wanted to apologize for destroying his peace. She'd thought her actions would help him find clarity, but she had shamed him instead. She needed to make everything right between them.

"Did you come to gloat?" he snarled.

"What?"

"Did you come to see if your little social work project was doing okay?"

Rosie could feel her own indignant anger rising. "You're not a social work project."

"Right, then why did you do it? Why did you bring my mother here? Why did you sleep with me?" Jacob demanded through clenched teeth.

He took a step toward her, his arms ramrod straight at his side, his fists clenched. Rosie moved back instinctively.

She spoke quietly. "I didn't do this to hurt you. I wanted to help."

"Well you didn't. You didn't help at all!" he yelled, bellowing the last two words. "AT ALL!"

There it was. The truth. Loss was a wave of hurt, and no matter how much his mind willed otherwise, the tide inevitably rose. He stood there, beaten and defiant at the same time. Rosie was compelled to go to him. She expected him to move away, but he held his ground.

She put her hands on his chest to comfort him, to comfort her. Instinct said to kiss him. She moved her mouth to his, stopping before touch. He didn't respond, but he allowed her to put her face a thread's width from his.

Jacob whispered, "Why couldn't you leave well enough alone?"

Rosie's lips formed the shape of barely spoken words: "Forgive me."

They stayed suspended, nearly touching.

Then Jacob kissed her, fiercely and passionately. There was a need that surprised her. This time their lovemaking was insistent. Jacob's mouth moved down her body, clothing falling away. Every place his mouth touched became alive. She welcomed him, neck, breasts, her softly rounded belly, the inside of her thighs.

Rosie's tears caught her off guard. For the first time in her life she was truly making love—taking and giving at the same time.

———◆———

Mo and Hava sat on rocking chairs on the back porch. It was a glorious late spring evening. They sipped iced tea and listened to the buzz of the cicadas.

"You know, Mo, in my tradition, I shouldn't be sitting here with you," Hava remarked.

"Why not?"

"A man and a woman. Alone. People would talk."

Mo laughed, a good deep belly laugh. "I don't think you have anythin' to be afraid of...two old goats like us."

Hava laughed with him. "It feels good to laugh."

"Nothin' wrong with it."

"Sometimes you think you'll never laugh again...but then out of the blue, something strikes you as funny, and off you go," Hava said.

Mo thought for a moment. "When Elsie passed, I didn't want to eat again. I thought it wasn't fair that I could still taste a warm apple pie, and she couldn't. That woman loved apple pie." He smiled. "I could use some of that apple pie right about now."

"We're programmed to go on—find joy, move forward," Hava responded thoughtfully.

Mo nodded.

"I make a mean apple strudel," she said.

"I'm sure you do."

After a moment, he changed the topic. "You know, Rosie and Jacob—"

Hava cut him off. "I know. I have eyes and I have ears."

They sat in silence, rocking.

CHAPTER 41

The following morning, Langston and Jacob were shooting hoops in the church parking lot. Langston had taken Jacob's instruction seriously and continued to improve. He was an intense child, goal oriented and competitive. Mastering basketball skills had become a priority, and practicing had become an obsession.

"Remember what I said. Put the ball where you're going, not where you are," Jacob instructed.

Langston broke away and passed Jacob, going all the way to the basket. He missed the layup, but his movements were fluid.

"Nice try."

Langston was disappointed. "I missed."

"But you took the shot."

Jacob was huffing and puffing from the effort of guarding Langston. "I'm getting too old for this."

"How old are you?"

"Old enough to know that you can outlast me."

Jacob sat down on a nearby bench. Langston scooted in next to him.

"Do you live with your mother?" Langston asked innocently.

"No. She lives nearby. A short bus ride."

Langston was quiet for a moment. "When I grow up, I'm going to live right next door to my mom."

Jacob smiled. Mothers and sons, an invisible cord. When he

was Langston's age, he tripped on the playground and banged his head on a bench hard enough to give him a black eye. Fearful of concussion, his mother stayed up with him all night—chatting about nonsense, playing board games, and nudging him to stay awake. As a boy, he was exasperated by her devotion. As a man and father, he understood completely.

Langston bounced the ball, shaking Jacob from recollection. He looked at Jacob. "Did your mom come to take you home?"

Jacob shrugged. "She'd like that."

Langston took the ball and dribbled toward his house. "I hope you stay," he called over his shoulder.

⸻⸱⸱⸻

Jacob sprawled on the cot in the caretaker's room. Because his mother claimed him, he could no longer pretend he belonged in Brent. He was grateful to Mo for giving him a home and to the choir for reminding him of his purpose. But it was Rosie—beautiful, intelligent, generous—who had reached him with her body when words could not penetrate. He was grateful for her kindness, yet ashamed of his desire. His mother's presence caused a swirl of conflicted emotion. In making love to Rosie, had he sullied his love for Julia? His wife hadn't been gone long enough for him to be with another woman.

His mother knocked on the door and opened it a crack. "Ya'akov?"

Jacob sat up, and Hava entered the room and sat down next to him.

She measured her words. "These are good people here. But they're not your people. You need to be with your own."

"All my life, you told me to be a good Jew. Look what it got me." His voice rose in agitation. "All my life, you told me to stay away from the *goyim,* like they would poison me. They didn't poison me. They nourished me."

She waited for Jacob to finish his argument, and then she stated firmly, "I want you to come home to Brooklyn."

"There's nothing for me there," he said flatly.

"Of course there is. You've got your students, your congregation. All your friends. Naomi's children." Then standing up she added, "your mother."

Jacob turned his face away.

"Tomorrow," Hava said gently. She shut the door behind her.

On her last night in Brent, Hava baked two desserts: apple strudel and cheesecake. Although Langston was usually a fussy eater, he ate both with gusto. After dinner, he did his homework at the kitchen table while Mo and Rosie cleaned up. Outside, Jacob and Hava sat on the porch.

Hava ran her hand over the rocking chair she sat on. "This is a lovely chair, Jacob. They taught you well in Israel."

Hava knew immediately that her reference to Jacob's rehab was ill timed. He was so distant this evening. He'd eaten his dinner in silence, not even complimenting his mother on her baking.

Hava kept up the chatter, hoping somehow to connect him to the present. "You got your father's handiness. I can't even sew a button on a pair of pants."

Jacob cut her off. "I got nothing from my father."

He saw that his words had pained his mother. Her cynical response caught him off guard. "Perhaps you're wrong about that. Maybe anger is inherited...or at the very least, learned."

The screen door creaked open. Jacob looked up to see Rosie silhouetted by the light of the house. The pinks and mauves of the scarf wrapped around her shoulders made her skin glow.

Rosie saw the two of them. "I'm sorry. I didn't mean to interrupt."

Jacob rose from his rocking chair. "We weren't talking about anything important."

Hava wanted to disagree—Jacob's relationship with his father was all-important, but she knew instinctively that she should make herself scarce. Jacob had hardly spoken all evening. The minute Rosie appeared, he came to life.

Hava excused herself. "I was going inside. The night air is delicious, but I've had enough. *Gute nacht, zisse kinder.*"

Rosie looked at Jacob for translation.

"Good night, sweet children."

Hava squeezed Rosie's arm, and then she kissed Jacob on the forehead and went into the house.

There was a long, uncomfortable silence. Jacob sat back down in the rocker. Rosie perched on the railing.

"Do you always speak German to your mother?"

"That's not German. It's Yiddish."

"What country speaks Yiddish?"

Jacob smiled. "All of them and none of them. It was the language of the Jews of Eastern Europe. My parents would speak it when they didn't want my sister and me to understand. So, of course, we learned it."

Jacob continued rocking in silence.

When he finally spoke, his voice was subdued. "Right before my family got on the bus, my daughter Miriam asked me to buy her gum. She wanted me to teach her how to blow bubbles. What harm would it have done if I had bought her the gum? Maybe they would have missed that bus..."

Rosie was unsure how to respond.

Jacob continued, "Why was that basketball game so important? I should have been with them..."

"Stop. You can go round and round with 'what ifs' forever. The universe is indiscriminate. Completely random. It had nothing to do with you."

Jacob sat with his anguish for a long moment. Finally, he asked, "What if I said that I wanted to stay here?"

Rosie studied his face.

"There's too much pain back there," he continued.

"The pain will follow you no matter where you live," she said softly.

She left her perch on the railing and sat on his lap. She put her head on his shoulder, and they rocked. The chair creaked gently as it cradled them. They were as comfortable with each other as they were with the silence of the Southern night around them.

"We did what we were supposed to do," Rosie whispered. "We breathed life into each other."

Jacob said nothing for the longest time. The truth screamed at him through the evening quiet. There was a pattern to his life. He had run when he wounded his parents, he had run when he used drugs, he had run when his family died. Fight or flight—and he always chose flight.

He stopped rocking and took a deep breath. "I'm going home." There—he said it. Until that moment he had been ambivalent. "I have to confront my grief. And I have to do it alone."

"I know," Rosie replied gently.

"We can keep in touch, phone, email..." he said hopefully.

"No. That will hurt too much...close your eyes," Rosie ordered tenderly.

Jacob closed his eyes, and Rosie kissed each one.

"Now me," she said. Jacob took her face in his hands and kissed her eyelids. It was understood. Only people who love you kiss your eyes. She leaned on his shoulder, and they rocked again in the still night air.

Jacob and Hava were scheduled to leave on the two o'clock train, so he had more than enough time to attend the Sunday service. Privately, Jacob tried to get Hava to join him.

"I'm not going to sit there with Jesus staring down at me," she insisted. "I've never set foot in a church, and I don't plan to start now."

"Come hear the music."

Hava was adamant. "The rabbis forbid it. A Jew cannot enter a church."

"Visiting a church doesn't make you convert to Christianity."

"I know that."

She felt the fear spread from her stomach to her chest. Jacob had changed, and she didn't know him. Her Jewish identity was all encompassing and uncompromising. She was deeply disturbed by Jacob's participation in church services, yet she didn't want to argue further. She didn't want to know how many prohibitions he had broken. All she had to do was get him back to Brooklyn, where no one would have to know.

She softened. "You go. Don't worry about me."

After breakfast, Hava watched Mo, Rosie, Langston, and Jacob cross the street and join the congregants arriving for the service. Hava went to the living room and turned on the electric fan. The morning was stifling, like Brooklyn in August. She stood in front of the fan, bending down so the moving air would cool her sweaty neck.

She set her overnight bag by the front door. Jacob had insisted they take the train back to New York instead of fly. The journey would give him time to adjust. When she looked out again at the church, she saw that everyone had gone inside. The service had begun.

Unable to contain her curiosity, she crossed the street and stood outside the sanctuary. Through the door, she could hear the pastor's impassioned sermon.

"Oh Lord," he began slowly. "You have tried my heart. You have visited it in the night. You have tested me.

"You—have—tested—me," he repeated, with emphasis on each syllable. "How many of us here have been tested by the Lord?" The congregation responded with mumbled affirmations.

"How many of us have overcome sadness, illness, disappointment, and loss?"

Hava wasn't sure she could ever overcome her own sadness, but finding her son had eased her anguish. Jacob had survived, brought from the depths of maddening grief by these kind people. She offered her own prayer and walked back to the house to wait for them.

———◆———

Mo carried Hava's bag to the truck. Jacob carried the coat that Mo had bought him at Walmart and a backpack with the few possessions he had accumulated. Rosie walked them to the curb in front of the house. She'd already offered the excuse of papers to grade so she wouldn't have to accompany them to the train station. She'd never liked public displays of emotion, and hers were in turmoil. Quickly, she hugged and kissed Hava and then Jacob, and turned back to the house. She didn't want Langston to see her so upset. It was important to keep up the façade that they would all see each other again.

By the time Mo's truck arrived at the station in Tuscaloosa, the train was pulling in. Jacob bent down to Langston's eye level to say goodbye.

"I'm going to miss you," he said.

Langston took a round gray rock from his pocket and showed it to Jacob. "It's slate."

"I used to collect rocks when I was a kid."

"This kind of rock comes from deep inside the Earth," Langston said.

"And now it's yours. That's something else."

"It's my lucky rock. I want you to have it." Langston handed him the stone.

Jacob carefully put the rock in his jacket pocket and hugged Langston close. "Thank you. I'll take good care of it."

He stood up and turned to Mo. Their handshake turned into a bear hug.

"Must be gettin' old," Mo mumbled, turning away. "Can't stop my eyes from leakin'."

Jacob and Hava boarded the train. Mo and Langston held hands on the platform and waved as the train slowly pulled out of the station.

———◆———

On a hill above Brent, Rosie sat in her car. From this vantage point, she could see the whole town. She imagined she could hear the far-off whistle of the train as it pulled out of the station. Rosie knew that Jacob had to go home. What she didn't know was that her heart would break.

CHAPTER 42

Jacob spent the first week back in Brooklyn at his mother's apartment, receiving guests and making small talk. He resumed the grieving process that was interrupted nearly a year before. People didn't ask him where he had been or why, but he knew they speculated about it behind his back. Rabbi Weiss came in the afternoons, and they studied a passage of the Talmud together. Reading the ancient Hebrew text was familiar and comforting. Still, when a section spoke of a benevolent God, Jacob could barely pronounce the words under his breath.

Like the biblical Jacob who wrestled with the angel, he struggled with his faith. He had observed the rules—and what did that get him? He was the "good boy," a dutiful son who'd turned into a "fine man," a devoted husband and father. Why the punishment?

Jacob struggled to work things out for himself. The rabbi told him that he had also experienced a crisis of faith as a young man. Jacob dismissed him. The rabbi referred to the normative questioning of a young adult, not the barren skepticism of a man who had watched his family perish.

Jacob's childhood friend David accompanied him one morning to visit the old row house he'd shared with Julia and the children. They walked through the silent house slowly, painfully. Jacob picked up the novel that Julia had been reading, the girls' hairbrush, Yossi's Yankees hat, hoping to find some comfort in the objects. Nothing.

David told him that his wife would organize a group of women to sort through the house and give the clothes and toys to the needy.

"Not yet," Jacob said. "I'll let you know when I'm ready."

Hava couldn't resist writing Detective Rosenberg a note. She debated whether to walk into the station with Jacob, or call Rosenberg on the phone. She wanted to see his face when he discovered that Jacob was in front of him, not dead from suicidal grief. She wanted to wag her finger and give a big "I told you so." She took out her box of stationery and wrote in perfect script.

> *Dear Detective Rosenberg,*
> *Through the grace of God, we found Jacob.*
> *He is home and healing.*
> *Thank you for all your concern.*
> *Hava Fisher*

Jacob put off contacting Barbara and Steve, Julia's parents, for as long as he could. His grief had subsided enough for him to function, and seeing them might tear the wounds open again. His palms were sweating when he finally dialed their number.

Jacob circled their Upper West Side block several times. He feared they would judge him for running away, and question why he stayed away so long. He couldn't possibly tell them about those months at First Baptist. What could he say about Langston—or Rosie—that would not sound like betrayal? He nodded to the doorman on his way into their building. No turning back. When the elevator doors opened on the sixth floor, Steve and Barbara, noticeably aged, stood waiting.

Jacob saw emotions tumbling over one another on his mother-in-law's face. She was excited to see him, and yet wounded that he was there without her daughter and grandchildren. Julia's father stood, shoulders pulled up around his ears, both hands shoved into his pants pockets. He looked like he was going to extend an arm to shake Jacob's hand, but instead both arms spontaneously enveloped Jacob. The two men held their breath trying to remain in control.

The three of them—once legally bound, but now permanently untethered—remained suspended until they could talk. Awkwardly animated, Barbara ushered them into the apartment, littering the hallway with half-finished sentences of concern and waiting coffee cake. Jacob prepared himself. Julia's parents had questions that needed to be answered. He owed them honesty.

———⊱◦⊰———

Jacob fell into a new routine. He moved back into his home. He couldn't bear to change anything. He needed to live with his family's absence, with the silence that penetrated his sleep. Although there were regular invitations from friends and colleagues, he preferred to eat at home by himself. His beard grew fuller.

He returned to teaching at the yeshiva. He was no longer the exuberant educator who acted out Talmudic arguments for his students' amusement. The boys, in turn, no longer shared gossip or invited him to shoot baskets after school. They were scared to say something wrong, to show too much joy or enthusiasm. They were all afraid of Jacob, as if his loss were an infectious disease.

As Jacob walked the streets of his neighborhood, he could sense people sidestepping. His tragedy was well known in the community. Grief was his constant and only companion—when he woke in his empty bed, sat at the vacant breakfast table, stood on the crowded subway.

He knew what his community expected of him—a new wife, eventually a new family. His mother's friends were biding their time, waiting for Hava to give them a signal so they could make a *shidduch*, an arranged marriage, with a divorcee or a widow, someone who would bring him a "new normal."

Being back in Brooklyn made him feel like he had never left. Sometimes, he'd pick up the phone to call his wife, and then remember that it was impossible. Even though so much time had passed, his internal body clock couldn't shake the rhythms of family life—early waking, before-school schedules, homework, bedtime rituals. Once he put animal cookies in his basket at the supermarket—and then remembered there were no children at home to eat them. He took long walks to tire out his body so he could quiet his mind for rest. Sleep seldom came.

He gradually adopted a "fake-it-till-you-make-it" attitude, returning to the practices of Orthodoxy—eating only kosher food, reciting blessings before and after meals, covering his head at all times. It was easier to go along with the community than stand against it. He suspected that he would never vanquish his doubts about God and accepted his inner debate as part of a lifelong process, an argument between faith and doubt.

Jacob also found himself thinking of Brent. He wondered if Mo's new medication for arthritis was working, if Langston had joined the peewee basketball league, if he was still practicing with the same determination. He wondered how the choir was managing without him. He often thought of Rosie, but he didn't reach out. She'd asked him not to be in touch, and he respected her wishes.

In all his confusion, he knew one thing for certain: love mattered. What he felt for Julia and his children had been real, and even though he could no longer touch them, he could still feel the pulse of that connection. He also knew that what he felt for Rosie, even in his sleepwalking state, was a kind of love.

━━◆◆◆━━

When Jacob felt strong enough, he returned to synagogue. His suit fit him differently—in the months away, he had grown leaner, more muscular. He put on his old black fedora and, with his mother, walked the three blocks to the synagogue. After months in First Baptist, the synagogue looked both familiar and strange. He was living in a time warp, alternating between feeling that nothing had changed and he'd been gone for only seconds, to feeling that everything had changed and his months away were a lifetime.

The service was already in progress when Hava and Jacob quietly entered. He sat near the back of the men's section, took out his prayer shawl, and reverentially put it over his shoulders. Hava sat with his sister in the women's section. Several women embraced her, and a buzz traveled through the sanctuary. Slowly, the congregation turned to Jacob.

The men crowded the podium as the sacred Torah scrolls were removed from the ark. Rabbi Weiss led a processional with the scrolls through the synagogue. As is customary, congregants leaned forward to touch the sacred scrolls with their prayer books and prayer shawls. When the rabbi saw Jacob, he stopped, leaned over, and extended his hand. Rabbi Weiss pulled Jacob from his seat and brought him up to the podium, where he could see the loving faces of his mother, his sister, his students, and his friends. There was value in this tradition.

CHAPTER 43

In the days after Jacob left Brent, Rosie had a peculiar burst of energy. She began by scouring the house from top to bottom. She moved furniture and vacuumed even the most neglected corners. She scrubbed walls until sweat poured from her face. She sorted through closets and made bags for the Salvation Army, culled through the bookshelves and gave old volumes to the church library. Then she began on the garage, a project she had postponed for over a year. She filled a dumpster with her parents' outdated and useless possessions. She found a box of her own childhood clothes and toys, but she didn't allow herself to wax sentimental. The stuff was tattered and stained, and it went in the dumpster with everything else.

When Mo tried to wheedle out the cause of the cleaning frenzy, she nearly bit his head off.

"Fine line between cleanliness and mental illness," Mo muttered. Luckily for him, Rosie didn't hear.

Truth was that as the days turned to weeks and the weeks to months, she threw herself into the whirl of activity for a reason. She wanted to forget about Jacob. Whenever she'd experienced tough periods in her life, cleaning had been the best therapy. But this time the therapy didn't work. If she sat still long enough, she realized how much she missed Jacob—his gentle face, his voice, his touch. She moved on, hoping that the next project would block out her feelings for good.

—◦•◦—

Robert had become a steadier presence in Langston's life. His girlfriend Denise had been a good influence, making sure he paid child support and showed up for parent-teacher conferences. Rosie allowed Langston to visit his dad in Birmingham one weekend a month.

One Sunday, Rosie was in the kitchen making dinner when Robert brought Langston into the house instead of dropping him at the curb. Langston gave her a perfunctory kiss and ran to his Xbox. Robert stood there awkwardly as she peeled the potatoes, making small talk about Langston's precocious abilities. There was no mention of his girlfriend. Rosie could see he wanted to talk. She asked, "How's Denise?"

Robert plunked himself down at the kitchen table. She could see the disappointment in his face, but she didn't really want to ask what had happened. It was none of her business.

"It didn't work out." He dropped his voice. "Is it me? Is there something wrong with me?"

Rosie wiped her hands and sat down across from him. "Why do you think that?"

Robert looked stricken. "I can't seem to maintain a relationship."

Rosie put her hand gently on his, suddenly aware that he needed her, and that she cared about him deeply. He no longer had power over her. She had let her anger go, and now he was an old friend from college who happened to be the father of her son. She could live with that. She let him talk.

—◦•◦—

Rosie got to Sunday services early and took her seat with the sopranos. She noticed that Edmond was not with the tenors and

wondered why he was missing worship. As Pastor Johnson welcomed the congregation, she saw Edmond enter pushing a wheelchair with Mrs. Fredericks, Hansom's grandmother. He parked
her on the aisle and took his place in the choir. Mrs. Fredericks
wore a paisley dress that pulled over her massive chest and house
slippers on her swollen feet. Hansom, his complexion improved
and wearing his Sunday best, took the seat next to her.

Rosie admired how Edmond had stepped in as advisor and
mentor. Edmond had rolled up his sleeves and become fully involved, and Hansom had blossomed under his attention. There
was an easy connection between them that allowed humor to
surface. That's how Rosie knew Hansom was getting better. She
heard him laugh, his tentative smile evolving into an audible hoot.

Rosie was eager to catch Hansom's eye. Since his return to
Brent, she and Edmond had been tutoring him. There was no
way he could return to school and the bullying that led to his suicide attempt. The twice-weekly sessions had allowed her to know
Hansom on a deeper level. He had revealed himself as much more
than a troubled adolescent. He was bright, responsible, and loving. He was learning how to manage emotions and create coping
mechanisms. She and Edmond agreed that if Hansom pursued
higher education, they'd make sure his books were funded each
semester.

As the choir rose, Rosie could feel Edmond staring at her.
When he caught her gaze, he mouthed the words, "Lunch?"

Rosie nodded. Why not give him a chance?

CHAPTER 44

The Jewish cemetery in Staten Island was impossible to reach. Jacob had to travel by subway, bus, and taxi. The journey had taken ninety minutes with traffic. When he finally did arrive, he was transported back to a ghetto in prewar Europe. A large cement arch with a wrought iron gate marked the entry to the burial ground. *Baron Hirsch Cemetery* and the year *1880* were etched into the arch. Inside the gate were containers of stones that a visitor could bring to the gravesite and place on top of the headstone, evidence that a loved one had been there. The custom of leaving a small stone on the grave came from the awful truth of long-ago burials. If the bereaved did not cover the gravesite with rocks, then wild animals could dig up the remains. Now, a stone was a calling card.

The graves were a tangle. Headstones leaned at odd angles, all different shapes and sizes—like the people they represented. Jacob's grandfather had purchased the family plot years ago. His grandfather had immigrated to New York from Poland in 1937, in time to escape Nazi atrocities. A few other survivors from his village relocated to New York after the war. These wanderers banded together and bought family plots adjacent to one another on Staten Island. Together in death, they re-created their long-abandoned village. The Weintraubs rested near the Plonskys, the Feinsteins overlapped the Goldbergs.

Jacob knew where his family was located—the far west corner, the corner facing Jerusalem. His grandfather was proud that he could pay extra for this choice piece of real estate. In life, the man rented a cramped tenement. In death, he faced Jerusalem—a landowner. He was, at last, a wealthy man.

Jacob came upon Julia and the children's resting place. He had been here only once, on the day they were buried. There was little he could recall of that day. He'd never seen their headstone. The family had put the marker in place when he was gone. The children had been buried with their mother.

One headstone spanned the graves:

> *Julia Fisher—Age 32*
> *Beloved wife, mother, and daughter*
> *Yossi—Age 8*
> *Miriam—Age 6*
> *Sarah—Age 4*
> *Beloved children of Jacob and Julia Fisher*

Generations from now, a stranger in this cemetery would look at the singular end date and know that they had all died together. They would shake their heads and wonder what tragedy could have befallen such a young family. The vision of an exploding bus assaulted him.

"I'll wave until you disappear," he heard himself say out loud.

Jacob lightly traced the engraved names of his wife and children. He kissed the granite, disappointed that it was inanimate. Jacob wanted to say *Kaddish,* the mourner's prayer. He had said it only once, on the day his family was buried. Was the desire to pray so ingrained that he would say the words even if he no longer believed? Validating God was the reason for the prayer. Orthodox Judaism required him to say *Kaddish* daily for a year after his family's death. The ancient rabbis knew that if they required people to recite the prayer each day—a prayer that never mentions the dead, but instead praises God—then those who hated God for taking their loved ones would be pulled back into the community by simply following the laws.

The laws. They were meant to tell you how to be Jewish, but more importantly, they were meant to keep you Jewish. Jacob was compelled to say the words of *Kaddish*, but without a *minyan*, the requisite ten men, he was breaking a rule. He'd been breaking rules for so long, this transgression didn't matter. His need to say the prayer—with only the sky as his witness—reached far beyond any religious restrictions.

He began reciting the mourners' prayer in a whisper, but slowly his voice increased in volume until the final phrases echoed his powerful voice throughout the cemetery. The word "amen" bounced off thousands of headstones. The dead served as his *minyan*. Here were his witnesses.

Jacob lingered in the cemetery as long as possible. There was a chill in the air as the sun went down. He spoke softly, telling Julia and the children all about Brent, the choir, and Mr. Day. He told them about Rosie and Mo and Langston. He sang the song he wrote for Gospel Sunday. He whispered words to his wife and asked her for understanding, pressing his face close against her engraved name. Before he left the cemetery, Jacob reached into his pocket and took out a stone, Langston's lucky rock. He placed the treasure tenderly on the headstone, turned, and walked away.

Once a week, Jacob joined his mother for dinner. Hava would take great care to prepare his favorite foods, and she'd pack up leftovers to tide him over for a few days. They were polite with each other, talking about safe subjects until they could go back to their own corners.

One night Jacob cleared the dishes and turned on the water to wash up. He stood at the kitchen sink, looking out at the Brooklyn night. His mind wandered. The tap water whined as it left the spout, the same sound it made in Brent. Jacob allowed his mother's kitchen to become Rosie's.

Hava approached and turned off the tap. "You're wasting water."

Deep in thought, he didn't react.

She touched his arm. "Your life is here."

Jacob shook his head. "I can't find my way back into this life. I don't fit."

Hava knew her son was tormented. His mental health depended on structure and familiarity. He needed to put one foot in front of the other and slowly walk back to some kind of normalcy.

"You know David's grandmother, Esther?" Hava asked. "She was the only member of her family to survive the concentration camps. Even after her baby was taken from her arms, she moved on. Even after her husband was killed, she moved on. She's ninety-one now, a lifetime beyond that horror. I once asked her how she had the strength to start over. She said, 'It has nothing to do with strength. People are meant to love.'"

Jacob took in the story. The message was clear. His mother and his community expected him to make a new life.

He leaned down and kissed his mother's cheek.

⬦

Jacob slept fitfully. The covers were askew and one arm was flung over his forehead. His face was knotted in concern. The recurring dream plagued him. Each time familiar, each time disturbing.

In his dream, Jacob made his way to Penn Station in a taxi and magically found himself on a train, like some chaotically edited movie. While he was waiting in line in the dining car for a cup of coffee, Yossi appeared next to him and asked him where they were going. His response was instinctive: "We're going home."

Jacob was shocked that he could ever—even momentarily—consider anywhere else but Brooklyn home, but that was the word that came out of his mouth, and it felt right. He took Yossi's hand and returned to their seats, where Miriam and Sarah sat coloring.

Even in deepest sleep, Jacob smiled.

The train slowly pulled into the station. His children were no longer with him. Jacob disembarked. He wore a simple white shirt and black pants. His beard was full, specked with first grays, neatly trimmed. He wore a black *kipah* on his head. As he stopped on the platform to breathe the loamy, damp smell of the South, he heard the insistent greeting from the cicadas. He shifted the cumbersome duffel bag on his shoulder and began to walk. Julia, suddenly at his side, begged him to slow down. She always complained when they walked together that his legs were so much longer than hers.

Now was the time he half awakened.

Now was the moment he willed himself to complete his mind's imagining.

Jacob slowed his gait to accommodate his wife's. Her smile was serene, and her eyes, reassuring. When they were shoulder to shoulder, she took his hand, and they walked through the magnolia-lined streets of Brent, past the diner and the market, past the familiar steps of First Baptist.

Finally, in a desperate haze of memory and heartache and restoration, they arrived. Together, they stepped into Rosie's welcoming embrace.

<hr/>

The growing light pulled him to the surface of reality. His body unfolded filling the mattress with a satisfying stretch. As he did each day, he sat on the side of the bed and permitted the nourishing dream to ebb.

His cellphone buzzed—his mother was texting him. She

must have forgotten the time difference. He'd answer her after coffee.

Purposefully, Jacob walked across the sparsely furnished apartment, opened the window, and allowed in the day. The air was fresh, the sky perfectly blue. He treasured the vitality of this hour, when beginning felt sacred. On the horizon he could see the sun glinting off the iron beams of the Golden Gate Bridge. No time to idle. A roomful of boisterous teens expected him. He taught his first choral class at nine.

ACKNOWLEDGMENTS

Our profound appreciation for the many hands, eyes, and hearts that contributed to our creative process. Thank you to our husbands, Sandy Weintraub and Avi Fattal, for support and feedback, to our children for inspiration and encouragement, to Terry Corbin and Theresa Barker for reading and rereading, to John Paine and Caroline Leavitt for their editorial skills, and to Michelle Brafman, Rabbi Steven Z. Leder, Jeffrey Richman, Margery Schwartz, Dorie Bailey, Caitlin Ek, and Anna Russell. Gratefully, we acknowledge Colleen Dunn Bates of Prospect Park Books for believing.

ABOUT THE AUTHORS

J.J. Gesher is the pen name for co-authors Joyce Gittlin and Janet B. Fattal. Together, Janet and Joyce have won several screenwriting awards, including the Geller Prize and the Screenwriting Award at the Austin Film Festival. Their first screenwriting collaboration was a Lifetime Television feature.

Joyce Gittlin has written and directed such television shows as *Frasier* and *Everybody Loves Raymond* and has written more than ten feature films for Disney, Paramount, and 20th Century Fox. She has an MFA from NYU.

Janet B. Fattal has a master's in comparative literature from UCLA and has taught literature and writing at the college level. She leads many Los Angeles–area book groups, including for the Skirball Cultural Center, Hadassah, and Brandeis.

Joyce and Janet both live in Los Angeles. You can learn more at www.jjgesher.com.